On the Bright Side

ALSO BY ANNA SORTINO

Give Me a Sign

On the Bright Side

ANNA SORTINO

G. P. PUTNAM'S SONS

G. P. PUTNAM'S SONS
An imprint of Penguin Random House LLC, New York

First published in the United States of America by G. P. Putnam's Sons,
an imprint of Penguin Random House LLC, 2024

G. P. Putnam's Sons is a registered trademark of Penguin Random House LLC.
The Penguin colophon is a registered trademark of Penguin Books Limited.

Visit us online at PenguinRandomHouse.com.

Library of Congress Cataloging-in-Publication Data is available.

Printed in the United States of America

ISBN 9780593697863
1st Printing
LSCH
Design by Nicole Rheingans
Text set in Arno Pro

This book is a work of fiction. Any references to historical events, real people, or real places are used fictitiously. Other names, characters, places, and events are products of the author's imagination, and any resemblance to actual events or places or persons, living or dead, is entirely coincidental.

The publisher does not have any control over and does not assume any responsibility for author or third-party websites or their content.

For Gabe

NOTE

THE ITALICIZED TEXT is an English translation of American Sign Language used by the characters.

CHAPTER ONE

Ellie

THE STATE SHUT down my school. Some crap about budget cuts. On my last day as a junior, I'm clearing out my dorm to leave. Except this time, I won't get to come back next fall.

I stomp my foot to get Kayla's attention. She's on the other side of our dorm, packing up her things. She looks my way. "*Do you have scissors?*" I sign, then gesture toward the door. "*You know, something that could . . .*" Clasping my fingers together, I make a prying motion, indicating removing our nameplates that are on the other side.

Kayla plays with the end of her long ponytail as she thinks. "*Maybe a fork!*" She cheerfully points toward the silverware we'd hoarded from the cafeteria that's still on the vanity in front of the mirror.

"*Right,*" I sign, tapping my hands together, index fingers extended. I try to match her enthusiasm, but that's always been difficult. My default range of emotions doesn't stretch that far.

Stepping outside the room, I forcefully remove the silver rectangle that says ELLIE EGAN beneath the Brandview School for the Deaf logo. No one's going to use this, so I'm taking it. I toss Kayla's to her as I shove mine into my overpacked suitcase, beneath my Sonic Boom alarm clock.

Our usually messy living quarters are now devoid of the decorations that made it a cozy home. With the absence of our belongings, the issues are more noticeable. The peeling gray paint. The stained carpeting. The crack across the ceiling that I'd watched slowly grow. All these amenities went unfixed because the government had no interest in renovations when they'd been long conspiring to kick us all out.

With each passing year, there were fewer teachers, textbooks, and resources. The state stripped away the essentials until we were left with nothing. Now we're being sent back to our home districts, left to fend for ourselves. But we shouldn't worry! Who needs a fully immersive Deaf school when I can have a random adult interpreter trailing me around Amber High? In case it isn't clear, I'm not looking forward to this.

The lights flicker twice, alerting us to someone at the door. Cody stands there, leaning against the open frame and casually waving for my attention.

Kayla takes this as her cue to leave. "*See you around,*" she signs, giving me a quick hug and my boyfriend the slightest of nods as she rolls out her suitcase. Their indifference to each other is likely why Kayla and I didn't hang out much outside of our dorm despite rooming together every year at Brandview. She never liked Cody, and he always had a monopoly on my time anyway.

Cody glances around the empty dorm. He's still in the same sweatpants and BSD football T-shirt he was wearing last night, possibly because everything else is packed away. He steps forward, slinging an arm around me, much like he did my very first day here, letting me know that this was where I was meant to be.

"*Want to hang out down by the tree for a bit?*" he asks.

"*Y-e-s.*" I sign the word *Y* to the *S* for added emphasis that a simple nod of my hand wouldn't have conveyed.

He plants a sweet kiss on my cheek. His bloodshot eyes suggest he hasn't gotten much rest. I can tell he stayed out with the guys much later after I went to sleep. All of us at Brandview want to stretch the time we have left here. Yet, by three o'clock today, Cody and I will be headed to opposite ends of Ohio.

"*Oh, I have this for you.*" I reach into my tote and retrieve the navy sweater I'd spent the last few weeks knitting for him.

"*Thank you, Grandma,*" he signs with a smirk.

I nudge him encouragingly. "*Feel how soft it is!*"

"*It's nice.*" But he places it back with my things. "*I don't have room. Bring it for me when you visit.*"

"*Sure.*" I should have planned to do that from the beginning. Of course he doesn't have space to take this right now with everything else he has to bring home. I just would feel better about the distance if we'd left with parting gifts of some kind.

I brush back his scruffy blond hair as he smiles, taking my hand. We walk through the maze of hallways to the heavy back door of the dormitory. Turning onto the worn trail toward a small shaded grove, he places his arm around my waist, squeezing me tight. This is our spot, where we'd sneak out to if our roommates were occupying the dorms.

Cody sits down on the grass. I sit beside him and reach for the spare bobby pins clasped on my bra so that I can pin back my auburn hair. This could be any other afternoon. Except it's the last one.

I turn to sign, "*It's all weird. It's still not real to me yet.*"

"I'll miss it." He glances around, taking everything in.

The large century-old brick manor where we had our classes. The eighties-era bunker-style building that housed our vastly outdated dorm rooms. The playground across the quad where the two of us had first kissed by the swings when we were twelve. Is he remembering all the same moments, too? So many of my memories at this place are intertwined with Cody.

I fell for him while discovering my love of sign language and Deaf culture. How do I maintain this part of me without him?

"I don't want to leave." Taking a deep breath, I fight to hold back tears.

Cody is stoic. *"I guess we were almost done here anyway."*

"Exactly. Why'd they have to take it all away from us now? We had one more year." I repeat, *"One."*

"There's no perfect timing." He stares up at the sky.

It's different for him. His entire family is Deaf.

But for me, Brandview was home. Not back with my hearing family who don't sign. I'm only myself here. How am I supposed to go from total ASL immersion to being probably the only Deaf kid at Amber High?

"Do you know anyone at your new school?" I was initially surprised when I found out that Cody would be mainstreamed next year, too. I figured his family might be able to send him away to another Deaf school somewhere, but not all of them are large enough to have their own competitive athletics programs the way Brandview did, so Cody ultimately chose to go to the public school back home in Powell Heights.

"Yeah, I toured and met the football team." He checks something on his phone and chuckles but doesn't tell me what it was. *"Because I've got training with the guys before playing in the fall."*

"That's nice." Cody hadn't told me he'd visited and gotten to know the team already. Did that happen when he went home over spring break? I hate the distance between us already. I'm jealous of his instant new friends and presumably busy summer schedule, since my spare time is occupied by solitary activities such as reading or knitting. *"Bet playing there won't be as fun."*

He shrugs. *"It'll be fine."*

We've been inseparable at Brandview. Wherever I go, he's there. Anywhere he goes, I'm there. Ever since I turned the corner my first week here, when—lost, overwhelmed, and a touch homesick—I ran into Cody. He sized me up with an amused grin and signed for me to stop crying. I hadn't been and was ready to protest, but as I fumbled to remember the basic ASL I'd learned during orientation, he stepped close and offered his hand. I took it without hesitation, forgetting my anger. Under his wing, I found my place at Brandview, even though I didn't come from a Deaf family or arrive fluent in sign.

But last night, I noticed the first crack, a tear at the seams between us that now threatens to unravel further. It made sense that Cody wanted time alone to say goodbye to the guys so that they wouldn't intrude on our final hour. However, he isn't giving me much to work with. I guess he's processing this last day differently than I am. I want to reminisce and cry over how much we'll miss each other. Meanwhile, he seems content to sit still and let it all wash over us.

"We'll still move back here, right?" I ask. *"After graduation?"*

I may be imagining it, but he pauses for a beat, then slowly signs, *"Yeah, we have our plan."*

Once we're done with high school, Cody and I are going to get a cheap place in the town of Brandview, deliver food for apps, and save money to open our Deaf-owned auto shop. That's not entirely where I always envisioned myself, but it's been our goal practically since we started dating. Always good with cars, he'll do repairs while I run the office. We'll be our own boss with no one else to answer to. It beats being stuck in some hearing-centric office somewhere, wasting away.

Sure, this area is a little small-town suffocating and religiously over-bearing. But because of the institute, lots of graduates stick around. It's a Deaf enclave . . . Will it still be once BSD is shut down? Where else are Cody and I supposed to craft our future? Maybe we could try a new city with a large Deaf population, like DC, Rochester, or LA?

For the next year, Cody will be with his family up by Cleveland, while I'll be with mine outside Cincinnati near the Indiana border. Two hundred and sixty-two miles. A four-hour-and-thirteen-minute drive. Doable for summertime visits, but more difficult for weekends. Not to mention expensive.

I keep telling myself we'll make it through. I know it.

What I'm not sure about is how I'll survive an entire year back in the hearing world. And I've lived so much of my life without parental supervision that it's going to be difficult to be trapped under the same roof as my family year-round.

At least it's only temporary.

"*When do you think you'll be able to visit?*" I ask, needing to get the logistics straight and to know it won't be long before I see him again. "*Or do you want me to drive up to you first?*"

"*Look.*" Cody's distracted and points to a truck that's pulled up alongside the manor.

We watch as a small crew methodically removes and loads all the classroom furniture to take away. Are they going to sell it, or is it headed straight to a landfill? I've checked several times, but there hasn't been any announcement about what they're going to do with the property yet. It'd be a shame if this beautiful building sat empty. Still, I'd rather that than it be torn down.

Whatever it turns into, maybe they'll have some sort of plaque in the entryway commemorating how long this building served as a school and some of its historical attributes. Maybe they'll leave the wall of class portraits of each graduating class, even though my own legacy here will never be framed.

Years from now, people looking at these artifacts won't see the whole story.

They won't understand how generations of Deaf students once made Brandview our own. And how easily those in charge were able to take it away from us.

I squeeze Cody's hand. At least by holding on to him, I'll be keeping part of this place with me when I leave.

CHAPTER TWO

Jackson

THE SCORE IS one to one. I kick the ball across the bright green field. With the goalposts ahead of me, I have a clear path to score, and then the championship is in the bag. I can already taste sweet victory. It's all but a guarantee now that Amber High varsity soccer will win state.

Walnut West is struggling. Their defense is exhausted, and their goalie has been on his heels all game. Double overtime will do that, and so will penalty kicks, but those won't be necessary when I make this shot. I dribble just inside the box, aligning and planting my left leg, ignoring the tingling sensation shooting up my calf. In a few short seconds, the ball will be in their goal, and the game will be ours. I swing my right foot back to make the kick.

Then I collapse.

"Shit!" someone shouts behind me, skidding to a stop to not topple over my crumpled body.

It's like the ground gave way beneath me. There are loud gasps from the bleachers. I blink as my head spins, trying to piece together what happened. But it's like there's a gap in my memory. One moment I'm about to score, and the next I'm sprawled out on the grass.

My teammates are left scrambling as our opponents take advantage of the situation. Falling isn't new to me—we knock into each other on the field all the time—but this time, no one else was around. It was just me and gravity, and for some reason, I'm down. When I'm finally able to catch my breath, I see Walnut West's forward on a breakaway to our goal. They must have played a long ball down the field while I've been on the ground. And now my cousin, guarding our net, fails to save my mistake.

"Nooooooo!" I shout faintly as Walnut West scores a deciding point.

Sweat drips down my temple and onto my jersey. *Is it hotter than usual?* I mean to stand up, but I'm hit with exhaustion, so I stay planted in the grass. Coach calls for a time-out.

"What was that, Jackson?!" Liam shouts, running my way. He towers over me, his light skin reddening with anger as he spits on the grass. It didn't seem to be aimed at me, but I can't say for sure.

Tucking his gloves beneath his arm, my cousin runs over from the end goal to help me up. While the rest of the team keeps their distance and joins the huddle, undoubtedly processing their feelings about the turn this game has taken, Darius is the only one who seems concerned about me. "Are you all right? What's wrong?"

"I—" I'm usually quick to bring the optimism, but the words are hard to find.

It's difficult to explain, because I do have a sinking suspicion about what happened. Shaking out my legs, I try to feel out if there's more numbness than usual. *When will this go away?*

They fell asleep a week ago, and I never imagined this many days later I'd still be waiting for them to wake up. What started as a strange vibration at the bottom of my feet quickly spread to my toes and up my calves until my entire legs were engulfed in some indescribable tingly feeling. I thought I could wait it out. *Fight through the pain*, as my dad always says. *Pain is just weakness leaving the body. Stop making excuses and try harder.* There was no reason I couldn't live with this numbness and play the rest of the season in spite of it, like it was some strange fluke.

I notice as my parents leave their seats and rush to the field. They're the holistic type, avoidant of making doctor appointments unless absolutely necessary. Which is why I hadn't told them about my legs. I could still wiggle my toes and walk normally. I didn't need a doctor. Now I'm not so sure.

Liam is still looming nearby, muttering some choice words, but he clears the area as adults hurry over.

"Messina!" Both my cousin and I look up as our last name is called out. Coach approaches, leaning beneath my arm to hold me up, gesturing for his assistant to grab my other side.

"I can walk it off," I insist, but Coach immediately puts a stop to that.

"This will *look* better," Coach whispers to me. "Let's get you to the trainer."

Right, because otherwise I look like the clumsy asshole who blew the game for no good reason.

Coach and Darius return to the team while I wrap an arm around the assistant coach's shoulder and hobble off the pitch. My parents trail closely behind us.

Mom seems to be talking to herself now, probably trying to figure out which one of her supplements I should have been taking to prevent this. "Are you all right, Jackson?" she asks.

"Yeah, yeah, it's fine," I say with no strain in my voice.

From my dad's scoff, I can tell he disagrees with this display of frailty. I really wish they'd let me walk off by myself. Yet, as I put one foot in front of the other, my legs drag heavily along the ground, and I stumble. I guess I'm playing into appearances even if I don't mean to. I'm *fine*, really—it's embarrassing to have this many eyes watching me struggle to get away.

"You can lie low for a bit," the assistant coach tells me reassuringly.

"Accidents happen, I guess," I say, mustering up a half-hearted grin. "They can get it back."

So close to summer break, it's not surprising to find the school is empty on a Saturday. We go in through the door nearest to the field, making our way through the dark hallway to the athletics office. I shrug off assistance. There's no need to keep up the pretense now that we're away from the curious crowds. "I can walk by myself."

But my gait is slow and meandering, and I reach to steady myself against the wall a few more times than I'd care to admit. I can't remember it ever taking this long to get through these corridors before. My parents observe me closely.

"It isn't swollen," my dad states, scratching a finger against his freshly shaven cheek.

Mom gathers her long brown hair over one shoulder and squats to check my legs, but I don't stop long enough to let her inspect. "No, it doesn't seem to be. But we'd need to get the shin guard off to tell." She tries to pull down a knee-high sock to get a glimpse.

"You're going to trip me." I shoo her away.

She stands back, hands resting on her hips. "Does it feel like anything's strained?"

"We're almost there; *relax.*" I wish they'd chill, but they have a tendency to hover. It's the major downside of being the only child of parents who have more time and money than they know what to do with. And ever since discovering CrossFit a few years ago, they think there's nothing heavy weights and protein smoothies can't fix.

After what feels like forever, we reach the athletic trainer's office. She is eating a granola bar and watching a movie on her laptop but jumps to assist immediately. There's obvious relief when she sees no blood or terribly contorted body parts.

I climb onto the examination table, and she inspects my ankle and leg, not seeming too concerned. It's awkward, lying here while my parents and one of my coaches stand around. I'm mortified there's nothing wrong. Like, obviously I want there to be nothing wrong, but at this point, a *little* something wrong would make this whole situation not a waste of time. Can there just be anything to prove this hasn't all been in my head?

"Hmm," the trainer says, bending my left knee back and forth, then switching to the right. "Does anything feel different?"

I shift to sit upright. "Like I've sat too long and my legs fell asleep."

She stands back, putting her hands on her hips. "And how long has this been going on?"

At least a week. But I see my parents—Dad's jaw tightening, while Mom frets. "A few days," I answer, wanting to convey the gravity of the situation while also not making too much of a fuss.

The trainer grabs her clipboard and makes a note. "You know, it could be a pinched nerve."

"Yeah, maybe." I nod like I know what she's talking about. "How would that work?"

"There could be too much pressure on a nerve somewhere like your lower back," she explains. "It can go away on its own with rest or massage. But if it continues too long or gets worse, definitely go see your doctor."

"I've got some potassium, Jackson," my mom says, holding up a bottle of capsules, since for some reason, she was already carrying it around in her purse. "And I can think of a few yoga moves that might help stretch it out when we get home."

"Okay." I stand from the table, wincing as I place my feet on the ground. As I expected, there's nothing to do but wait it out. No use worrying about it. But I do need to start brainstorming excuses so that I won't have to sit in on an exercise class full of bored housewives.

The game must've ended pretty quickly after my fall—there'd only been a minute or so left on the clock—since Darius is now walking into the room.

"Did we—" I start to ask, but my cousin's solemn shrug gives it away.

We lost.

We should've won, but we lost. The teams were too evenly matched for Amber to gain back any momentum in so little time.

"Well, I'll meet you at the car," I tell my parents, eager to get away from my father's unamused gaze.

"Are you doing all right, though?" Darius removes the sweatband from his forehead, shaking out his Persian curls inherited from my aunt. "Want me to grab your stuff?"

"Nah, I got it." I shrug, not sure how to explain what happened. "And I think I'll be fine." We head to the locker room while the assistant coach hangs back to chat with the trainer.

"Dang, Uncle Roberto was not having it," Darius comments once he's sure my parents are long out of earshot.

"I once caught him in the garage trying to stitch up a gash on his own leg. And then he just," I say, while gesturing with my arms to display how ridiculous I found the situation, "continued his home workout."

"That's intense."

My dad and I look similar—brown hair and eyes, tan complexion, lean and strong—but we couldn't be more different. Though he's never explicitly voiced it, I can tell my dad thinks soccer players tend to act fragile, feigning injury to get sympathy from referees. That's not his style. He comes to every match to watch me play, happy to celebrate when we're victorious, but he acts above it all whenever things don't go our way.

As we rejoin the team, I regret not letting Darius grab my stuff for me. The guys are finding it impossible to hide their disappointment. We should be out celebrating a state championship, not moping in the locker room. With a mixture of confusion, resentment, and concern, my teammates glare at me, their towels hanging around their necks post-shower. A few dudes pat our shoulders as we walk past to our lockers, but since I lost the ball and my cousin let in the game-ending goal, it makes sense that the team isn't exactly overflowing with sympathy right now. The sting of defeat is still too fresh.

"You look fine to me," Liam says, getting up in my face.

"Sure . . ." When he doesn't step aside, I shove against his shoulder.

He pushes back, causing me to lose my balance and crash back into the row of metal doors. "I'd go cry to the trainer, too, if I messed up that bad."

What a jerk. I clench my teeth, telling myself to let go of it. I hate being a people pleaser. The kind of guy who never has a bad thing to say about anyone. Even if I might think it. "Yeah, sorry, I don't know what you want me to say, man. We'll be back next year."

"Who's gonna trust you on the field anymore?" Liam crosses his arms.

"Maybe you shouldn't have let the game get that close in the first place," I say. The next words tumble out of my mouth before I can stop myself. "They were crossing you up all game."

I can tell my burn landed because Liam sneers, fumbling for a comeback. I grab my stuff and hurry out.

Part of what Liam said echoes in my head since I worry that he's right. Can I trust myself on the field anymore? I thought I had everything under control, that I had what it took to play the match, and then my body just . . . gave up.

I have no doubt the team will make it back next year, but will I?

CHAPTER THREE

Ellie

ALL SUMMER, MADISON and I share a room, as we usually did whenever I was home for break. By the end of the season, however, it's never been more painfully clear that we aren't the closest of sisters. What's worse is that nearly every conversation of ours devolves into ceaseless bickering.

"What's Amber High like?" I ask, sitting cross-legged on the thin folding mattress that's my bed until Madison vacates hers. She ignores my question in the midst of her indecision about which five jackets she wants to bring to college, even though she'll be visiting home long before the weather calls for that many options.

Madison says something as she walks into the closet.

"What?" I ask.

She ducks her head back out to repeat, "I don't know; it was just like a normal high school."

"That's super helpful, thanks."

With a small shake of her head, Madison adds, "Well, I guess you've never actually been to a *normal* school before, so I don't know what to tell you."

I roll my eyes and nod toward the pile of winter coats. "Just take one for now . . . You can swap them out later."

"Oh, that works."

"Mom will make you take—"

"—take a scarf anyway," Madison says, finishing my thought. We share a knowing look.

Then a noxious smell fills the air. "Ew, your roommate is not going to appreciate that."

"It wasn't me!" She bends down and scoops up Cheese, dropping him into my lap. "Take care of my baby. Make sure you feed him."

"He's not *your* cat." I cross my arms. "Of course I'll feed him. Why wouldn't I feed him?"

When we first moved into this house, there was a Post-it Note on the back door that said *Cheese makes him gassy*. We had no idea what it was about until this fat long-haired black cat showed up in our back-yard later that evening. I was the one who hid him inside for a week before anyone found out. My parents weren't thrilled at first but came around to him eventually, as long as we both promised to take care of him. Madison and I were equally obsessed, and it broke my heart to be away from him while I was at Brandview. But now that I'm back, I'm never leaving this cat ever again.

Madison finishes packing, and I follow as she lugs her suitcases downstairs, where our parents are waiting. They make us take a picture together to commemorate the occasion. Madison's starting at Indiana University. It's hard not to be jealous that she's the one who gets to leave this fall, while I'm stuck here. At least I get the house to myself the weekend before starting at the new high school.

"Okay, now one with just Madison," Mom calls out, motioning for me to step aside. *Story of my life.*

Dad is quick to explain when he sees my expression sour. "We'll get one of you on your first day at Amber. Don't you worry, Ellie-door."

Yeah, when I was little, I couldn't hear my name correctly and pronounced *Eleanor* as *Eledor*, which spurred this oh-so-hilarious nickname my father won't drop.

Mom says something to me about "emergency numbers on the fridge," but I don't ask her to repeat. It's not like I'm going to call anyone anyway.

"I'm glad we got to spend time together this summer before I left," Madison says, pulling me into a hug.

"Yeah, me too." We did have our nice moments, however sparse.

"Aww, well, *good luck* at Amber."

Just like that, something about her infantilizing tone sets me off. She constantly belittles and treats me like I'm significantly younger than her even though we're only a year apart. You can't tell me that my parents raising us as "the perfect one" and "the disabled one" has nothing to do with this dynamic.

"You *always* do that," I snap.

Madison sighs dismissively. "Stop getting upset over nothing. I can't say good luck? Whatever."

"Now, girls—" But the rest of what Dad says is drowned out by the roll of suitcases clunking down the two front steps toward the driveway.

I give a curt wave before locking the front door behind them, then go upstairs to the bedroom that's supposedly mine now but still feels temporary. Madison left her movie posters on the wall and plants dangling on the window sill. It's all hers, every decoration in here.

Clearing off the desk, I shove the clutter in with the rest of her stuff in the closet so I can place a few items of my own, finally trying to settle in as best I can. The nameplate I brought home from Brandview. A stuffed octopus Cody won for me at a summer fair. The sweater I knit him, which he kept sneaking back into my bag whenever I visited this summer. I want him to accept the gift already, but he seems to think he's turned this into some silly game of giving it back to me. I still need to print out photographs, since the smiling faces on the wall staring back at me are Madison and her friends.

Couldn't Madison have at least given me some guidance about Amber High? The only time I've ever been inside was for her graduation. That day, my sister strutted through the halls, and I should've paid closer attention to my surroundings. I was still in denial back then. Amber was always supposed to be her school, never mine.

I spend the weekend curled up on the couch with Cheese, watching movies at full blast. The first thing my mom does when she and Dad get back Sunday afternoon is lower the TV volume. "You've already got the captions on; surely you don't need it this loud."

It's clear my parents aren't sure how to operate when it's just the three of us. After a mostly silent dinner, my dad pulls out a board game, but I extract myself after a half hour of confusing rules that I couldn't hear the specifics of.

I retreat to my room and climb into bed, grateful to no longer be relegated to the folding mattress. I'm scrolling through my phone when it vibrates. It's Cody, video calling. *Finally.*

We've kept missing each other these past few days. He had his big family reunion this weekend, which I usually join him for, but since

I start school tomorrow, the logistics just didn't work out. He must know I'm nervous. He always gives the best encouragement right when I need it.

Quickly opening my laptop, I accept the call from there, blinking rapidly in the bright light. "*Hey!*" I sign enthusiastically.

Cody nods, his expression plain. He signs with one hand, holding his phone out in front of his face with the other. But he's a blur, and the connection glitches.

"*Again?*" I ask him to repeat.

He's being shifty, his eyes darting off to the side to avoid the camera. A knot forms in my stomach, twisting harder the longer I wait for him to get out what he wants to convey. After all these years, I can read Cody easily. It's clear that something's wrong.

Lowering my eyes, I ask, "*What are you signing?*"

"*We're just . . .*" He takes a deep breath. "*Really far away, you know?*"

"*Yeah, I wish I could have been there this—*"

Cody slaps his hand toward the camera, cutting me off. "*Things are different now.*"

I'm immediately defensive, fighting the creeping suspicion that the worst is about to drop. "*It's one year. That's nothing.*"

But it's not. We've been more than distant lately. It's been four weeks since I last visited him, which was my third drive north this summer. Meanwhile, he hasn't been down here at all because he hadn't been able to borrow the family car. Everything's a hassle. That's how it's always been during breaks, but we'd come together no problem when school started up again. He's still on summer vacation for another week and supposed to be driving down to see me in a few days. We'll be able to smooth things out then.

Cody bites his lip. "*You know . . .*" He takes an incredibly long pause. My chest tightens in anticipation. "*I don't think I want to go back to the Brandview area.*"

We can work with this. We can adjust our plan. "*I can move to you. Or we can pick some other city. We can start to figure it out when you come later this week.*"

He looks off to the side as he signs, "*I don't think that will work, either.*"

"*Why?*" I sign, almost as an afterthought, but my lowered eyebrows clearly convey the question.

Cody stares at me blankly. I don't recognize where he's at, but someone walks by, knocking into him, and he turns to reveal a party in some basement. Cody's having no trouble adjusting to being back home. Why is he not sharing things with me? We never met up with people or went to any events whenever I visited him. He just kept me to himself. Does he not want me to know his other friends?

Suddenly, I don't know the person before me. I feel like a switch has flipped. And the world is upside down. The Cody I knew at Brandview would never do something like this—*would he?* He doesn't feel like the same person anymore. Somehow the person I thought I'd be with for my entire life is now a total stranger.

Because I realize exactly what he is trying to tell me.

"*Seriously?*" I raise my eyebrows and give him a pointed look. "*Are you for real doing this? Right now?*"

"*It's not what I want anymore,*" he signs somewhat apologetically.

His brow crinkles in a way I used to find endearing. Now I see it for what it really is. Condescending.

"*And you don't want me.*" My teeth clench as I shake my head. "*Anymore.*"

He sighs, giving a small nod. *"I think that—"*

I smash my laptop shut.

I jump up and pace the room, replaying the conversation in my head and trying to piece together where it all went wrong. Part of me wants to call him back, just to have the argument.

Yet there's no way I'm subjecting myself to any of his excuses. Five years of my life, and that jerk doesn't even have the decency to drive out here and do that shit in person. Or at the very least in private. He's at a *party*. Probably dumping me so he can hook up with someone else. *If he hasn't already . . .*

I grab the cheap carnival stuffed octopus from my desk and tear it apart. Limb by limb.

The next victim of my rage is that sweater that was supposed to be his. Hours upon hours to weave the threads together, seconds to pull it all to shreds. I sink to the ground, defeated, while Cheese prances around in the wreckage.

Like I'm in a trance, I hold tight to my phone, scouring social media for any hint of what Cody is up to tonight. His accounts, his tagged photos leading to friends' accounts, his siblings' updates, as well as any of his new recent follows. I'm a total wreck, while he's out there somewhere having the time of his life.

I scroll for the next several hours until my body physically can't stay awake anymore.

But I find something I wish I hadn't seen. In the background of a photo posted by his brother's girlfriend an hour ago, there's Cody. He's lounging on a couch, arm around some other girl. Not the slightest bit upset.

I was just a convenience to him, not worth the trouble now that someone else is more readily available. And yet, for me, he was everything.

Like that, it's all completely over. My plans for the future crumble. I lost Cody. I lost Brandview. I don't know who I am anymore.

The next day is Monday, my first at Amber High. I wake up with my head throbbing and eyes crusty. If only it had all been a terrible nightmare, but I've got a screenshot with evidence right there on my phone. *As if I'd need reminding.* Today was already going to be hard enough. Now I'm supposed to face a brand-new school after my entire existence has been pulled out from under me?

If Cody is going on and thriving without me, I'll have to try to do the same. I don't want to give him a second thought.

Which is easier said than done.

Dark clouds encroach as I drive the fifteen minutes to Amber, the high-traffic suburban roads littered with tired commuters heading into the city for a morning of work. The wispy branches of the blue ash trees slash around in the strong wind. When I get to the school parking lot, the only spots left are in the back, so I sprint across the pavement, entering the wide brick building mere seconds before heavy splashes of rain fall from the sky.

There's so many people moving around me, knowing exactly where they need to go. I lock eyes with another poor lost soul—obviously a freshman—yet she's immediately claimed by a small gaggle of other fourteen-year-olds, all eager to find kindred spirits in their new environment. I have no such support. Everyone else my age already has their friends, favorite meetup spots, and place in this school.

I don't belong here.

I make my way through the crowds to the front office, where, after taking one glance at me and the devices on my head, the receptionist calls for someone on the intercom and gestures for me to take a seat. A few minutes later, a woman with a name badge that reads MS. LILY—GUIDANCE COUNSELOR comes to greet me. She's a petite thirtysomething-year-old whose enthusiastic smile could give my old roommate a run for her money, wearing a bright yellow dress that clearly didn't get the dreary weather memo.

"Welcome, Eleanor! Your interpreters aren't"—she overmouths her words, unsure how to speak to me—"here yet."

I just nod in response.

"Locker." She points down the hall while handing me a slip of paper with a number and lock combination. "Meet me back here at—" She holds out eight individual fingers across both hands, then just her index finger, then all five on one hand, looking quite proud of herself.

"Okay, thanks," I say out loud, not really wanting to give her the satisfaction of signing one of the only words she might know in ASL, before heading off to wander the halls.

There's so much clatter around me—doors opening and closing, shoes shuffling across the floor, and students shrieking with excitement to catch up with friends they haven't seen all summer.

Back at Brandview, I usually went without my hearing aid or cochlear, especially for classes that were conducted entirely in sign language. I prefer the world without all this unnecessary noise. From the app on my phone, I mute my devices and use them to stream some rage breakup music instead.

Except, when I find my locker, the girl who's at the neighboring one gives a little wave and says something after gathering her books. I scramble to turn off the music so I can hear her, but when I look up, she's already walked away. That probably wasn't a good first impression. Today is not great. *Ugh, just got to keep my head down and power through.*

At 8:15, and not a second earlier, I circle back to where Ms. Lily is waiting with my assigned interpreters. It's two women, both in long-sleeved black shirts. They almost look like a mother-daughter pairing, but they're too close in age for that to be the case. They're both pale, blond, and super smiley. The older one—Kim, I learn is her name—is short and plump, while the other, Pamela, is tall and slim.

Following our initial introductions, Kim signs, "*Nice to meet you.*"

"*Yes, same!*" Pamela chimes in.

"*We're both part-time,*" Kim signs, explaining something about their current childcare schedules. "*Going forward, Pamela will work your morning classes, and I'll do the afternoon. And then we'll cover for any of each other's absences throughout the semester.*"

"*Okay, thank you,*" I sign, and catch Ms. Lily's eyes lighting up in recognition, just as I expected.

"Thank you!" Ms. Lily says and signs, but her motion comes too close to signing "fuck you" instead. Classic.

I stop in the bathroom to get a moment to myself before class. Up first is physics, which is taught in one of the labs, apparently on the total opposite side of the school. I rush, getting there with only a minute to spare, and find that a seat has been reserved for me at the front of the room.

Pamela is already in position, waiting to interpret. She's in a folding chair only a few feet away, facing me, frowning as she reads something on her phone before sliding it into her purse. Other students stare at the two of us as I slink into my predetermined spot.

Back at Brandview, we often sat in circles or rectangles so everyone was visible. It's not great to have a bunch of classmates behind me where I can't see them. My neck hurts in anticipation of all the craning I'll have to do.

Despite the sound I can hear through my hearing aid and cochlear, I need an interpreter for class. That way, when the AC unit is too noisy—or the teacher is facing the board and I can't read their lips, or a classmate is asking a question I can't catch—I'll still get the full context of the lecture through the accommodation.

I *could* voice my own responses if I wanted to. But for now, I'd like to make it clear that communication should flow through my interpreter. I rarely voiced at school after learning ASL, even though I have to speak at home because of my family.

"Class, as you see, we have a special guest," the physics teacher says, and Pamela signs. "A sign language interpreter for our new Deaf student."

I grimace. It'd be one thing if we were going around the classroom doing first-day introductions for everyone, but we're not. Instead, it's like I'm some demonstration science experiment that all my classmates should get a good look at.

"Ellie, would you like to tell us a little bit about what your old Deaf school was like?" Pamela interprets the teacher's request.

"Well, it was falling apart, but it was our school, you know?" I sign, trying to smile and seem somewhat friendly but keeping it real all the same. I didn't choose to be here, but Brandview wasn't perfect, either. Yet the interpreter fails to convey this nuance. I watch Pamela's lips as she says, "You know, our school was falling apart."

Um, that's not at all what I was saying, but maybe I misheard. I drop my fake pleasant expression. *"Because of all that, I needed to go to a new school, so it's not exactly like I'm happy to be here, but nice to meet you all."*

Instead of addressing my classmates, I turn and watch the interpreter to confirm my suspicions. "I'm happy to be here at this new school. Nice to meet you all."

Is Pamela not understanding my signing? Or is she intentionally changing the words? From what I heard from the teacher earlier compared to what she relayed to me, I know what she's translating into ASL is passable. But she didn't voice what I signed correctly.

Ordinarily, I'd try to be discreet with my correction. Unfortunately for her, today is not the day I tolerate any of this.

"That's *not* what I said," I say—well, sort of shout—my Deaf accent coming out loud and strong. From the shock on my classmates' faces, I realize the teacher had already started to speak again and now I've interrupted him.

I turn back to Pamela, my hands flying, but she sits there, not doing her job. Her lips quiver and eyes glaze over.

In fact, she starts crying.

"*What are you doing?*" I ask, unable to hide my baffled expression. Why is she this upset? She's the one butchering my words; the least she can do is correct her mistakes and explain what's going on to my classmates. "*Tell them what I'm signing!*"

I can feel the weight of everyone's attention from behind me, eagerly watching how this plays out, even if they don't understand what's going on. This is absurd. And completely unprofessional.

Pamela stands, grabs her purse, and hurries out of the room. I'm left to sort through this disaster myself.

"Well," I say out loud.

My classmates have broken into rapid whispers. The physics teacher is frozen, unsure how to proceed. "Ellie," he says hesitantly, clearly unsure how to communicate with me now that the interpreter isn't there. He gestures for me to come to his desk, where he scribbles on a piece of paper, *Why don't you go wait in the principal's office while we get this situation taken care of?*

Now *I'm* getting kicked out? How did I end up in trouble? I could theoretically try to muddle my way through the rest of class on my own, but that would take too much explaining, and I don't want to be here now anyway.

Ignoring the pointed and suspicious looks from my classmates, I grab my stuff and leave.

Pamela's already at the front office, having pulled herself together enough to be speaking low and fast to the administrator across the desk. When she turns around and sees me standing there waiting, she signs with a huff, *"I'm having a rough morning. They'll see if Kim can come back early before her afternoon classes."*

And then Pamela pulls a huge umbrella out of her purse and leaves.

I'm ready to walk out myself, but the receptionist ushers me to wait on a couch. Now I'm too far into this office to ditch school without someone noticing.

There's absolutely nothing that could turn this day around.

CHAPTER FOUR

Jackson

ON THE FIRST day back at school, I'm able to avoid Liam all morning until he bumps into me on the way into the cafeteria for lunch. "Hey, Slip, surprised to see you walking," he taunts me.

I survived a summer full of supplements and yoga until eventually I regained feeling in my legs. Everything went back to normal.

Yet it's apparent I still haven't won back the soccer team. It's not my fault I had to sit out the summer workouts. Coach insisted I needed a break in order to return during the school year in top form. He didn't consider the team dynamics and the fact that I was going to continue working out on my own anyway. Rest is a foreign concept to me. I've been itching to get back to the weight room with the guys.

"Just ignore Liam," Darius says as we head to our usual spot at the soccer table. He's carrying his food tray, while I've got my gray reusable lunch box from home.

But among the other players, Gavin and Karl don't look too happy with me, either. I hate this animosity and don't know how to make things right with the team. "They all know Coach forced me to sit out, right? I wasn't *allowed* to go to training."

"I tried to remind them of that." Darius shrugs. "Posting a few less pictures from the resort probably would've helped."

Okay, the team may also be mad that, while they were doing sit-ups in a musty old gym, I was lounging around the Amalfi Coast. My parents saw my forced soccer hiatus as the perfect opportunity for a long family trip. Italy's always the go-to spot, but this visit was solely for vacation, rather than catching up with our relatives there.

By then, I had regained all normal feeling in my legs but was still building trust in them again, worried they could give out at any moment. I was particularly nervous doing some challenging spots on the Path of the Gods hike, where the cliff's edge was an easy trip and fall away, but, whew, I survived. And the views from up there were worth it.

"Well," I say, "my parents *did* rent a boat for a few days, and I was captive with only my phone to keep me company."

"Wasn't Anthony there?" Darius asks, mentioning our older cousin who's starting his final year at the University of Cincinnati.

"Only for a week and with his girlfriend, so I never saw him. I wanted to explore, but not by myself."

"You gotta start doing things on your own."

"Yeah, yeah, but also, you should've just tagged along for the trip."

"I couldn't. I had summer workouts," he teases.

I shake my head, and we stall a few feet away from the lunch table. "Really thought things would have blown over a bit by now."

Darius winces. "I mean, it was *state*."

"I guess I'll avoid the soccer table for a while . . ."

Looking around the small, crowded cafeteria, I realize that, aside from the soccer team, I don't really have anyone. Sure, I've got tons of acquaintances. There's Ashley, who's always in the student government office working on projects when I'm there. And Sean, my go-to partner in gym. Plus, plenty of others who I would easily pair up with for class assignments and to have a good time. But none of them are friend-friends to hang with outside of school or anything. There's not really another group that I could plop down with at lunch without it being weird.

"I'll be okay sitting by myself for today," I say, glancing at some space across from a girl with red hair I don't recognize. She's alone, reading a book, but Darius shakes his head.

He nudges my arm. "Heard some stuff about the new girl."

I give a blank stare, puzzled, trying to avoid peering at her too obviously. "Like what?"

In a pronounced whisper, loud across the chatter, he says, "Apparently she's pretending to be deaf."

"Who would do that?" I ask. "That's so weird."

"She started screaming in class earlier." Darius shrugs, signaling that's all he's heard. "Best to avoid."

I stare back at her, trying to make sense of what kind of person would do that. Or if I should believe the rumor. Her eyes are locked on her book, not missing a beat as she turns a page or eats a cracker. I would be totally uncomfortable on my own like that, peering off to see if anyone was staring at me—for good reason, I realize, and withdraw my gaze—but she doesn't seem to care at all about being alone.

Odd, to say the least.

Darius and I are almost the last ones still standing now, as our classmates rush around us to fill in the remaining seats. "Where'd you hear all that from?" I ask my cousin.

"The guys were texting about it earlier," he says. *Ah, I can guess who was leading the charge.*

Liam is vocal and forms fast opinions. You're either with him or against him, and he's pretty good at convincing the rest of the group to feel the same way he does. A year or two ago, I might've been able to crack a well-intentioned joke and brush past all this. But now, the team sees me as a weak link. Even though I was home for the majority of the summer, I was pretty obviously left off the group chat. I see how it is.

"Where are you going?" Darius asks as I turn around.

"I'll catch up with you later," I say, taking my lunch outside the cafeteria.

There aren't many other feasible places to sit, so I settle for the bench outside the admin office and get weird looks. The staff has been really against loitering lately, even though I'm just trying to find a quiet place to eat. I'm only halfway through my meal when Ms. Lily walks by. She's the guidance counselor who helped me squeeze an extra science class into my schedule last year.

"Jackson Messina, what brings you here?" she asks.

No, not right now, please. I should've gone to the student council office instead, despite it being full of sophomores on their free period. I gesture to my head as I swallow a bite of food. "Thought I might be getting a bit of a migraine, but it seems to be clearing up."

Although, now that I mention it, I do have a headache. Water might help, so I take a quick swig from my bottle.

"I see." She nods toward the new banner hanging in the front lobby. "I should congratulate you for bringing home the conference championship last year."

"Right, well, thanks." Since it was the state victory we really wanted, the display only reminds me of my failure.

"It's always an accomplishment to make it that far." She nods slowly, double-checking a list of names on her clipboard. "You have study hall next period, right?"

"Yes, I do."

Presumably, that aligns with what's on her paper. "Wonderful. While I have you here, there's something I could use your help with. Do you mind if I borrow you for a few minutes?"

"Sure." I stand, tucking my unopened bag of kettle chips back into my lunch box.

I've always been involved in school, but somehow I've become the go-to guy for the administration. I'm seemingly always the first they ask to volunteer during parents' night, or to tutor underclassmen, or to show visiting alumni around. My parents think this will bolster my college applications so I can get in somewhere like Duke, Notre Dame, or their alma mater, the University of Dayton. And, of course, that does contribute to my reasons for doing these things, but I'm not sure they understand that I actually *like* helping people. Well, that, and I sort of like being anywhere but home, where my parents try to involve me in all their things. On the other hand, always volunteering means I've built up this reputation where I feel like I can't say no; otherwise I look like a jerk. So I take another sip of water and make myself available.

"What would you like me to do?" I ask. Being busy with something will at least ensure that I'm not still sitting here when the soccer guys exit the cafeteria.

"Walk with me." I follow Ms. Lily down the hallway as she explains, "We have a new disabled student who could use some help navigating the school. It would be great if you could show them the ropes and how best to settle in." With a sympathetic look, she says, "Mostly they could benefit from a friendly face. Even without any extra hurdles, transferring to a new school senior year is difficult."

"Right, of course."

I don't fully understand what Ms. Lily is asking of me, but it can't be that difficult. I'm not sure what to expect of the student. My mind flashes to various disabilities I've seen on TV. Maybe some dude in a wheelchair who I can help push around and play accessible basketball with.

But as the guidance counselor turns the corner, waiting for us at a locker ahead is not who I was expecting.

Standing next to a stout middle-aged woman is the girl from lunch who Darius was telling me about. She's wearing a light gray dress and worn boots, as well as an attitude that screams she'd rather be anywhere else. Once closer, I notice a brown attachment on the side of her head that blends into her short red hair. And there's something in her left ear as well.

Her dark brown eyes narrow skeptically as Ms. Lily and I approach. Like she's sizing me up, already judging me, and for some reason, I'm desperate to prove wrong whatever she's thinking.

"Nice to see you again." Ms. Lily speaks, and the woman begins to interpret her words into sign language. "I thought it might be nice for you to have someone to show you around so you feel more at home here at Amber. This is Jackson Messina." Ms. Lily gestures toward the girl. "And Jackson, please help me welcome Ellie Egan. As well as her interpreter Kim."

"Hi," I say, gesturing hello because it feels like I'm supposed to do something with my hands. Pointing to myself, I say to Kim, "You can tell her I'm Jackson."

Ellie reaches out and waves a hand in front of my face, redirecting my attention to her eyes. What's this about? Maybe she is a little . . . *something*. I try to keep my expression neutral. She completes a string of signs that the interpreter voices as "She's not the one you're trying to talk to. I am."

"The ASL interpreter will facilitate the conversation," Ms. Lily says. "But you can talk to Ellie as you would any other student."

The obvious difference being I don't have to have an adult relay my words when I talk to any other student. I shrink, feeling much less confident about this whole thing. Another type of disability might have been easier to work with, since there wouldn't be a communication situation. That's probably not great to be thinking.

I just say, "Right, yes. Thank you."

Ellie gives me a look that shoots daggers and pierces my very being.

The bell rings, and the interpreter alerts Ellie to the sound.

"You both have study hall this period, so maybe you can sit down somewhere and get better acquainted. Feel free to drop by my office anytime," Ms. Lily says before walking away.

"Um." I awkwardly hold up my lunch box. "I need to put this away in my locker, but that's on our way."

Ellie and Kim trail silently behind me, and I try to think of more to say but come up short. Whatever. They know I'm not showing them around yet. Finally, we get to the empty classroom on the second floor.

Sitting next to the new girl and her air of intrigue, as well as a middle-aged woman, brings a lot of eyes onto me as others trickle into study hall. I'm uncomfortable with the looks we get from our classmates, but Ellie seems indifferent, holding her head high, just like I saw her at lunch. She must be used to all this. I'm both impressed and sorry for her.

"Yeah, welcome to Amber High," I say, tapping my hands restlessly on the desk. "I can give you a tour of the school soon and help with any questions you have, or even with tutoring. Since I'm one of the student tutors here, we can always set up time for that, too."

There's a brief delay as my words are interpreted. I watch Ellie's face carefully as it contorts into a mischievous smirk. I give a nervous grin, a little terrified but unable to resist matching her smile.

"What makes you think I'll need tutoring?" she says with a strong Deaf accent.

I'm caught off guard and immediately say the first question that comes to mind. Probably the *wrong* question. "Oh, you speak?"

Whew. Because that would make things *a lot* easier for me.

Ellie runs a hand through her hair, clicking her tongue as she slides back in her seat. Her feet accidentally knock against mine. She signs to the interpreter, who nods politely, gets up, and leaves. Then Ellie pulls out her phone and ignores me.

How is this supposed to work? Does she not need an interpreter right now? Will she be able to tell what I'm saying?

I wave my hand in her direction, not quite as aggressively as she did earlier but in an effort to show that I'm trying to pick up on what the right course of action is here. It's not my fault she's sending all sorts of mixed signals. She keeps her head down but raises her eyes from her phone to look at me.

"Can I ask you a question?" I say, loud and as slow as possible to make it clear.

"Just speak normally," she says, irritated.

I'm taken aback. "Yeah, normally. Can you hear what I'm saying, then?"

She watches my lips as I speak. "Yes. And no."

"Cool, cool." I wait for her to elaborate, but she doesn't. "Does that implant thing bring your hearing back?" I ask, painfully aware that I'm using all the wrong terminology. "So you don't always need the interpreter?"

"It's been a long day." Her exhaustion is palpable. "I'm not in the mood to educate you right now."

That's fair. What was it that Ms. Lily said her last name was? Egan, right? There was another girl who graduated last year. I'm searching for any way to make a connection here. "Any chance you're related to Madison?"

Apparently, this was also the wrong thing to say. "My sister," Ellie grumbles.

I worked with Madison on some student government projects last year. I kind of recall her mentioning a sister away at school, but I'd assumed that meant an older sibling at college.

Ellie adjusts some settings on her phone, then pulls up a Spotify playlist and selects a song, totally checking out of the conversation. *Geesh, at least help me help you.* Straining to listen, I can detect the faintest hint of music leaking out from her cochlear thing. Oh wait, no. I think that's what the one on the other side of her head is called. This must be a hearing aid.

We sit uncomfortably side by side for the rest of study hall. Up close, I notice the faint freckles strewn across her cheeks. If she wasn't so intimidating, she'd be cute.

Scratch that, she's attractive in part *because* she's intimidating.

Spotify must play a song Ellie doesn't like because she scrunches up her nose and skips to the next track. She throws a side-eye glance my way, aware that I'm watching her. But I don't back down.

We hold each other's gaze.

I try to figure out what she's thinking. She stares at me for a moment and lowers her eyebrows ever so slightly, as if posing a question.

One I wish I had the answer for. But with a small shake of her head, she breaks away. She probably thinks I'm another jerk in a school full of them.

If only there was some parting sentiment that could restore good faith here, but at the end of the period, I carefully alert her to the bell ringing. She nods, then walks away, probably not giving me another thought.

Everything about Ellie is intriguing. There's so much personality behind her expressions when she signs. It seems that's when she gets to be herself, and I wish I knew what she was saying. I can't help but feel like I'm missing out.

Damn. I wish that had gone better.

CHAPTER FIVE

Ellie

I PULL OUT my hearing aid and cochlear receiver and take my time walking inside my house after school, avoiding the water pooling in the small indents on the driveway. The rain is still drizzling down in this clammy heat. I need to shower off this terrible day. An involuntary half grin curls up when I notice Cheese watching me from the bedroom window, but remembering today quashes that would-be smile immediately.

Gossip must've gotten around after first period, because I was stared at all day long, more so than usual. The guidance counselor tried to take pity on me and assigned some guy to sit with me during study hall. And he thought I'd need a tutor? Not even for any particular subject, just assumed I must be bad at school. *Ugh, how embarrassing.* My mood simmers, yet I know as soon as I step inside the house, it will come to a raging boil.

Everyone is acting like everything about this is normal, but it's not. I should still be at Brandview. This place doesn't feel like home to me. There has to be some better alternative than sticking me in a new school for my final year. Honestly, I'm eighteen, so do I legally even need to be going to Amber?

I enter the code to open the garage and am relieved to find no cars inside, meaning my parents aren't home. Dad's schedule is all over the place depending on what plumbing repairs are needed each week, and Mom really has to work hard to justify a vacation day to herself, even when she has plenty to spare at her corporate marketing job.

Two hours later, I hadn't even realized they were home yet when Mom appears in my bedroom doorway, already irritated with me somehow. When she says something that I don't hear, she points to her ears, so I reluctantly reach for my devices and put them back on.

"I *said*," Mom continues, "that food is ready."

I look back down at my phone. "You could've just texted me."

"Or you should keep your hearing aid and cochlear on," she counters.

"But my head hurt."

Ignoring this, she walks back down the stairs, shouting over her shoulder. "Come on. It's getting cold."

Tired of waiting at the table, Dad decided we're eating dinner in front of the TV. He's on the couch watching some nineties movie, but there's no captions on. I sit on the other end, bowl carefully balanced in one hand while I wordlessly reach for the remote to rectify that. Dad mumbles something about "turning off when you're done."

We eat the room-temperature pasta without saying much. After a while, Mom tries to start up a conversation, but I'm too exhausted from a long day of listening fatigue to be in a chatty mood.

"What?" I ask a little sharply.

She's immediately defensive. "You should hear me now. I *said* how was school?"

"I hate it." I keep my voice level while sharing this truth. Matter of fact. Straight to the point. "I want to drop out, honestly."

"You are *not* allowed to drop out." Mom makes sure she gets her point across.

Dad is usually calmer but still strict, trying to level out my mom's reactions. Except no matter how they present their opinions, they're always in agreement. One unit, resistant to change, unwilling to accommodate or comply with anything that would make my life easier. He says, "I know it's not what you wanted. But you can't just quit."

They should give me some valid reasons, then. "Why not?" I play coy.

"Because we're not going to let you," my mom says, standing to clear her plate, and when she returns, she doesn't resume sitting in the side chair, as if this will physically give her the upper hand in this conversation.

"You didn't have to send me to Madison's school." I get up, too. "You could've homeschooled me for the year, or found somewhere else, or, I don't know, anything other than making me the freak who has to start senior year at a new school!"

"Homeschool you?" Mom laughs like I've just told the world's funniest joke. Her voice goes level and quiet so that I only catch "you really think" and "time to teach you on top of."

"So, you don't really want me home, then," I counter, understanding the poor logic of this argument, but I'm backed into a corner.

"Not while we have to be at work, no."

Dad grabs the remote to pause the TV. Seems like we're being too loud for him.

"You'd rather I was still gone." I cross my arms. "Me too."

"Yes, this is a big inconvenience to everyone. The universe really conspired to do you wrong here." Mom's tone is part mocking, part sympathetic. But my read of it is cruel. "We didn't shut down Brandview. You still have to go to school."

"I'm eighteen, so." I let that linger.

Dad tries to salvage the moment. "Now, Ellie-door, if—"

I cut him off. "I really don't."

Mom shakes her head. "And then what will you do? You have to go to school if you're going to live here."

"Maybe I'll find somewhere else." Except, these days, I have nowhere to go.

I can't crash with Madison, not that she'd welcome a disruption at college anyway. None of my friends are living in the Brandview area now, and I couldn't afford an apartment by myself. I would have run off to Cody in a heartbeat, but he's moved on so fast that I'm still reeling from having to reevaluate everything I ever thought about our relationship.

"You just don't get it!" I shout at my parents. "You never have." My voice falters, but I don't dare let it break into too much emotion. "You never tried."

"What can we do to make things at school easier for you?" Dad asks.

"Nothing." I storm upstairs, slamming the bedroom door shut behind me.

I'm still hungry, having barely touched my dinner, but I spend the rest of the night locked in my room, refusing to confront my parents again. I check under the bed, but Cheese isn't here with me. I'm all alone.

The next morning, Mom drags me out of bed. I didn't set my deaf alarm clock, but she unlocked the bedroom door with a bobby pin— seriously—and made sure I was awake on time. We ignore the argument from last night. I begrudgingly get ready.

My head hangs low as I return to Amber. I brace myself for immediate stares as I walk through the main entrance, but fortunately, it seems everyone's already moved on to the latest thing.

When I get to my locker, there's a note taped on the door telling me to stop by the front office.

Surprise, surprise, Pamela dared to show up again today. She is clutching the strap of her crossbody bag tightly, like she's not ready to use her hands to sign anytime soon, and refuses to look at me directly. Kim is seemingly still in pajamas and standing by a baby stroller that she keeps shushing at even though my devices aren't picking up on any crying. Maybe her child is just threatening to break out into large screams at any second. What a relatable mood. Kim seems irritated to have to show up at Amber before her shift for the second day in a row.

"We had a meeting to discuss yesterday. It's unfortunate to have a difficult start. Sometimes it takes time to settle in. To that point," Kim says, redirecting her attention to me and speaking for the avoidant interpreter, *"we're going to make sure that we address any of your clarification requests immediately. But, moving forward, please bring additional feedback to us outside of class time."*

Right, because, once again, yesterday was my fault. *I'm* the one who didn't handle that situation correctly . . .

If I don't use interpreters while mainstreamed, my grades will probably suffer. Despite disliking this school and all my fuss about wanting to drop out of Amber, I do really love learning. I was a top student at Brandview, somewhere that was set up for me to thrive. But I could quickly be considered a bad or problematic student at a place like this.

Not to mention, if I stop using my accommodations now, my class-mates will probably think I was faking. Even though that's just, like, not a thing. Abled people accuse disabled people of faking at an extremely disproportionate rate to the very small number of people who might actually lie.

I walk fast, trying to get a few more minutes to myself, but Pamela closely follows me to first period. In the room, I can sense my class-mates are expecting a show. The physics teacher takes a deep breath and asks, with Pamela interpreting, "*Are we all good today?*"

"*Probably,*" I answer, not wanting to give my interpreter the satis-faction of voicing a *yes*.

Waiting for class to begin, Pamela pulls out a bright-colored flyer from her bag. "*I saw this earlier,*" she signs, leaning forward to drop it on my desk. It's for the school's ASL club, which has its first meeting of the year this afternoon. I didn't realize they had one here. Madison didn't think to mention that? "*I know it's hard when things change. I thought you might find some new friends there.*"

Is this supposed to be a gesture of goodwill? I might be more open to considering it a nice act if I weren't so keen to hold a grudge.

When school ends for the day, I'm exhausted. Plus, I had to endure a meeting with Ms. Lily during study hall to make sure all my credits had transferred over correctly. But since I don't want to go home yet, I'm desperate enough to check out that ASL club. No one at Amber has approached me trying to sign, as intro ASL students often do in public, so I'm not sure how many people I expect to find there.

I peer into the math classroom where the meeting is held. There's a bunch of hearing students, mainly freshmen and sophomores, chatting and ignoring the VOICE OFF message scrawled in big letters on the whiteboard. I'm about to turn around and leave when the teacher waves for my attention from across the room, where she's been rearranging chairs into a circle.

"*Hey, you're new! And Deaf?*" the cheery young Black woman in jeans and a Cincinnati Bengals shirt asks, hurrying over. "*I'm S-h-a-y,*" she signs, also supplying her sign name, an S clearly positioned for the dimples she has when she smiles.

"*Yes.*" I realize the familiarity in her movements even though she isn't wearing any hearing devices. "*And you are, too? Whew!*"

"*We're good.*" She smiles wide, understanding my relief. I introduce myself as well, and then she gives a subtle nod to the others. "*Most of them aren't conversational yet, but we'll get there soon.*"

A student walks over to ask Shay something, but when they don't sign, she simply points to the policy on the board, reminding them not to speak. "*Sorry, sorry,*" the student signs apologetically but then seems stumped as to what to do next. They turn to me and sign, slowly and stilted, "*You're. Really. Fast.*"

"*I mean, I already know ASL,*" I respond at my typical speed.

"*A-S-L,*" the student signs, nodding enthusiastically and gesturing toward my ears. "*Deaf!*"

"*Yes.*" I'll try to be nicer because I do appreciate the attempt.

Once Shay gets the club situated, opening with a round of new vocabulary for the week—holidays and weather—she has them break off into pairs. And I get to hang with her for a bit—two Deafies shooting the breeze. Shay takes the teacher's chair, so I sit on the desk.

"*I was a student at Amber a few years ago,*" Shay signs. "*They didn't have an ASL club then. I had to both found and teach it.*"

"*That's annoying,*" I sign, chopping my hand into the opposite between my thumb and index finger. It doesn't surprise me that she had to be the one who went through all that effort. They'd hire teachers for foreign language classes, yet Shay had to fight just to get a club for ASL started.

"*But we got enough interest that, when I graduated, they hired me on part-time to keep it going. You know, their diversity initiatives and all.*"

"*Seems a nice enough job.*" I nod toward the board, where she'd added notes from her lesson. "*Plus, you're good at teaching it. Not everyone has that skill.*"

Shay beams. "*And now it's more fun that we can chat together! Let me guess; are you coming from Brandview?*"

I raise my hands, theatrically shaking them to convey my upset before signing, "*I only had one more year.*"

"*That's awful. I was always so jealous and wanted to go there. But my parents chose mainstreamed, which, whatever.*" She shrugs.

"*My hearing sister just graduated from here. Seems like she never came to the club . . .*" I emphasize my skepticism, giving side-eye as I scrunch my fingers outward twice, signing *vee-vee.*

"*That!*" Shay tosses the Y shape down, in complete understanding of my family dynamics.

It's great hanging out while everyone else practices their ASL. I can tell they are all trying to figure out what we're discussing, but none are advanced enough yet to keep up.

"*I don't really know any Deaf here in town,*" I admit.

"*We can change that. There's a small group of us taking classes at ACC now. You know?*" she asks, making sure I'm familiar with Amber Community College. "*You should come meet up sometime.*"

"*Definitely!*"

I'll never admit it to Pamela, but I'm glad to have found this club and Shay. Maybe I'll be able to make it through this year if I can carve out one little space in this school where I can be myself. I don't want to seem desperate, but I really hope I'll get to hang out with Shay and her Deaf friends.

Out of the corner of my eye, I notice someone at the door. It's Jackson, that kid who knew my sister and said he'd tutor me.

Ugh, what does he want?

He walks into the room wearing one of those dark zip-up jackets I've noticed several other athletes wearing, with yellow stripes down the side and a small Amber logo on the front.

To my surprise, Jackson notices the VOICE OFF sign and immediately abides by it. He avoids eye contact but steps closer, and closer, until he's only a few feet away from me. His hand gives a small shake as he scrambles to type something on his phone. Is he nervous?

As much as I hate to admit it, it is kind of cute watching him squirm. He's tall and lanky—tan from whatever sport he plays in the sun—with dark eyes and unkempt light brown hair. Jackson sways a little as he holds out his message to Shay. She smiles and flashes me a knowing look before teaching him the ASL for the sentence he'd written down.

"*I*," she demonstrates, and he copies. "*Give.*"

A flush rises at my cheeks, and I'm not entirely sure why. I turn away and pull out my phone. If I ignore whatever's going on, then maybe it won't involve me. I'm not registering anything I scroll past on the screen, though.

After he's learned whatever he asked Shay to teach him, Jackson waves for my attention. He's standing there with a goofy, lopsided grin.

"*I have give-you tour school not-yet.*" He looks unsure of himself as he has to use his mouth and tongue for the *not yet* sign, but he powers through.

I'm starting to smile. I can't let a hearing boy get to me this easily.

CHAPTER SIX

Jackson

"*–YET,*" I SIGN, watching as Ellie fights a smile. I must look ridiculous. When I asked the instructor for this sentence, I didn't realize I'd have to use my freaking tongue? To shake my head with my mouth open wide so my tongue can rest up against my teeth. I close it, eager to move on. "*Can I show-you soon?*" I ask, finishing strong.

The other students are all staring at us. I'm sensing some jealousy that I'm not even in the club but I'm getting to sign with the Deaf girl. If you can call what I did signing. Ellie hadn't been in study hall today, but when I passed by this classroom and saw her sitting there on the teacher's desk up front, laughing and smiling with the ASL club teacher, something came over me. She seemed happy, and I wanted a second chance to win her over. Enough people at this school are mad at me. I don't want the new girl to be, too.

Ellie's still sitting there, head tilted, staring at me. By now, the grin on her face is really betraying the serious look she's trying to put on.

She bites her lip and signs something casually, lowering her eyebrows and tapping her thumb and index fingers together on each hand.

Hmm, that isn't one of the eight words I know. The instructor is watching me like I'm a kid trying something far out of my league. So no help there.

Then Ellie laughs as she slips off the desk. She walks straight toward me and holds out her hand. It takes me a second to realize what she's asking for. I dig my phone out of my pocket and give it to her.

She's writing something on the notes app. There's a small twitch in my leg that I chalk up to uncertainty. This might have been too showy. Should I have waited for study hall tomorrow?

Ellie hands me back my phone. I half expect to see some sort of "get lost" message.

But instead, it's her number.

She matched a move I hadn't even realized I'd made. Now it's my turn to restrain my expressions. I whisper the word *okay* and give a quick nod.

After I wave goodbye and thank the instructor for her help, I slip out of the classroom. Half not wanting to overstay my welcome in the ASL club, half not wanting more opportunity to embarrass myself in front of Ellie.

Before going home, I make my way down to the gym for a quick workout. The soccer team has optional conditioning sessions most days after school.

Walking down the hall, I find myself clapping my hands together, repeating the signs. "*School.*" Two fingers trailing through the air. "*Tour.*"

Someone turns the corner and walks by, so I reach up to grip my backpack straps, acting like I wasn't just talking to myself. It could be good to learn—to help folks like Ellie, and probably for college applications and all.

Since, well, I've got her number now, it's probably best to figure out more of this ASL thing.

I climb the narrow set of stairs to the weight room, which is on a second-floor balcony that overlooks the basketball courts. There's a volleyball practice going on down there. Of course, Liam is leering over the edge of the rail, watching the girls play. Some of the other soccer guys are in the corner, spending more time on their phones than exercising.

While I do a few quick stretches, my cousin breaks off from the group to join me at a bench. "Good to see you here," Darius says while loading the other side of the bar for a warm-up set. "You're officially allowed to join us for offseason training now?"

"Pretty sure. Coach only mentioned skipping the summer, so I don't see why not." I lie on the bench and reach for the bar. Still adjusting my grip, I admit, "You're all doing club soccer in the offseason, yet I'm stuck sitting out because registration was due before my legs seemed better. I don't know what to do with all this free time."

"Right, soccer is life."

I lift the bar, hold for a moment, and bring it down to my chest. *One.* I push the weight up and, ten reps later, rerack the bar. I shake out my arms, feeling really in my element. Maybe I'll keep up with the others despite missing the team's summer workouts.

"You're in a good mood, though," Darius comments.

"Happy to be back," I say, though my cousin's look is clearly pressing for more. I sit up on the bench, adding, "And, um, well, Ellie just gave me her number."

"*Her* number? Ooooh, dude." He claps his hands together, then stops. "Wait, who is Ellie, though? Do I know her?"

I stand, trying to act casual. Has it really been forever since I went out with someone? "The new girl who—"

"Oh." He leans back, dipping his chin down. "The crazy one."

"I wouldn't say *crazy*." I hold up a finger and start to ramble. "Also, I don't think we're supposed to say the word *crazy* anymore—"

"You know," Darius cuts me off again, "she's kinda cute if you can deal with all that. And you haven't gone out since, what, freshman homecoming with Rachel—if that even counts?"

"Nah, that was junior-year homecoming. Stop acting like I haven't dated."

"Mm-hmm . . ." He stares me down. The gold chain he always wears rests over his sleeveless top. Sure, my cousin's relationship status changes more often than I can keep track of, but that doesn't mean I haven't dated enough. Darius just has the sort of energy and aloofness that seems to effortlessly draw in girls—whereas *effortless* has probably never been an attribute of mine.

"Give me a break. I've been busy. If I'd known you were gonna roast me, maybe I would've skipped and done homework instead," I joke.

Darius scoffs. "You always get good grades. You could do a little of my homework if you want. Do you know how many pages I'm going to have to read for Advanced Lit every week?"

"It's not my fault you signed up for it. Have fun with that while I do a three-sentence poem for my creative writing class."

"What a joke. I should switch into that." He adjusts his hair tie and sits on the bench.

"Gotta balance my AP Chem workload somehow."

"All right, all right." Darius knocks out his ten reps easily, then jumps up to head over to the weight plates. "What's on there already? Fifteens?"

"Yeah, plus the bar. Next let's add a pair of twenty-fives," I call out. "And keep building to a one-rep max."

Arms at his sides, Darius carries the plates over, swinging one up for me to grab to load onto the other side of the bar. I grip the top with my right hand, but it slips from my grasp when he lets go.

I save it easily with my other hand as if I'd intended to do so. But my toes were in danger of being crushed for a second there. Instinctively I search the room to see if anyone else noticed. I stretch out my palm, wondering why it betrayed me. The guys are all on their phones, of course, and Liam is still creeping on the volleyball team.

Almost dropping something. That could happen to anyone. I caught it. All good; nothing to see here.

I can't let myself get bothered about every little thing. It was my legs that were the problem, and now they're completely fine. Like, I could go out and run ten miles right now. I *should* go for a run. I've got to get out of my head.

"Wanna do a couple laps after this?" I ask Darius while clipping the weight into place.

"You know," he says, nodding back to the guys in the corner, "if you hadn't shown up, today would've been an easy day. Like, super easy. Coach isn't even here."

"So you don't want to?" I grin, knowing what's coming next. Because Darius is always game.

"I'm good for it. I'm just saying I could've been lazy."

"Nah, this summer was torture. I can't be doing lazy."

I hate getting knocked down. I'm someone who needs to be constantly moving, be doing something—*anything*. All summer, even when I wasn't supposed to be exercising, I found something to do. Because on the days when I didn't and was home from vacation with nothing else going on, what was left? Being alone. General restlessness. And a ton of depression naps. (Not that I'd admit those to anyone.)

I wake up the next morning feeling like I got hit by a truck.

What is this strange achy exhaustion?

Wiping the crust from my eyes, I roll out of bed and manage my morning sit-ups, but they're *rough*. I take a warm shower, hoping that will help me feel better, but it does the opposite. Now I'm so tired it's difficult to keep my eyes open. If I were anyone else, maybe I'd try to call in a sick day.

But I'm the guy who brings home the perfect attendance award every year. I know that's kind of cringey, and it's definitely not something I go bragging about. Yet, at the same time, it would suck to break the streak at this rate.

Anyway, a nurse would take one look at me and think I'm clearly not sick, assuming I'm faking to get out of school.

Maybe I pushed myself too far yesterday. It didn't feel like it at the time, but maybe my body isn't ready to jump back into the usual routine. It's annoying how quickly we lose muscles if we're not using them. Which is *exactly* why I didn't want a forced break all summer. After the coastal hikes, I should've hit the hotel gym with my parents, but I hadn't wanted to let on that the elevated climbs somehow left me more tired than it did them. I'm going to have to fight to get back my gains.

I get to school all right, but everything still feels a little *off*. Even though my legs aren't exactly sore, I'm walking slowly. Like I'm fighting through the air to get where I want to go.

During first period, I zone out through most of the AP Chemistry lecture. Mr. Miller is going over the chapter he assigned as homework.

I read the pages last night, but it's like nothing got absorbed. Quietly I flip through the textbook, trying to refresh my memory. Especially because Mr. Miller is the type of teacher who calls on people randomly.

"A mole is an important unit of measurement." Mr. Miller writes $6.02214076 \times 10^{23}$ on the board. "Who can tell me what this number is called?"

Oh, that's an easy one. It's Avogadro's number. Whew, good thing I've already got the answer if he calls on me.

"Jackson." But then Mr. Miller keeps rambling with his question. "It converts between the mass of a substance in grams and the relative atomic mass. So, what do we refer to this by?"

Shit. What was the name? I *just* had it. On the tip of my tongue. I literally just had it.

Crossing his arms, Mr. Miller pushes me for an answer. He takes his class very seriously and is quick to get strict. "We're waiting, Jackson . . ."

"Please come back to me later," I say, sitting stiff as I stare ahead.

"It's the name of the *number*." Mr. Miller won't let me go despite my struggling here. I flip back a page in the textbook, trying to quickly find it. "Don't look it up," he snaps.

"I'm sorry." I shrug, not knowing what to do. I lost the answer.

"This is why we do the homework, class. You must come prepared. Otherwise, I don't think you're worth a spot in my advanced section." Mr. Miller gestures to me specifically. "Last year, Jackson was one of my best students. But skip the homework and see how easy it is to look like one of the stupidest."

Shit. I could evaporate on the spot. Gritting my teeth, I'm surprised how offended I feel. I'm *not* stupid. Am I not allowed to have a bad day? Not in Mr. Miller's class, apparently.

My other classmates seem to be shrinking in their seats as well, worried they could be the next victim. I'm still racking my brain for the answer, but it vanished into a black hole.

"Anyone else?" Mr. Miller asks, tapping his foot. "Or should we do a pop quiz to make sure you all did the reading?"

Someone behind me nervously calls out, "Avogadro's."

Right, that's what it was.

The bell couldn't ring fast enough. I'm ready for this day to be over, and thankfully, I manage to keep a low profile in the rest of my morning classes.

I need to think of some other excuse to avoid the soccer guys at lunch again today. Yesterday was a real low: I circled the cafeteria and ended up hiding out in the bathroom. I'm sure their jokes will blow over soon, but honestly, I'm embarrassed about the whole thing. I let them down.

I swing by the student council room. Though I've never run for office, I'm support staff, and there's always something I can take on. I find a stack of orange flyers promoting this weekend's 5K fundraiser, one of the events I help organize every year. We have a good number of sign-ups, but this will encourage last-minute joiners and remind everyone to show up this Saturday. There's a note on the stack that says they need to go up Wednesday, so I grab them.

I stroll through the hallway and stop every fifteen feet or so when there's a good spot. Holding the stack of papers in my arm, I rip a few small pieces of tape, then put up each poster.

After several of these, my arms start to get annoyed with me. Must be sore from yesterday, I'm pretty sure. Though I do need to sit down. It's lunch, after all. I must be hungry. I'll feel better after I eat something.

I'm near my own locker, so I sit on the floor in front of it, eating a quick bite. When a teacher walks by, I just gesture to the flyers stacked beside me, and they continue past.

My parents are big on philanthropy, donating to every school fundraiser, mostly because they get a kick out of writing a very large check to boost my name to the very top of the donor list. Not that they truly feel passionate about the cause or care what the prize is. They just appreciate the way people fawn over them to thank them for their generosity. Do they actually care about cancer or ALS or—I glance at the flyer—MS? Not really.

Ugh, I should get back up. There are too many posters. I'll have to keep working on these during study hall, too. Crap . . . which is probably when I should give Ellie a tour. We never actually set a time or anything.

I just put up a flyer next to one for the sign language club that has an illustration demonstrating how to sign the word *learn* on it. That's something I could text Ellie. I hold out my phone and sign with my right hand, drawing my fingers up to my forehead. I make sure to keep the poster in frame so she understands where I got the inspiration for this.

JACKSON:

> How about the tour during study hall tomorrow?
> I'll try to LEARN some more by then.

I attach the video and hit send before I can second-guess myself. Did I really need to record myself probably totally messing up that sign?

I'm in the middle of putting up my next poster when she replies.

ELLIE:

> Sounds good
> And close enough

I smile. I wouldn't have expected any other response.

CHAPTER SEVEN

Ellie

MY PARENTS INSIST I join them for dinner again tonight. I oblige, rather than hoarding snacks in my room or coming downstairs for cold food once they've finished eating. They must have run out of things to talk about without Madison here.

There's a big bowl of some Instant Pot dish, but I go straight to the fridge to grab lunch meat for a sandwich instead. The kitchen table is long and rectangular, with three of the chairs typically gathered to one end, while the fourth chair is all the way on the other side. That's where I always sit, far away from the others.

Cheese sits at my feet, eager for any food I can spare. He's especially enticed by the turkey, though that makes him the gassiest. I'm looking down at him, while eating my sad little meal, as Mom says something. I don't look up. Dad clears his throat loudly but doesn't respond.

"Ellie, please," my mom says, voice raised. "You can't be this miserable all the time."

"*I don't know; can't I?*" I mope, signing one-handed while taking another bite.

"This is exactly—" Mom turns her entire body away from me, continuing her complaining to my dad. "She always—" *Something, something, something.*

Boring.

Mom faces me again. "Maybe we never should've sent you to that school."

This we can agree on. "Exactly, I don't want to be there. Just let me drop out. I can take online classes or—"

"No. That's not that." She purses her lips into a tight, straight line. "I meant Brandview."

Those are fighting words. I narrow my eyes, hinging my head forward. My parents don't exactly know the facial movements of ASL, but they can understand that I'm upset.

"It was hard being the only Deaf kid at school. Going to Brandview was the best option," I try to explain.

"You weren't like *this*," my mom says, waving a hand toward me, "before going there. You could sit at the dinner table and have a decent conversation."

"A decent conversation?" My phone buzzes in my pocket. I ignore it. Full of rage, I stare down my mother. "A *decent* conversation?"

I've never been an active participant in family dinners. Ever. Madison was the star of the show, eager to fill any silence with lengthy stories about her own life. The three of them would chatter and speak over each other, always leaving me in the dust. Whenever I was home for holidays or break, it was like I was a guest in their home and not another member of the family. I don't know what fantasy my mom is making up in her head, but dinner was never an idyllic mealtime situation.

At least, not for me.

"Decent, where you'd speak to us and participate in conversation, not hide behind those hand gestures." Mom puts her utensils beside her plate and crosses her arms.

"It's a language," I correct her. My parents nod along, not contradicting but not fully understanding me. I smirk, signing what I really want to say. "*Stop being such an asshole about it—and yeah, I'll sign that right to your face.*"

My mom doubles down on her argument. "I know French, but you don't see me using a language no one else at the table understands."

Dad leans back as if subconsciously conveying that he's not in full agreement with her line of reasoning. I stare straight down across the table at the both of them.

"That sounds like a *you* problem," I say. "If you bothered to learn—"

"I didn't get any sort of contract that said that was a requirement of being a mom."

"No, you just gave birth to a Deaf kid."

"Eleanor," Mom says, "we've been over this. It's fine to know sign, but you don't need all that."

Dad steps in, trying to bring his rational approach to things, but instead makes it all so much worse. "It's helpful, of course, but you know, you're not *deaf* like that."

It all comes down to this. The nagging point that must've been lurking in the back of my parents' brains all these years. The fact that I'm not the kind of child they wanted.

Mom winces at my inscrutable expression and extends a hand down the table toward me. "We don't mean it like . . ." She trails off.

Softly I ask, "Like what, exactly?"

My father takes a deep breath and sits up straight. "You know we always wanted what's best for you. And we never stood in your way."

"We were happy for all you got to learn at Brandview," my mom says.

Dad agrees. "We would never stop you from having that experience."

"I just sometimes *wish*," Mom continues, attempting to choose her words carefully now that they've dug such a deep hole, "that all of that hadn't come at the expense of you being away from us for so long."

"Right." I roll my eyes. *Like that would have changed anything.* At least with living away from here, I could sometimes forget my constant resentment. "Well, thanks for another fantastic evening being back home." I stand and take my plate to the sink. "Really makes me think of all the great nights I must've missed while I was gone."

Dad says something as I walk away, but I don't bother. I did my part by showing up. It's not my fault the dinner went that way.

If I were younger, I would've stormed off, screaming, stomping up the stairs, and slamming the bedroom door shut. Well, sort of like I did the other night. But instead, I move slowly. To let them know that they can't get to me anymore.

I close the door to my room softly and slump to the ground against it. I need to plan a way out of here. Soon.

My phone vibrates again.

I finally check it and find a follow-up text from Jackson.

JACKSON:

> Sorry, that was kinda dorky. I meant for the video to be funny, but now I'm thinking it was really weird. I'm just really getting into this for some reason.

Above it is another video message like the one he sent earlier today. I was curious when he was missing from study hall, wondering when we were supposed to do a tour. This time, he's learned the word *spaghetti*, demonstrating the curling movements with his pinkies while slurping an actual strand of pasta.

Why *is* he suddenly interested in learning ASL? It probably won't last long. People are always so eager in the beginning, but eventually, if they don't have any sort of personal connection (or even if they do), they lose the initial interest and dip out.

ELLIE:

Nice, that looks better than my dinner

He responds fast.

JACKSON:

Oh no, what'd you have?

ELLIE:

A sandwich and an argument

He's typing another message. Then stops. Yeah, that was a difficult text to respond to. He's trying to be friendly, and I'm giving him absolutely nothing to go on here.

I'm half hoping that he's looking up a quick bit of ASL to respond with another video. I try to come up with something to casually double text, just to soften my last message and seem more approachable. But it's been too long since my last message, and now it doesn't seem right to send a follow-up. I'm hoping he'll still reply.

And yet there's not another text from him tonight.

Since the weather's nice today, I wish I could spend lunch outside, but Amber High doesn't let students leave the building during the school day. I'm alone at a far corner table in the cafeteria, reading some dry thriller that's not the least bit thrilling. Still, I jump when I realize someone is standing beside me saying something. It's Jackson.

Are we doing the tour now? He'd said study hall in his text, right? I already know where all my classes are and don't really care to learn much more about Amber High. "Is Ms. Lily making you do this . . ." I say bluntly. Maybe I should've led with a *hey* or something.

Jackson waits for me to look up from my lunch again before speaking, starting with something about "making me do this." Did he say *is* or *isn't*? "But I don't want to bother you if you'd rather—" He gestures to the book I've put down.

"That's okay."

I pack up my food, close my book, and stand—then look down to see Jackson has sat and opened his lunch box.

"Um." Jackson is flustered. "If you didn't want me to . . ." He trails off, mumbling.

"Oh, we're eating first?" I realize my mistake. Now it's my turn to feel awkward. I take a seat again and lift the plastic flap off my microwaveable soup that still has the spoon inside. "And then the tour during study hall?"

"Yeah." He takes a long sip of water. Jackson's lunch is meal-prepped chicken and rice with a side of veggies and a bag of kettle chips. Before he dives into anything, I try to insist that he doesn't need to be here. He's more than fulfilling his obligations to help the new student, and he doesn't have to sit with me just because I'm all alone at lunch. Like, yes, he's nice, and I'm surprisingly enjoying his company, but I don't want it if it's coming from a place of pity.

"Really, I'm fine by myself. I don't want to keep you from your friends." The next part slips out of my mouth before I remember we do not have this level of familiarity yet. "That is, if you have any."

Half his mouth curls into an uncertain grin. "The checks must have stopped clearing." That was a joke, I think. An attempt to level out the rather rude statement I just made. He's still saying something as he nods toward a group of guys sitting a few tables down.

Some of them are wearing similar athletics jackets to the one I've seen Jackson sport.

"You're usually there?" I ask.

It's impossible to know what he's saying. My hearing aid and cochlear implant are no match for the raucous cafeteria. Even when the technology tries to autofocus on what's in front of me, I don't get a clear picture, especially because Jackson and I are sitting side by side and not across from each other, which means I have to keep turning to read his lips.

My resting bitch face now has an added "I can't tell what the hell is going on" frown to it. It's definitely going to scare Jackson away.

I hope it doesn't.

"My teammates," he says, facing me now. "They've been the worst lately."

"Oh, really?"

He opens a small Tupperware of green beans. "I don't know if I should tell you this . . ."

I wait, impatiently, but he doesn't continue. "Now you kind of have to," I pry.

"That one"—Jackson points to the preppy-looking guy dominating the conversation between players—"seems to be the one who started the, well, rumor."

My eyes narrow. I hate that I know what's coming.

"That you were faking, um . . ." Jackson's jaw tightens.

I save him from having to explain further. "I figured. The way people were staring at me after that shit class."

"I'm sorry."

"Why are you sorry? 'Cause you're friends with him?"

Jackson laughs. "Um, not really." He then starts telling me something about a soccer match—but his words are going a mile a minute, like he'd rather not be sharing this. There's "and after the game," "I tripped," and "cost us" somewhere in his story. Jackson takes a deep breath, ending with "They don't seem to want me around right now."

"Oof. Well." I try to come up with something reassuring. "You're better off not being around an ableist jerk anyway."

"A what?" It's Jackson's turn to question what he heard from something I've said.

"Ableist. You know, someone who discriminates against disabled people."

"That makes sense."

"The type of person who spews some crap and doesn't understand that anyone can become disabled at any time." I instinctively reach out to sign one-handed, flicking my middle finger out from against my thumb. "*Awful.*"

Jackson's eyes go wide.

"I don't mean that as, like, a threat," I clarify, realizing that, to non-disabled people, what I just said could be construed as fairly morbid. "Just a fact of life."

"Yeah," he says, his voice low. He mumbles something else. "I mean, we all get old eventually," he concludes.

"That, too." I'm not sure he fully gets my point, but I won't belabor it.

"If I hear people bringing up that nonsense rumor again, I'll tell them to cut it out. I wasn't sure if I should let you know, but I thought, if it were me, I'd want to be aware."

Maybe it's better that I know, but it stings all the same. "I'm not sure it'll help you with the team to be seen sitting with me, then."

He waves a hand like it's nothing. After finishing a few bites of his chicken, he says something about "bigger dreams out there."

"Like what?"

"Studying business at—" he says, losing me at the college name, then mentions something about joining his dad's company, which I think he says was founded by his grandpa, and another tidbit I miss entirely.

"Wow, it's all planned out. Are those your dreams or your parents'?"

He's taken aback, like he's never considered this. "Both, I think."

"What'd you say the family business was?"

"Manufacturing plastics." Jackson shrugs, clearly not passionate about this at all. "My dad is trying to be more hands-off these days, but he has a hard time stepping back. Until he hands it over to me one day, I guess."

"And what? You're, like, the heir to this plastics company? The prince of plastics?"

I'm delighted when he laughs, an amused, full-chest response. "Please never call me the prince of plastics ever again," he says. "But what about you?"

"My plans?"

I honestly haven't thought that far ahead. I'm still in my whole "re-configuring my future" stage. When you've got everything plotted out and it blows up in your face, it makes you hesitant to commit yourself to too many future endeavors. "First things first, I'm counting down my days here, for sure."

"And where were you before this?"

"Brandview. It was a Deaf school. So, like, classes in ASL and such."

"That's cool." His response is neutral. "I bet it was hard leaving your friends."

I shrug with indifference. But the more I think about it, who was I actually close to there? Since breaking up with Cody, no one has been in touch. I lost our shared friends in the breakup. They were more his than mine, apparently. I probably should've spent time with other people, like my roommate, Kayla. I wonder how she's doing living at home now.

"The worst part is being back with my parents," I admit. "They were happy to ship me off to the Deaf institute, but now that I'm back here, they act like all the years they missed while I was away were *my* fault."

Jackson listens intently. "I get that. My parents—" he says, talking about his own gripes, and I miss most of what he says next. I wish I'd been able to hear more about the "multipage Christmas-card letter," though. He asks me another question about my old school.

What did I like doing? I think that's what it was.

"Hmm, my boyfriend and I," I start to say, and Jackson's attempt to disguise his reaction doesn't slip my notice. "I mean, *ex*-boyfriend." I hold up the letter *X* for emphasis, unsure if Jackson knows the ASL alphabet. "Still not quite used to that one."

"Right." There's transparent relief in his eyes. Why does that make my stomach flutter? "Yeah, that can be tricky."

"Well." I push forward, realizing most of what I have to say about my time at Brandview involves Cody. "We'd hang out on the grounds. There was a lot of space to spend time outside. I hate that we can't do that here. It's claustrophobic to be stuck indoors all this time."

"I wish that wasn't a rule," Jackson agrees. "It's pretty packed in here."

"And *noisy*," I say, also signing for emphasis.

A realization dawns over him. "Have you been hearing what I'm saying? I'd hate it if I was rambling about," he says, along with *something, something, something,* "and you were just being polite?"

I shake my hand side to side, like so-so. Most people wouldn't think to ask, so I appreciate that. "A quieter spot would make a huge difference."

"I can try that! Ms. Lily could—" He continues his thought, but I'm out of the loop again.

"What was that?" I ask.

"Get us lunch somewhere else," he repeats, signing *lunch* in the L shape circling by his mouth.

Smiling, I suggest an alternative version of the sign that he's less likely to accidentally sign as something else. "Or like *eat-noon*," I say while demonstrating. "But really?"

"If you'd want. You wouldn't have to talk to me every day, or anything like that, if you don't want to." He fidgets with his fingers. "Somewhere you can read more comfortably and I can avoid the soccer table for a while longer."

"Honestly, that sounds great."

CHAPTER EIGHT

Jackson

ALTHOUGH IT STARTED awkwardly, lunch with Ellie was nice. She's easier to talk to than I would've thought, in the *we could have more in common than I would've expected* kind of way, since I'm not sure how much of my talking she was able to hear. I think I'm drawn to Ellie because she's the only other senior who is out of place this year.

We swing by our lockers during passing period to drop off lunch boxes and grab books for our next classes. Once the hallways clear out, we've got all of study hall for this tour. And I have *no idea* what to show her.

"These are the labs," I say, walking backward, gesturing over my shoulder to the stretch of rooms behind me. My sneakers squeak across the linoleum flooring. Then I stumble but catch myself before I fall. Might be easier to take a sidestep approach instead. "All the science equipment. If you were a prospective student, I'd have to brag about the microscopes and Bunsen burners, since they were new at one point, but that was a few years ago."

Ellie nods through my rambling. She points to one of the closed doors beside us where we can see the teacher lecturing through the window. "That's my physics classroom." Rolling her eyes, she adds, "Which they're making me retake, since something about that course didn't transfer."

"That sucks." Well, there's no reason to linger in this science corridor. I backtrack and lead us around to where we can go to the second floor.

Approaching the stairwell, Ellie stops. "I've got English and history up there."

"Of course." With a slow nod, I say, "You already know where those are. Not getting lost or anything?"

"No." Ellie gives a sympathetic smile. "It's not that big of a school."

"We could go down by the gym?" Which she also already knows about because of PE class. Fortunately, a better idea comes to me. "Or actually, the library."

"I've been there, too," Ellie teases me, but she eagerly rushes down the hall with me.

I pull open the double doors. "There's something you probably haven't seen yet," I say, too loudly, as we walk past the checkout desk. The librarian gives us a friendly but pointed look. I turn back to Ellie, whispering, "We'll need to be quiet."

Ellie smirks and responds to me in ASL.

I offer a sheepish thumbs-up. "What's the sign for this place?" I whisper. When she moves an *L* in a circle, I go, "Oh, almost like one of those signs for *lunch*. That's a little confusing."

The small library has a welcoming vanilla scent emanating from the tall stacks of wooden bookshelves that have been here longer than we've been alive. The new carpeting's initial chemical odor has finally faded. There are a couple students here doing homework at the long rectangular tables near the new YA display.

What I want to show Ellie is on a ledge along the wall. The windows above don't have an amazing view—it's just the parking lot—but they let in plenty of light to help four little planters of marigolds grow inside this otherwise dim place.

"I know it's not the outdoors," I say to Ellie as we both lean against the counter, "but you can smell some flowers here."

Smell some flowers here? I'm being so cringe it hurts.

Ellie is sweet about it, though. "This is nice," she says sincerely, looking from the marigolds to the sky outside. The sun shines across her freckled cheeks and lights up her eyes.

"I should've started the tour here." Unaware of the time, I'm caught off guard when the bell rings. "Wow, the period is over."

"Already?" she asks.

We wasted so much of the time wandering around the hallways that this stop flew by in a flash. I reluctantly lead us out of the library and back into the hall. "Well, I think we've established you know your way to your classes. What do you have next?"

"AP English. Are you headed that way?"

"Yes," I say, so relieved she was the one to ask that I fall into step with her before remembering that my calc class is on the other side of the building. "Maybe tomorrow we—"

I reach my hand out and catch a locker door that someone threw open before it hits Ellie in the face, since she'd been reading my lips rather than watching where she was going.

"Ope, sorry!" the student calls out as we speed past him.

"Good catch," Ellie says, grateful. A few paces later, we come to a stop at the English room. "Thanks."

"Yeah, I'll, um, see you later."

As soon as she enters her classroom, I haul across the school, moving as fast as I can without running, and slide into my desk with only a second to spare.

The following week, I'm helping in the student government office because it's all hands on deck during free periods to gear up for elections. There are ballots to print, the voting box to assemble, and candidate speeches to schedule. I'll never run myself, since I prefer to stay behind the scenes.

With all those activities and my course load getting heavy and after-school soccer workouts, I've been swamped. By the time I'm home every day, I need to crash for a nap before I can manage homework. Then I end up lying awake in bed the rest of the night, only to repeat it all the next day.

Which means it's not until next Friday after school, while I'm waiting for my EasyRide in the parking lot, that I run into Ellie again. I'm staring at the phone screen when she taps my shoulder gingerly.

"Are you avoiding me?" she asks, with the confidence to know that's not the case. I don't think anything could faze her. Her hair is styled differently today, wrapped into a braided bun, though some strands have broken free after a long day of classes. She's getting more settled in here, hopefully feeling more at ease now than during her difficult start at AHS.

"Sorry, I've been busy." Knowing that could be construed as an excuse, I add, "Really."

"I know, I saw you sitting at that voting table today during lunch with those student government kids."

She noticed me? "I don't remember seeing you."

Ellie squints in the afternoon sun. "Maybe I should've stopped by to say hi."

"Yes, that or, you know, to vote in a *very* important election that's not at all a high school popularity contest," I joke. I understand that, starting at a new school senior year, she has very little incentive to care about Amber High student government.

"Does that make me a terrible person if I didn't?" she says playfully. "Don't worry; I intend to cast my ballot for non–Amber High elections, I promise. I care about the world, just not the theme for a prom I won't go to."

"You don't think you'll go to prom?" I ask before I can stop myself.

I know it can't just be me feeling this. Is she picking up on the vibes? Because I already have a hunch who I might want to ask in the spring. Ellie looks away, a faint blush on her cheeks. I'm not imagining this, right?

Staring out into the parking lot, she asks, "Are you going somewhere now?"

"Just home."

She glances at my phone, which I'm holding out, keeping track of the driver on the map. "Why are you taking an EasyRide?"

"I don't have a license," I say matter-of-factly, knowing people can have a wide range of reactions to this.

"But you're eighteen, right? And there's no other reason you *couldn't* get one?"

"Nah, I've just always had a ton of other ways to get around, so I never dedicated the time to it."

"If you're going to tease me about not participating in the *very important* student government electoral process," she says with a smirk, calling back to what I said, "then I can definitely give you grief about not having a driver's license yet."

"Fair enough." I don't mind at all.

"It's just—you seem so on top of things. Like the type of person who grows up and thinks filing their taxes or scheduling doctors' appointments is fun. You know? Like you'd be extra eager to get that license so you can run all sorts of errands."

"Let's get one thing straight." I pause for effect. "I'm perfectly happy to let my mom continue to make my dentist appointments forever," I joke, if only slightly. Obviously, one day I'll take care of it on my own, but that doesn't have to be anytime soon.

"I got my license the second I could," Ellie says. "Even if you don't plan on driving yourself most of the time, don't you want to have the option? To be able to get yourself wherever you need to go, not rely on anyone else?"

"When you put it that way. But cars do kind of suck."

"True." She tilts her head, considering this. "I'm ditching mine as soon as we get high-speed rail."

My ride pulls up along the curb, and for a change, I wish the car had taken longer to arrive. "Well, this is me. I'll see you soon," I say, waving goodbye and getting in the sedan, but before the driver pulls away, I roll down my window. Despite all the hectic election preparations this week, there is something else I managed to arrange.

"I forgot to say that I found us a new lunch spot!" I shout as Ellie crosses the lot to her car. "I'll take you there Monday."

"What?" she calls back, hand cupped behind her hearing aid.

The driver does me a solid and slowly passes near her on our way out, so I repeat, "I got us a new lunch spot!"

Ellie smiles. "I was starting to think you'd forgotten about that."

CHAPTER NINE

Ellie

ON MONDAY, I wake up eager to go to Amber High. Something I never thought possible. The contrarian in me doesn't want to admit it, even to myself. I don't snooze my earthquake of an alarm clock five times this morning. Only twice.

But then I arrive at school and remember I have to slog through morning classes with Pamela. The initial catastrophe might have been her first-day jitters or something, because she's been *fine enough*, I guess, but the lingering distaste continues to be mutual. We're professional but not friendly. I know I should be better about trying to hide my obvious preference for working with Kim, but I still can't shake that disastrous first day. It wasn't just my first impression of Pamela. It was also my classmates' first impression of *me*. A major setback at a new school.

During lunch, I'm not sure where to go, but I find Jackson waiting for me near the cafeteria entrance. He's holding his lunch box at his side, scanning the hall as other seniors rush through the doorway while juniors exit.

"Hey," I say, waving for his attention.

"All right!" Jackson gets right to business, motioning for me to walk alongside him. "Okay, it's an *interesting* new lunch spot," he says, swerving to dodge oncoming students. I hop at his heels to do the same. "Don't judge it too harshly."

He leads us to a narrow hallway between the school library and the teachers' lounge, where there's a small circular table with two chairs. I choose the spot facing the hallway, not realizing there'd be plenty of people in front of and behind me, with faculty and staff trafficking in and out of their break room leisurely. Several of them give us strange looks for being here, but no one questions it. At least, not that I can tell.

I notice the door to the lounge is ajar and whisper to Jackson, "Are they saying anything about us being here?"

He scrunches his lips to the side, listening intently, before texting a message out on his phone.

JACKSON:

> Yep, but Ms. Lily's in there, so she keeps being like, "It's the best spot for our new disabled student and her friend. What? Am I supposed to stick two students alone in some classroom? You all know how that ends up going."

"*Right,*" I sign, mouthing my words so he hopefully follows along. "*It's like, if two people are alone, then . . .*" With my index fingers extended, I bring my hands together, motioning like a couple making out, all while emphasizing it with a kissy face. It's super casual, the way I'd gossip with friends.

Yet Jackson's face grows beet red. He's flustered. I forget he's probably not used to such visual descriptions. I drop my hands as another teacher passes by, eyeing us suspiciously.

Jackson's looking off to the side—did he realize I was joking? Or is he still listening to whatever commentary is going on in the teachers' lounge.

"Now what?" I whisper again.

He shakes his head, amused. "Just lots of laughter," Jackson mouths back. Thinking for a moment, he adds in sign, "*I don't know.*"

"*Nice,*" I sign back to him.

"What was that?" Jackson asks, speaking at regular volume now. Being here in the quiet hallway instead of the cafeteria is like night and day.

"Nice," I say, fingerspelling out the word. "*N-i-c-e.*"

"You know I was trying to say 'I don't know,' right?"

I smile encouragingly as I unpack my lunch. "A little stiff, but correct, yeah. The way a lot of beginners look."

"Stiff? How so?"

"You don't need to be a robot. Let your hands move naturally. And you can kind of accent it with however you're feeling, using facial expressions." I demonstrate, making an uncertain face and a small movement for *I don't know*. Then I do it again with a bigger motion, a flare to go along with an angry face. "You see?"

It's strange being the one teaching ASL when, not too many years ago, I was the student. Brandview got me up to speed quickly, but it was Cody who filled in all the missing blanks. Who taught me the slang, the nuance, the beauty of all the different ways my hands could communicate. I used to watch him in awe, jealous that he'd known sign his entire life, while I was still playing catch-up. But after half a decade at Brandview, I left more confident than ever in my abilities— something I worry about losing now that I'm predominantly back in the hearing world.

Sometimes I think I miss Cody.

His physical absence yet lingering presence in my mind is something I need to reckon with. A change of scenery does a lot, but nothing will ever be the same. I hate how something as essential as signing is tinged by his memory. Thinking about what Cody and I had, a lot of what I miss is stuff that comes with any relationship. The closeness. The way the other person can tell what you're thinking just by exchanging a look. The knowing exactly who you want to see and hang out with every day. How do I untangle my life before now from Cody?

Breakups are so confusing.

Because I like sitting here across from Jackson. He's sweet and attentive in a way I've never really experienced before. And he doesn't pretend everything is effortless, like that somehow makes it cool. He pauses for a moment with his hand held up. "*Yes, I understand,*" he signs, a bit looser, taking my feedback into account.

"Whoa, he's got more tricks up his sleeve!" I smile widely, impressed he's been looking things up on his own. Gotta say, good for him. It's the basics, but I hadn't expected him to be working on learning ASL. Let's see if he keeps it up.

"I'm trying, I'm trying." He's clearly pleased with himself. "You never know what I'll come up with next."

CHAPTER TEN

Jackson

DESPITE OUR VERY early start, the sun rises in the sky, bringing the heat during a soccer pickup match Saturday morning. All the running was a lot easier at the beginning when it was cooler out, but by the time we wrap, I'm drained. I can't wait until next semester when we're in season and back in practice mode.

When it's time to go, I pull my shirt over my face to wipe away the sweat and walk around to the front of the school to meet my dad. He parked the SUV along the curb and is standing there waiting for me, arms out to the sides, twisting his torso to crack his back. Dad is wearing fresh athletic shorts and a clean sleeveless shirt, so he hasn't gone to the gym yet, which can only mean one thing.

"Hey, kid. Let's stop at the Box on the way home," he says, hopping in the driver's side.

Despite spending less time at the company these days, Dad is still restless. He decided to fill his late fifties with CrossFit rather than turning to golf like my nonno did. It seems to be the first hobby Dad's ever enjoyed, which is why I don't find his dedication to it utterly ridiculous. I just hope I don't wait that long in life to find something I want to spend my time doing.

I groan and slink into the passenger seat, chugging the last of my lukewarm water from the green reusable Gatorade bottle. "Can you drop me off first?"

"Come on; you're young! Bursting with energy." Dad shakes his head and puts the car in drive. "We need to keep you on your toes."

After listening to a playlist including "Eye of the Tiger" and a few other classic rock songs to hype us up, we pull up to the CrossFit gym, a large brick warehouse with several people from the previous class time still running laps around the building. As Dad maneuvers the SUV carefully to avoid hitting someone, several of his buddies wave hello through the windshield.

In the waiting space inside, Dad begins to stretch. The nearby bench is holding everyone's bags, so I plop to the floor, legs out and back slumped. I don't have the energy to even pretend to be eager for this. On the nearby whiteboard, the WOD—workout of the day—is scribbled out.

It looks rough. One hundred squats. One-thousand-meter row. Half-mile run. Thirty burpees. Today's record time: nine minutes, twelve seconds. *RIP me.*

"Small group," my dad says, nodding toward the two others who have joined us for the class. A dude in his thirties and a woman about sixty. Both regulars. Both about to smoke me in this workout.

"All right, 10:00 a.m., let's go!" the instructor in a tight gray shirt calls out. "Rob, my man," he says, greeting my dad. "Was wondering where you were this morning."

"I thought I'd bring my son with me today." Dad nods toward me. "You all remember Jackson?"

After saying hi to the others, I tell my dad, "Really, I'm exhausted." He usually works out while I'm at my own training. Why today of all days did he think we needed to do this together?

"You got this."

We start with some warm-ups and strength techniques before moving on to the competitive workout. Dad is eager to get the record time today, even though what someone from an earlier class already attained seems impossible to me right now. As the trainer starts the clock, Dad claps while dipping into his first squat. "Let's go!"

My first ten squats are fine. But they continue on and on. Dad knocks his out no problem and moves on to the rowing machine. The woman goes next. It's just me and the other guy remaining.

"Keep it up, man," he says, slapping my back as he, too, runs off to the next station.

I take a deep breath and mutter the count out loud to myself. "Ninety-eight. Ninety-nine. One hundred."

The back and forth of rowing is nauseating. Since I'm on the far end of the line of machines, I try to bump down the resistance when no one is looking. Even with that relief, everyone else moves on to their run long before me.

Pull, release. Pull, release.

"Come on, Jackson!" Dad shouts as he hurries past me to do his half mile outside. The others cheer and holler as well. The counter inches to the one-thousand-meter mark. By the time I let go of the handlebar, they've all returned and are quickly knocking out their burpees. Soon I'll be the only one still going.

I rush out to the parking lot, where no one can see me, and then slow to a jog, planning to cut this short at a quarter mile. Dad would say doing so is only cheating myself, but I don't care. I want to go home. He's probably embarrassed that I'm the last one done anyway.

As I finally stagger back into the Box, Dad calls out, "Let's go, son!" I hobble over to the center of the gym for the final exercise.

Fortunately, the old woman is sitting on the bench mixing a protein shake, but the other guy, my dad, and the trainer are all standing around waiting for me. The worst burpees of my life with three sets of eyes staring at me. I throw myself down to the ground, fully extend my legs, hop back up, then jump.

"One!" the instructor calls out. At least I don't need to remember the count.

By the halfway point, I've given up on form. I just lie down for a brief relief and drag myself back to standing. The smallest of hops.

I'm going to be sick.

But my dad never takes his eyes off me. "Let's go!" he shouts, more commanding than encouraging.

The trainer counts out my final burpees. "Twenty-eight! Twenty-nine! Thirty!"

After the final jump, I sprawl out on the floor again, completely broken. Dad offers a hand to help me up, barely giving me a moment to rest on the floor. "All right, kid. At least you didn't quit," he says in a tone that conveys it wouldn't have been an option. "Good thing you've got months before soccer officially starts back up."

Totally wiped, I'm relieved to get back home. Dad hangs his car keys on the hook, and I immediately go to chug several glasses of water. My stomach rumbles as I scoop almonds from the jar on the counter and grab some chocolate chips from the pantry.

Mom rushes across the living room, shaking her head as she sees me about to sit at the kitchen counter stools. "I've told you, please shower first."

"Right, sorry." I straighten up. "But we're having lunch soon, right?"

"Yes, just something light since we've got that fundraiser dinner tonight."

I definitely need something more than light. "Should I order something later, then?"

She shakes her head. "I bought a plate for you, so you're coming with us. We leave at six."

I trudge upstairs to wash up. The last place I want to go tonight is some fancy dinner. At least I can pass out after lunch for a few hours first.

It would be nice if Mom would ask before committing me to these events, but she likes when all three of us can go. The happy, healthy family there to help "those poor dears," as she'll say multiple times throughout the night, regardless of what the fundraiser is for. It doesn't matter, since all of them are on her social calendar, especially when she's friends with the organizers. I know she feels proud of herself for doing what she can and considers charitable work her job now that I'm grown up.

I check my phone and see a recent text from Ellie.

ELLIE:

> Hey, do you know where I can find quizzes on the AHS portal? I need to do one for AP English and can't find it anywhere.

I type out some instructions, but I'm not sure how clear they are. The whole website is confusing and pretty glitchy.

JACKSON:

> Let me know if that works. Even I'm not doing homework on a Saturday morning

ELLIE:

Just getting it over with

Mom drops by my room carrying a pressed suit, which she hangs on the back of my closet door. "This is for tonight. Any tie will do."

"Okay, thanks."

I take a quick shower and head back downstairs, sitting at the table and absolutely starving as Dad cooks salmon on the stove. I hadn't noticed a second text from Ellie.

ELLIE:

What are you up to?

JACKSON:

I'm considering a nap. My dad made me go work out AFTER a scrimmage set, and now my mom wants to drag me with them to some charity event tonight.

ELLIE:

Double yikes

JACKSON:

I think my parents love the idea of who I *could be* a little too much, probably some instinct to shape a successor in their own image, and all that

ELLIE:

I feel this—my parents definitely wish I was different, more like them

JACKSON:

That would be boring and repetitive

ELLIE:

You don't have siblings, right? Because that's how you get definitive proof that they'd prefer if you were a different way

Mom sets the table as Dad brings over the salmon, green beans, and potatoes. "No phones at mealtime, remember, honey?" she says.

"I'm helping someone with a homework question," I say, quickly sending another text to Ellie. "One second."

JACKSON:

Yeah, but a sibling or two could really deflect some of this constant attention

CHAPTER ELEVEN

Ellie

I THOUGHT THAT, after a little while, Jackson would get bored of hanging out by the teachers' lounge and return to having lunch with the soccer guys. But several weeks later, even though he seems friendlier with some of his teammates when they cross paths, he's still sitting with me every day.

We don't always talk the entire time, but the silence has become comfortable, not awkward.

On Wednesday, I'm spending study hall knitting while Jackson struggles with some calc homework. I stream music to my hearing aid and relax into the repetitive stitches and soft cotton blend.

A few minutes later, Jackson shrugs off his jacket, tossing it over the back of his chair before running a hand through his hair. He frowns at the math worksheet and gives up. "What's that you're making?" he asks me.

Every instinct in me is to downplay my craft. After all, Cody didn't think much of it, always poking fun at my hobby and commitment to leveling up my skills. "I know, I know, I'm such an old lady to be knitting right now."

"No, it's cool. I'm guessing that's a . . ." He glances at the small patch of a soon-to-be-long brown rectangle that I'm only about fifteen rows into. "Pot holder?"

I laugh and nod toward the big ball of yarn that I'm spooling from. "What will eventually become a scarf. I can do more intricate stuff, but this is an easy way to keep my hands busy."

"I wish I knew how to make more things." His warm brown eyes closely watch my next few stitches. "When did you learn how to knit?"

"A couple years ago, mostly from YouTube tutorials. It took a while until I was comfortable with a pattern or freestyling something simple."

"Can you—" he says, asking a question, but I only catch his hesitant smile.

"What?"

"Can you knit me something?" he repeats.

"Really?"

No one has asked me that before. I've given knitting projects as gifts that others seem to accept out of obligation, even though my stuff usually turns out super high-quality if I may say so myself.

"Oh, I mean," Jackson says, backtracking, "you don't have to. It's probably so much work."

"No, no, it's fine. I'll make you something." I'm already debating colors in my head, so Jackson's getting something knit, even if I'm not sure exactly what yet. There's no way I'm making a sweater for another guy anytime soon. "It's just the last person I gave a piece to, well, he totally hated it."

Jackson obviously realizes I'm talking about my ex. "I promise to appreciate it even if it sucks."

"It won't suck!" I hold up my small sample and show it off with a flourish. "I know it's only a few rows so far, but look at this impeccable stitching. What do you want—a scarf? Maybe a hat? Socks?"

"You can do socks?"

I chuckle. "Yeah . . . I can knit socks."

"*Yes, please,*" he signs, with a sweet grin on his face.

CHAPTER TWELVE

Jackson

IT'S A CRISP late-September morning as racers gather outside Amber High for the Running for a Cure 5K. There was a lot of rain yesterday, so fallen leaves are clumped together along the curbside. Participants and spectators gather near the school entrance. There's a couple hundred people here. My parents usually run as well, but Dad had a work convention in California that Mom tagged along for, extending the stay to soak up some warmer weather. I guarantee my dad will check the times posted after the race. Anything to scratch that competitive itch.

Standing beside my cousin, I rub my hands together for warmth. I've got a light jacket on, but it's not glove weather yet.

"Very ready for those doughnuts and hot chocolate after this." Darius glances over his shoulder at the tables waiting to greet everyone by the finish line. "What do you think, thirty minutes or so?"

We'll be starting with the running heat at 8:00 a.m., while walkers hit the road about a half hour later. The course doubles back on itself, so the organizers want to let most of the faster runners clear the route first.

Gently rolling my ankles, I stretch my neck from side to side. "I'm going to break twenty." *Something that my dad won't be able to give me grief about.*

"Really?" Darius asks incredulously. "You want to do a sub-seven-minute mile?"

"Always striving to beat that PR."

A snide laugh comes from behind me. "If your legs are up for it," Liam taunts.

"Shut up," Darius says to him. "You could stand to shave off a few minutes yourself."

The newly elected student government president grabs a microphone and stands beneath the inflatable archway to thank everyone for coming to the race. I twist at the waist, cracking my back. Then the countdown begins. I lean forward, ready to go.

Three.

"Seriously, don't even bother," Liam says, lining up beside me.

Two.

"What? You're not gonna say anything?" he continues.

One.

I leave Liam in the dust.

I'm at the front of the pack, but soon, the fastest runners—the couple cross-country kids who can do a six-minute mile in their sleep—pull into the lead. I may not end up on a podium, but I love race days. With the course marked out, I don't have to think about what route to take. Just put one foot in front of the other, feeling the wind in my face and passing the world by, almost like I'm on autopilot.

We exit the school parking lot, cut through a residential neighborhood, then circle through a nature park, orange leaves falling to the ground around me as I go through.

From the park, the course essentially runs parallel, doubling back through the houses to return to Amber. Which is how I know I'm going to beat Liam by at least five minutes, since I'm passing him entering the park right now as I'm already on my way out.

In the distance, I can see the small crowd of family members and other onlookers are in the high school parking lot, waiting for the walkers to begin. There's a bunch of cheers when the cross-country kids rush toward the finish line. A few minutes later, I increase my pace for a final burst, crossing beneath the archway as the clock reads twenty minutes and thirty-four seconds.

Damn, so close.

I slow to a jog, shaking out my legs.

Now, didn't Darius say there was hot chocolate somewhere? I navigate through the sea of people to find my way to that table. I glance behind me to see if he's back, too, but he must still be running.

Because the number of walkers is easily four times the number of runners, I'm stuck wading through the crowd lining up to begin the course. Craning my neck high, I'm searching for the snack table when someone waves for my attention. It's Ellie.

I smile and jog over to her. "Hey, you're with the walkers? I didn't think this was your kind of thing."

She shifts her weight from one leg to the other, hands resting at her hips on her oversized maroon sweatshirt. "I can get behind a good cause. Also"—Ellie points toward the group of ASL students and their teacher—"I'm trying to get to know Shay better so I can hang out with her and her Deaf friends."

The club is gathered a few feet away. Someone signs something to Ellie *extremely slowly*. I can tell it's testing her patience a bit.

She responds quickly, then turns back to me. "Are you ready to walk?"

"I just finished the run."

She narrows her eyes at the bead of sweat rolling from my forehead. "I was wondering why you were so sweaty."

I jump on the opportunity to hang out with Ellie outside school. "I can walk through the course, too. If you want me t—"

"That'd be great," Ellie says before I've even finished offering.

"Just give me one second." I hold out a finger, then jog away toward the refreshments table, since a path has finally cleared, and return with a maple long john and hot chocolate. "For the road."

Ellie tilts her head, and I understand by now that means I need to repeat what I said.

"To take it with me." I hold up the drink and snack in both hands. "For the road."

She nods, the recognition of what I said now clicking. "And you didn't want to bring me one?"

"I don't think you've finished the race yet . . ."

With a laugh, she concedes. "Fair enough."

The student government president now calls out for the walkers to start. Ellie and I catch up to her group, and I'm glad to have my breakfast to keep me occupied, because they immediately rope Ellie into conversation. After finishing my doughnut, I'm left slowly sipping hot chocolate to have something to do with myself since I have no idea what anyone is saying.

I thought I was picking things up fast with the words I've learned, but if these students are all beginners, I'm not even there yet. I need to step it up.

Ellie seems most happy signing with Shay, conversing rapid fire, but sometimes she will acknowledge when someone else asks her a question and reply to them more slowly. They all seem desperate to get in conversation time with her.

After some sort of joke, Ellie erupts into a loud burst of laughter. Noticing that I'm clueless, she turns to me and explains, "They said I'm like this group's new celebrity."

"I see it."

Shay signs something, gesturing toward me. Ellie waves away whatever her comment was, but then slows down so the two of us can fall a few paces behind the others.

"Need a break?" I ask. "Everyone's so eager to sign with you."

"Sorry, what?"

I immediately worry that I've crossed a line or something. But I realize she's asking me to repeat what I said.

I point to the club. "You *are* a celebrity. They really want to sign with you."

"I know." She lowers her voice. "It's nice and all, but a little tiring. Shay appreciates that I can help, but I'm not the teacher here."

"What was she signing about me?"

"That you haven't come back to the club." Ellie's expression is unreadable. I can't tell if she's upset about that.

"Oh, um, well."

"No, it's totally fine," she says quickly. "It's a bunch of freshmen. And you usually have soccer stuff at the same time."

"Yeah, next week we're supposed to help scrimmage again with the girls' team since they're in season now. It's not mandatory, but since I'm not playing club like everyone else is right now, I need all the practice I can get."

"I understand."

"I really do want to learn, though. I was just thinking I need to make time to look up more words." I glance down at my shoes. "You don't mind that I'm not trying it right now?"

Did disappointment flash across her face? It's more like she's not surprised. And that feels worse.

"That's fine," she says, also signing the word.

"*Fine*," I copy, poking my thumb into my chest. "There's one for today."

Ellie smirks. "Word by word."

"Yeah . . ."

"It's whatever. We can talk today."

Walking together, we don't speak or sign for a little while. I just know I'm disappointing her. But with everything I've got going on, I couldn't possibly have learned a whole language fast enough for us to communicate naturally already. I'll be better about it, though.

As we're approaching the park entrance, a member of the group waves back to Ellie again. She returns the motion but doesn't rejoin them.

Meanwhile, my phone buzzes in my pocket. It's a text from my dad. I cringe, anticipating his feedback, but it's just a picture of the beach.

JACKSON:

Nice, hope you're having fun!

DAD:

It's great.

Also, you should work on cutting down those thirty-four seconds.

There it is.

There's no pleasing him, I guess. I stop off to the side and lift my shoe to remove the time tracker, but I'm unsteady on just one foot, so Ellie hurries over to hold my elbow. I tear it off and toss the slip in a nearby garbage can.

"Everything all right?" Ellie asks.

"Yeah," I say. "Just didn't know if this would mess with the system going through a second time." More like I wouldn't want my dad to see my time update or something. I don't think that would happen, but whatever.

Ellie squints ahead down the marked route as we approach the park. "Well, we've lost the club."

"We can jog to catch up?" I say. Her face falls but then rises when I suggest an alternative. "Or we could ditch them entirely."

I'm growing less intimidated by Ellie's laser-sharp focus. The way she watches my lips closely as I speak. How she reaches for every word. I'd repeat them all for her as many times as she needed.

Ellie's eyes grow wide. She's intrigued. "Don't we have to get to the finish line?"

"Yeah." I nod off to the side of the path we're on. "But that would be a shortcut."

"Is that how you completed the race so fast?"

"Come on now." I raise my arms in an exaggerated shrug. "Do I really seem like a cheater to you?"

She considers me carefully. "No. But I guess I haven't always been the best judge of character."

"Let me guess . . . that ex?"

Ellie winces. "I've talked about him too much, haven't I?"

"Talked about *who*?" I smile, eager to bypass the subject if she wants. Though having heard bits and pieces about him in conversation, I am curious what the full story is.

"All right, let's go."

It's not like anyone is keeping a close eye on the walkers, 'cause there's no important timing to keep track of at this rate, but I look ahead and behind before guiding us off the paved road and onto the forest trail.

Except the path turns left and runs by the outskirts of the park as well.

"Are you sure this is a shortcut?" Ellie asks skeptically.

We continue forward, trying to cut straight through the loop to get to the other side. I'm *pretty* confident that this will work.

"Yeah, see the clearing right there? Just gotta—" I look down and realize there's a stream we're going to need to pass. "Um, we have to cross this first."

Ellie's still looking down at the water and probably didn't hear me. "Do we need to go through this?"

"Um, ideally over it?" It's only a few feet, and the other side of the bank is dried out and looks stable. "I'll go first."

I make the jump without a problem, but my legs are a little longer than Ellie's. She shifts her weight side to side, gauging how to best approach this.

"It's like that *Hidden Spies* trailer," she mumbles. "Have you seen that yet? I'll be able to jump across, but some snake will lunge out at me halfway through or some shit."

"There's no snakes. I promise." But I chuckle at her hesitation. "I'm excited for that movie, though." With my voice already trailing off, I add, "Maybe we could—"

"Same, it looks terrible in the best way." She must not have heard me. It doesn't seem like she interrupted me on purpose.

Ellie takes a step back, rushes forward, and leaps across, landing solidly on her feet. But I reached a hand out in case she needed to grab it, and somehow *I'm* the one who's lost their balance.

I skid a few feet down into the bank and plunge butt first into the frigid water, sending a shock through my system. Sitting upright, I brush the dirt from my arms and try to keep my composure. "Well, shit."

"Oh no, that's the worst," Ellie says, trying to hide her laughter. She reaches down to help me up.

Her hand is warm in mine as we lock our palms together. I step back onto solid ground, groaning at the squish of my wet socks.

"That wasn't at all embarrassing."

"Are you okay?" Ellie's still holding my hand, waiting to make sure I've found my footing. "Your hands are freezing."

"Sure." I let go and straighten out my shirt, which had ridden up beneath my jacket. All I can think about is how badly I need to take off these drenched socks. That, and about the fact that Ellie is standing incredibly close to me.

She pulls a small twig off my coat. Tossing it off to the side, she looks back up at me. Her dark eyes linger, peering into mine. She exhales, and her breath billows up in the cold air, tangling with my own.

"Thanks," I mumble.

Ellie reaches forward, her hands wrapped into the sleeves of her sweatshirt as she takes hold of my fingers. "Seriously, you're frozen." She gives a small squeeze. "Are you sure you're not too cold?"

That is *not* the temperature I'm feeling right now, since a warmth is creeping up my chest. I'm really glad I ran into Ellie this morning. Though my heart rate is beating faster now than it did running the course earlier.

Ellie watches my lips, waiting for me to speak. "I'm not cold," I say, fudging the truth as I slightly lift our joined hands. "Are you?"

"Maybe a little . . ."

Still holding on to me, she pulls me toward her a smidge. I don't lose my balance again, but I am leaning into her.

Is *she* moving toward me?

Then a loud bird squawks somewhere in the trees above us. I jump a little and glance up to make sure it isn't swooping down on us.

Ellie takes a step back, too. Though the sound must not have fallen on her radar.

It's like we snapped back to reality. I don't know how to close the distance between us again. My hands are cooling back down fast with the absence of hers.

I awkwardly point up, wishing I could undo the last few seconds. "I heard a bird or something . . ."

Shit. Had that been a moment?

I usually have a better read on things. Like, I very clearly understood when my homecoming date leaned forward during the slow dance. Or my first girlfriend stared at me during a movie. But with Ellie, I don't have anything figured out.

Is she just tolerating my presence? It really could just be that I'm the only senior friend she's made so far. We're friends at least, I think. I don't want to overstep. But there was something about the way she took my hands and looked up at me.

Did she want me to kiss her?

She starts to laugh again, using her hands to sign and visually recreate my fall. I chuckle, finding her amusement endearing.

"Definitely an interesting path to take," she says. She gestures to the forest around us. "A lot of pretty things to see."

Even though I don't want to, we need to get moving again. My toes are at risk of frostbite if I don't get out of these wet socks soon. Ellie takes the lead, so I follow her toward the opposite side of the park, back to the 5K course.

"Yeah, beautiful," I say, watching her walk ahead, knowing she didn't hear a word I said.

CHAPTER THIRTEEN

Ellie

FOLLOWING AN INTERESTING shortcut through the woods, Jackson and I dip back onto the course among the walkers and make it to the finish line in no time. Okay, I need to be real with myself—did I come here hoping I'd see Jackson? He's Mr. Every Extracurricular under the Sun, so there's no way he wouldn't be at the race. I barely spent time with Shay, which was my plan, so what am I doing running off with Jackson?

And I think I almost kissed him?

He couldn't have leapt away fast enough, making up something about a bird, and I almost ruined things with my only friend at this school.

We stand around after passing the finish line. Jackson shuffles his feet and looks down, clearly uncomfortable. After whatever happened in the forest, things are awkward now. At least he isn't running away from me. "What do you have going on after this?" he asks.

I tell him my boring plans, wishing I had something more interesting to share. "I'm supposed to take my car for an oil change. It's long overdue for one at this point."

"See, another thing I don't have to worry about without a license."

"Oh, but you're missing out on all the fun maintenance chores . . ." I sigh. "I'm all about being a strong, independent woman, *but* it can be really hard to hear people, and I don't feel like dealing with that, which is probably why I keep putting it off."

One reason, at least. The one I feel comfortable sharing with Jackson right now.

"Maybe I'll tag along," he says casually, but he grows more confident when he notices my eyes light up. "See what the fuss is about."

Oh, hey, things between us seem to be just fine. "Only if you really want to." Wanting to encourage him to say yes, I add with a smile, "I'd definitely appreciate it."

"Awesome, I'm down. But . . ." He steps from side to side with his soaked feet. "Any chance you finished knitting those socks yet?"

I wince sympathetically. "Enough to maybe cover one set of toes?"

He nods to the school. "I'll run in and change in the locker room. Want to get your doughnut and meet me back here?"

"Sure," I say and sign. I watch him jog away, then head over to the refreshments table, where I find Shay again, helping herself to a hot chocolate.

"Where'd you run off to with that boy?" she asks with a knowing grin.

"Nothing like that . . ." I sign back, taking a bite of my glazed doughnut.

She purses her lips, like *mm-hmm*. *"I've got to run, but want to tell me about it tomorrow? My friends and I hang at the Coffee Garden on Sunday afternoons. You know the place?"*

"Yeah, I've driven past it."

She holds out her phone for me to share my number. "*Cool, I'll text you once we know the exact time.*"

When Shay heads home, I wait near the school doors for Jackson. He shows up a few minutes later, changed into his dry gym clothes.

"Feeling better?" I ask.

"Much."

Does he really want to go with me to get an oil change? I don't question it too much because I need to get this done before my car explodes or something. We walk through the thinning crowds over to my little old two-door sedan, and I drive us to the auto shop a couple minutes away.

Jackson fiddles with the radio trying to find a decent song but gives up as we pull into the parking lot. "So, what do I need to ask for?"

"Just a regular oil change."

All right, admittedly, the main reason I haven't taken my car in for service is that I've never had to do it before. Ever. Cody used to always do the work himself since he had an uncle who taught him everything about cars, which is why we thought about opening our own shop one day. Cody could probably still go ahead with the plan if he wanted. He never really needed me. Someone else could handle the management stuff.

I park at the end of the check-in line, and a worker arrives with a clipboard. I'm happy to let Jackson do all the talking for me. We wait at a table inside, where a TV is blasting local news. A few minutes later, Jackson nods toward the desk, letting me know there's a worker calling us up. I glance at the invoice and hand over my card. Gotta say this whole thing was much cheaper when my ex did it for free.

As I sit back down, Jackson asks the worker something, getting a nod in response, after which he reaches up to turn off the television.

"Oh, thank you," I say in relief.

"And they said only a few more minutes," Jackson adds, taking a seat beside me.

"That's pretty fast."

"Yeah." Jackson taps his fingers on the table.

We wait in silence for a bit. "Thanks again. I was really dragging my heels on this."

"Anytime." He gives a soft smile.

It's funny how much I was dreading this, but just like being at Amber in general, Jackson made it a lot easier.

A little while later, he stands, gesturing toward the person at the counter. "They said it's ready."

We get my keys and hop back into the car. I'm not sure what happens now. "Do you want me to drive you home or—"

"Are we near your place? I could get an EasyRide from there."

"Okay, yeah."

Do I invite him inside my house? It's not like he expects to spend more time together today. Or does he? I can't glean much from our conversation on the way there, since we're just small-talking about the weather.

As soon as we pull up to my driveway, I notice my mom and dad getting out of their car, home from wherever they went this morning.

"Shit." I tap my fingers on the steering wheel, pondering how to navigate this.

"What's wrong?" Jackson asks. "That's your parents?"

I have no idea how my parents are going to react to Jackson being here. I don't want to introduce him to them. "Yeah, but you don't have to—"

Jackson has already stepped out of the car, and my dad greets him with a handshake. How the heck did he get over there so fast?! They're fully doing introductions now while I'm still glued to the driver's seat.

It's okay, it's okay. Right, it's— Who am I kidding? I haul myself out of the car. Shit. This day is slipping away from me, fast.

"We were at the 5K," Jackson is saying when I catch up to him.

"Well, come on in. I'll make some brunch," my mom offers, immediately more friendly to Jackson than she ever was to Cody. *Not that I'm dating Jackson or anything like that.*

"He was just leaving," I say, to surprised looks from everyone. I stare daggers at my parents, then turn and try to give a reassuring glance to Jackson. It's not that I *don't* want him here. It's just strange how my parents are being so friendly and inviting. It's uncomfortable because I know they're putting on an act for him. I'm not used to seeing them this way.

"It's all right," Jackson says congenially. "My EasyRide should be arriving any moment now." He lies so smoothly to diffuse the tension I created.

"Well, it was nice meeting you," my mom says.

"Yes," my dad adds. "You're welcome here anytime."

"Great to meet you, as well," Jackson says.

"Glad we all got to know each other," I quip toward them while ushering Jackson to the end of the driveway.

Looking bewildered by the exchange, Jackson says, "Sorry, I figured I should just—"

"No, it's just things have been rocky with them lately, and it all caught me off guard."

"We're okay, right?"

"Yeah," I say. "Really, it's just they're so . . ." I turn around to make sure my parents have gone inside, but I decide against getting into the details now. "Anyway, I'm sorry."

Jackson gets out his phone to actually order the EasyRide now. "There's one a couple minutes away."

"I'll wait with you." I shift onto my toes, then back down to my heels, regretting my actions a little bit. Would it have been *that* bad to let him talk to my parents? Now that he's leaving, I realize how much I want to spend more time with him. "It was great running into you today."

Jackson squints, like he can't totally figure me out. "Literally. Good thing I ran fast enough to catch you before you started walking the course."

"I'm glad you did."

He's about to say something else when his phone lights up with an alert. "A minute away."

"I'll see you Monday?"

"At lunch," he affirms.

Guilt washes over me as I watch his EasyRide drive up. He gives a small wave and hops in the car, then I head into the house. I don't know what's going on with the two of us, but I do know I don't want it to be ruined by my parents. They didn't seem to care when I ended a five-year relationship. I'm not ready to bring someone else home and into this mess.

Mom is standing at the kitchen counter waiting for me. "He seems nice."

"Yeah," I mumble.

"Easy to talk to," my dad agrees.

"Right . . ." I clench my teeth, holding back since I'm not in the mood to fight. But I can't help adding, "You'd hardly have to make any effort."

I retreat upstairs, but my dad's words replay in my mind. *Easy to talk to.* In general, a compliment at face value. But I know *exactly* what my parents mean by that, even if they don't realize it themselves.

$\searrow\swarrow$

I wait in my car at first, staring out at the Coffee Garden and feeling nervous to go inside. The place is busy for a Sunday afternoon, and I was lucky to have grabbed this parking spot. The car that keeps circling around clearly hopes I'm about to leave.

Through the hazy double-door windows, I see Shay there with her two friends, who seem to be a couple. They're chatting about some sort of homework assignment, but I don't have a good enough vantage point to fully "eavesdrop" from here. But dang, just watching them all sign and hang out makes me nostalgic for Brandview.

Should I make my way inside now? They all know each other so well already, and it's hard not to feel like I'm intruding on their group. Maybe this was a bad idea.

But my phone vibrates, and it's a text from Shay.

SHAY:

Did you get lost or something?

Finally turning off the car and dashing all hopes of the driver stalling behind me, I quickly type out a response.

ELLIE:

Just parked!

SHAY:

Nice, I got you a coffee.

Walking through the parking lot, I don't hear a truck zipping around the bend and have to jump back to dodge the reckless driver. *What the f—* And that guy is so convinced he's in the right that he flips me off. Even though he's in a gigantic contraption and I'm the tiny human he almost smushed. I scowl back at him, waiting for his pickup to be out of sight before I hurry into the coffee shop.

Shay and her friends must've been watching, because when I pull open the door to the cozy purple shop, all three are wearing relieved expressions. I sidestep around several giant potted plants and a small flower cart to join their table.

"*Damn, they almost hit you!*" Shay signs, pulling out the tall chair beside her at the round table.

I sit and sign one-handed, "*Seriously, never hear them coming.*"

"*Drivers are the worst,*" the girl with dark curls, full brows, and red lipstick on the other side of me signs, while the other one, with thin bangs and freckled arms, pats her shoulder.

"*E-l-l-i-e, this is I-s-a-b-e-l and A-l-e-x,*" Shay spells out.

"*I-z-z-y,*" Isabel adds with a shrug, offering up her and Alex's sign names as well. They both give official hello nods now that we're all acquainted. Like Shay, Izzy doesn't seem to wear any devices, while I notice a pair of hearing aids behind Alex's blond hair.

"*You went to Brandview?*" Izzy asks. When I sign *yes,* she adds, "*Me too!*"

"*Really?*" It was a small school, and Izzy couldn't be more than two or three years apart from me. But I don't recognize her.

"*Just my first year.*" Izzy sips from her coffee, so I do the same, grateful that Shay grabbed me a cup. "*Because I missed my family, you know? Wanted to be home more.*"

"*Then you all went to Amber for high school?*" I venture a guess, which they confirm.

"*I helped Shay start the ASL club,*" Izzy signs. "*Because there was a girl with hearing aids who I had a crush on, and I hoped she'd join.*"

"*And I did.*" Alex gives a wide grin, clearly relishing in the retelling of how they met. "*Though my ASL was so terrible at first.*"

"*It's kind of a struggle still,*" Izzy teases.

Alex scrunches up her face and shakes her head playfully. "*Only because I learned all your bad habits.*"

"*That's adorable,*" I sign. "*I'm jealous you all had each other. I've been keeping an eye out, but I think I'm the only Deaf one there right now.*"

"*Yeah, but you also still ended up having a meet-cute at ASL club,*" Shay signs. "*Why am I out here doing all the work but never finding love?*"

"*A meet-cute?*" I lean back, scrunching up my face, playing coy. "*Wait, do you mean J-a-c-k-s-o-n? He just had to give me a tour of the school.*"

Shay has her counterpoint at the ready. "*Just like he had to give you a tour of the 5K?*"

My cheeks are warm, and I'm running out of ways to deny that something is going on with us. "*Maybe . . .*" I let that linger for dramatic effect. "*But I'm not sure I'm really over my ex, honestly. We were together for years, the entire time I was at Brandview.*"

"*And the ex doesn't live nearby?*" Izzy asks.

I shake my head. "*By Cleveland.*"

Alex winces. "*That's a long drive.*"

"*Sure, okay,*" Shay signs, her lips pursed in disbelief. "*Maybe it takes a while to get over him. But you told me he was not great.*"

"*Right, true, true,*" I agree. Cody was the worst in the end, so why has it been impossible to get him entirely out of my head? Something as small as having to go get an oil change really shook me up since he used to fit in my life so perfectly.

Cody constantly sneaks back into my thoughts, slithering like a snake and forever contaminating my memories of Brandview. I miss being there so much, which, in turn, makes me think I miss being there *with him*.

The others have moved on from the topic to discuss something about classes at ACC, so I sit back for a while and just appreciate the easy conversation and being surrounded by Deaf folks.

Yet, since Shay brought it up, my mind does wander back to yesterday's 5K and Jackson. I wouldn't exactly call our conversations *easy* because of the hurdles, but, in spite of myself, I'm enjoying his company. With him, I can get out of my head a little. He's a welcome distraction that makes starting at a new school a little less impossible.

For some reason, communication that is usually taxing work doesn't feel as difficult with him. He's always eager to repeat himself, making sure I've understood. Like he's taking on a little bit of the barrier so I don't have to carry all the burden. And while I'd never expect he'd actually learn sign language *for* me, it would be nice if he continued the effort. Maybe restore my faith in hearing people a little bit.

Shit, I think, stifling a giggle. I felt so bad when he fell in that stream. He took it in stride, though. While he seems to generally walk through life all confident, the glimpses behind that facade make me think I'm getting to know the real him.

CHAPTER FOURTEEN

Jackson

WHEN I TAKE my seat for class on Monday morning, my knee bumps up against the desk. It hurts more than it should with such soft contact. I roll up my pant leg to discover a huge bruise already there. It must be from my fall over the weekend.

Walking down the hall to lunch, I run into Darius by the bathroom. "Yo, Jackson!" he says. "When are we ever going to see you back at the soccer table?"

"I think I'm fine in my new spot. Don't worry about me."

"By all those teachers?" He doesn't seem convinced. "If you say so. You know the guys aren't that mad anymore. It's kinda weird that you aren't there still."

"I guess since I'm not playing club right now, it feels like I don't really belong. Even when I'm doing just fine during conditioning or scrimmages, I can still *feel* the resentment a bit."

"Come on, man, it's not like that." Darius shakes his head. "Truly, if you wanna chill with your girl during lunch, that's all good. But don't feel like you gotta keep your distance anymore, all right?"

A few minutes later, when I see Ellie waiting for me at our table, I know that I'm sure. I was a little anxious to see her again after this weekend, especially after that weirdness with her parents, but we ignore it and settle back into our usual routine today and the rest of this week.

Ellie's class before lunch often runs late, so I'm usually the first one at the table, making small talk with the faculty passing by. When she shows up and makes the obligatory joke about me being a teacher's pet, we eat our lunches and hang out until it's time to walk down to study hall.

During study hall on Friday, while Ellie's doing some assigned reading, I look up an ASL alphabet chart on my laptop, finally thinking I've got it memorized. It's taken a while, especially since I always mess up *F* and *D*. But feeling fairly sure of myself, I wave an arm out for her attention. "Are you busy?"

Her eyes widen, eager for a distraction. "Not really," she says, dropping her highlighter and abandoning focus.

"I learned the alphabet." I give a small smile.

"What was that?"

To clarify, I hold up my right hand. There's a slight blood-rushing, tingling feeling as I move it. I guess it was resting weird while I stared at my laptop screen. Anyway, I sign, "*A, B, C.*"

"*Nice,*" she responds, sliding her hand across a flat palm. I recognize this one. She signs something else before repeating, "*A, B, C.*"

"Yes," I say, continuing with the next letter, but it's clear we've already hit the first hurdle.

"Actually, *D* is like this." Ellie slides her chair toward me. Leaning forward, she takes hold of my palm, folding down the pinkie and pushing the index upward. My hand shakes a little at her touch, and it's obvious my fingers are frozen compared to the warmth of hers.

I avoid her eyes as I finish the rest of the letters. Aside from mixing up *M* and *N*, I think I do all right.

Ellie deems it satisfactory. "Pretty good," she says and signs.

"I figured I should get the basics down." I clench and unfold my fist. "Now I can at least spell out some things to you."

She smiles. "It's a start." Obviously, she's not going to be blown away by something as elementary as the alphabet. I know there's still plenty more to learn.

"Yeah." I sigh and raise my arms up into a stretch. My fingers are still tingling, and there's no reason for that to be happening. Ugh, I hate how weird my body has been lately.

I'm about to start my chemistry homework, but Ellie is in a talkative mood. "Do you have Sanders for history?" she asks.

I shake my head and say, "But I took a different class of his sophomore year."

"He's offering extra credit if we go to a museum." Ellie holds up the paper. "We need to take a photo of an exhibit and then write a paragraph about it."

"Yeah, he loves doing things like that." I squint to read the details without taking the page from her. "Huh, just any museum?"

"It doesn't specify, but I assume it has to have some relevance to history, though I guess most museums do." Ellie does a quick Google search. "I'm not sure which to go to. Do you have any favorites?"

"Hmm." I press my tongue against my teeth as I try to think of something that could impress her. "Oh, I know. What about the Sign Museum?"

"Sign Museum?" she asks, confused. "I don't know that one."

"It's not like ASL," I say almost apologetically. "It's a bunch of neon signs from old businesses and stuff. It's all illuminated, kind of like walking through Times Square. It's a cool spot."

"That sounds nice." Ellie seems convinced.

I'm ready to offer to go with her, but is that too much? I'm not sure where we stand after last weekend. "We could—" I say, then stop, realizing she's started speaking, too.

"Do you—" Ellie pauses as well.

I twist my pen between my fingers, trying to play it cool. *Will she ask me?* "It's an interesting place. I'd go again."

Ellie understands what I'm trying to say. "Would you want to go with me?"

"Sure, let's go." I sit tall in my chair, trying not to wear my excitement on my face. "I think it's closer to where you live. I can meet you at your house. Don't worry; I won't have to say hi to your parents."

Tapping a thumb to her chest, she seems encouraged by that. "That sounds fine. Just text me."

"Sweet." I face my laptop again, and, thinking I'm saying it quietly to myself, add so softly there's no way she heard me, "It's a date."

Yet Ellie slowly leans forward, a smile curling up as she places a hand on my arm. "You know I can read your lips."

My mouth hangs open, and I'm at a loss for words. *Is she going to say anything else or just leave me hanging now?* Fortunately and unfortunately, the bell rings at that moment. I point to the ceiling to let her know. Ellie stands to leave but quickly leans beside my ear on her way to whisper, "I can't wait."

CHAPTER FIFTEEN

Ellie

AFTERNOONS ARE ALWAYS the better half of the day. Following lunch and study hall with Jackson, I spend my time with my interpreter Kim, who is always so great and professional. I could fall asleep at my desk and she'd keep on signing. I think one time that actually happened.

It's the morning classes with Pamela that are still the bane of my existence. Today, I was a few seconds late to first period, and she was so irritated. When I went to check my phone, she scooched her chair half an inch toward me as if to command my focus again. It's not her job to make sure I'm engaged in class. All she's supposed to do is provide access, and I can do whatever I want during class, like any other student.

"*You need to pay attention,*" she signed while the teacher was writing something on the board.

"*Relax.*" I rolled my eyes but put my phone away, lest she cause another scene.

Being watched so closely really keeps me on edge. She's judgmental, especially at eight in the morning. She's also way too friendly with my classmates. Whenever I ditch her between periods, she's chatty with people in the hallway. *What do they possibly have to talk about? And why is my interpreter more popular than me?* It's a lot.

Yet right now in AP English, I've already shared my thoughts on the *Pride and Prejudice* chapters we covered this week, so I can zone out while Kim carefully details my classmates' contributions that clearly show many of them didn't read the pages.

Which, it's a good thing I don't need to be engaged on the subject at the moment because my mind is anywhere but the many literary merits of Jane Austen.

Jackson asked me out.

I haven't been asked out . . . ever? Cody and I started dating so soon after we met as middle schoolers. There was never a does-he-like-me-or-not phase. We suddenly just *were* a couple.

I'd be reading too much into whether we are just going to the museum as friends, but Jackson said it himself—this is a date.

I've got a date with Jackson tomorrow.

CHAPTER SIXTEEN

Jackson

I WAKE SATURDAY morning feeling poorly rested, but I don't let that stop me from my usual routine. It was hard falling asleep last night since I'm a little nervous about going to the museum with Ellie.

We didn't text much after school yesterday. I suggested a time to meet at her house. What kind of date takes place at 9:45 in the morning—*and* is centered around a homework assignment? Maybe, if this goes well, I can get another chance to impress her with something more interesting.

I prop myself on my elbow, trying to muster the energy to get out of bed, but my eyes are still closed. How did I not get enough sleep? *Oof*, I must not have had enough water yesterday. That's gotta be it. It's going to be one of those mornings where my start-of-the-day warm-up is a slog.

Barely opening my eyes, out of habit, I slide down to the carpet beside my bed to do sit-ups.

One.

Blegh, I'm hating this. It usually helps me get a good start to the day, but not if I must deplete all my energy fighting through it. I lie with my head on the ground. Taking a deep breath, I start again.

Two.

Nope, I'm dizzy as hell, as if I just stumbled off an amusement park ride rather than attempted a single sit-up. *What is going on?*

Lying down again, I realize I'm having difficulty seeing. The light fixture above me seems to be moving. It's lurching back and forth across my vision. I take a deep breath. *I'll open my eyes again, and everything will be fine.*

It's not.

I stare ahead at the doorknob, not moving my eyes. I'm not moving my eyes at all. So why the hell does the handle keep darting off to the side like I'm in some sort of low-budget horror movie?!

I try to stand. Another bad idea.

The world has twisted. *What kind of nightmare is this?* The dizziness is all-consuming now. I can't find my center of gravity or hold myself upright, even while sitting. Swaying forward and back, I bury my face in my hands, willing whatever this is to end. I press against the bedframe, hoping to steady myself.

Something is wrong.

I open my mouth to call for my parents, but no sound comes out. I don't have the energy to vocalize. Grabbing the mattress, I try to pull myself up, opening my eyes a squint. I make it to the edge of the bed, which isn't a victory because I can tell this is about to get a whole lot worse. An unpleasant sensation swirls in my stomach.

Yesterday's dinner returns with a vengeance, shooting up my throat and pooling on the floor. I slide to the ground, narrowly avoiding the puke.

My parents must have heard something. I think they're calling me from downstairs. *Help*, I try to say. But I can't force the word out.

I lean to the right and vomit again. Smaller chunks this time, added to the mess.

The door creaks open, but I don't dare open my eyes. I'm glad my parents have found me. Dad says something, but I'm not processing anything. I think my mom left the room.

It's liquid this time, warm and stinging my throat on the way up.

Mom is back with a warm towel. A water bottle. And a bucket. She puts it in my lap for me.

More liquid. My eyes squeezed so tightly shut that all I see are red swirls. They spin. My brain spins. Everything is spinning.

Finally, it seems like my body has nothing left to give. I peek to find Dad offering me the water. My vision is still moving.

Despite sitting absolutely still, the world is still moving around me. I'm not in control of my eyes.

What is happening to me?

My hands shake and struggle to hold up the metal bottle. I drink in slow, small sips with my eyes closed, still swaying. I'm about to drop the water when my dad grabs it.

"Honey, what's going on?" my mom pleads, and I finally register what she is saying. "Are you sick?"

No shit.

My head lurches forward. Welp, there goes the water. Sloshing around in the bucket. I couldn't even keep it down.

"Let's go to the doctor," my dad says without hesitation. That's how I know something is *really wrong*. He loops his arms around me, helping me stand. I force a swallow to try to prevent more vomit.

Since I'm only in shorts, Mom runs to my closet and grabs a shirt.

She lifts my arms, sliding the soft tee over my head. She attempts to be gentle, but with my eyes closed, I feel so pushed around.

We get to the bottom of the stairs somehow. Then out to the car. Which might as well be a roller coaster. I clutch my seat belt to my chest. My head ducked down, too heavy to hold up. Every single turn. Start. And stop. Makes me sick. *Sick*, right into the plastic bag one of my parents must've given me.

We get to Urgent Care. Mom checks me in. Dad grabs a wheelchair. Too many bumps. The ramp winds so much.

We must be inside now. "We have to wait awhile," my mom says, patting my arm.

"Don't." No one touch me. I can't handle any movement.

I've never been so out of control of my own body.

When will this stop?

I just need it to end.

CHAPTER SEVENTEEN

Ellie

I'VE BEEN MESSING with my hair all morning, not sure exactly how I want to wear it. I'm in a flowy summer dress paired with a cardigan, but I'm questioning this outfit, too, and there's no time to change it. Jackson will be here any minute now. We decided on nine yesterday. And he seems the type to be punctual.

I pull open my bedroom window curtain and peek outside, but no EasyRide has pulled up to the house yet. Maybe there was a delay? And how much is he spending on all this travel? I should've just offered to pick him up, even if he lives out of the way.

Sitting on the couch, I distract myself with my phone, not wanting to seem too eager should Jackson catch me looking out the window. I need to play it cool. It's only 9:05; I'm sure he'll be here any minute now.

I bite my lip and send Jackson a quick text asking for an ETA at 9:15.

By 9:37, there's still no response.

Maybe Jackson didn't even want to go to the museum. I was the one who brought it up. He must've thought he *had* to offer just to be nice. It makes sense if he'd rather sleep in or do something more interesting with his morning. Still, it's so rude to make a plan and not follow through. And not a single text to cancel?

But he'd seemed excited, right? In a dorky, cute kind of way. The boy who blushed head to toe when I read his lips isn't the type to ghost me, right?

At 9:45, I send another text and quickly check his socials. No response or recent posts. Is everything all right?

Yet as time passes, I start to feel more upset. No one is two hours late. I have a sinking feeling in the pit of my stomach. It's funny how quickly my emotions and thoughts turn.

Maybe Jackson and that asshole from the soccer team who started the rumor about me are hanging out, having a big old laugh at my expense. Or maybe I'm drifting into some serious paranoia to try to spare my own feelings here. Should I go to the museum without him anyway?

I've never been stood up before. I guess there's a first time for everything.

CHAPTER EIGHTEEN

Jackson

I HOLD MYSELF as tight as I can in the wheelchair, totally unaware of the world around me as I try to keep still and fight the dizziness. After waiting what could have been either ten long minutes or two even longer hours, I'm wheeled into a small exam room.

"Can you get him up there?" the nurse asks.

My parents each grab an arm, helping me climb up to the table. I'm gonna be sick again.

The nurse has already supplied me with a barf bag. I retch. Almost nothing comes out.

My parents answer questions. Someone might have taken my pulse. I lie back on the exam table. "The doctor will be with you shortly."

"Mm-hmm." I pull my knees to my chest and curl up tight.

\/

"Jackson, honey."

My eyes flutter open as I hear my mom's voice. I brave lifting my head ever so slightly. The doctor is here now, and I'm feeling a bit better. I can see more clearly. My eyes seem stable.

But now how do I explain what the problem was if it's gone? How do I prove what was happening?

"Can you tell me what's going on?" the doctor asks while doing a cursory check of my ears.

"I woke up, and it was like my eyes were moving on their own." I motion with my hands to try to convey how my vision was acting. "And then I got *really* dizzy. And threw up. A lot."

The doctor examines my eyes next. We do a test where she makes me lie down quickly and turn my head to one side. Nothing happens. I do it again but with the other side. This time, a small flutter. The threat of dizziness. But nothing more occurs.

"We'll get you on an IV with some anti-nausea medication." She makes note of something on a clipboard. "This could be positional vertigo, which has to do with some calcium crystals in the inner ear getting stuck where they don't belong. There are some exercises you can do at home to try to treat this."

"What sort of exercises?" my mom asks, probably already envisioning the yoga mat rolled out on our living room floor. She's got blocks she'd lend me, too. Unlike the summer, this time I'm probably not getting out of her remedies. But just the idea of dipping my head in downward dog right now makes me want to barf again.

The doctor is encouraging. "They're simple. I'll print out instructions." She finally looks back from my parents to me.

"Okay." I'm not sure what else there is to say. My mouth is incredibly dry.

"You can lie back down." The doctor moves to the door. "The nurse will be back with the IV and papers."

Once we're alone in the room, my parents both breathe a sigh of relief. "Just vertigo," my dad says. "Must've been from your sit-ups somehow."

"I guess." I'm just glad the room isn't spinning anymore.

I lean my head back against the exam table. It's been years since I sat on one of these with my parents in the room. I probably actually fit on here back then, instead of having my legs and arms hanging off the edge.

Wait, shit.

Ellie.

"Where's my phone?" I ask, patting my pockets. I glare at my parents. "You didn't bring my phone?"

"It must still be in your bedroom," my mom says, not understanding the urgency. "You can borrow mine."

"No, I—" Closing my eyes again, I start to wonder how to explain this to Ellie. "I had plans today."

She must've texted me. I'm sure she did. Why does she think I haven't shown up? Ellie has no way to know where I am. At least we were going to meet at her house, so she wasn't alone at the museum waiting for me. But it was for her extra-credit assignment. Did she end up having to go without me?

There's a knock at the door. "Come in," my dad answers.

The nurse wheels the IV bag into the room and positions it beside me. "Which arm?" she asks.

"Uh." I've never had one of these before, though I did donate at Amber High's blood drive last spring. I hold out my right arm since she's already on that side anyway.

The nurse puts on a pair of gloves and then ties a tourniquet around my biceps. She taps the inside of my elbow a few times, sizing up my vein, before reaching for the needle. I look away and take a deep breath, trying my best to ignore the pinch. Once finished with the insertion needle, she tapes the plastic tube into place.

The fluids start working immediately. Finally, there's enough saliva back in my mouth that I can lick my dry lips.

"That feels much better," I say, propping myself up a little bit with my other arm.

"Yeah, you must've been really dehydrated," the nurse says.

"How long does this take?"

"About forty-five minutes or so."

There's no way I'll still be able to meet up with Ellie today, but I want to be able to text her. She's probably spiraling about why I'm not responding.

"Can I get you a blanket or anything?" she asks.

"No, that's fine. Thanks, though." Except I regret that as soon as I say it, because I am cold.

"All right, I'll be back to check on you in a few."

My parents are slumped in the two chairs along the wall. I've been in and out of it all morning, so I don't really have a grasp on how long it's been, but they've been sitting there for a while. Plus however long we were in the waiting room.

"What time is it?" I ask.

My dad checks his watch. "Almost two."

"Seriously?" There's no way it's been that long, but my stomach does rumble. "Two o'clock?"

"I'll make something to eat when we get home," my mom says, not looking up from whatever she's googling on her phone. "It says to avoid caffeine. And junk foods, but we would've figured that much already," she says, sharing a look with my dad. They've already been on a healthy-eating kick for a while, but something like this could make them take it to further extremes.

"At least they're going to help you fix this with just exercise," my mom says approvingly. "We don't need unnecessary antibiotics or anything like that. I mean, we had to vaccinate you for school, but I've always wondered if that was the right move."

Dad nods in agreement to appease my mom. I roll my eyes. They sometimes doubt medicine, and yet they rush me to Urgent Care. Make it make sense.

Is it time to go yet?

I need to text Ellie. And these forty-five minutes, alert and alone in a room with my parents, are turning into agony without having my phone as a distraction.

Eventually, the nurse comes back with papers that she hands my parents. She removes the IV, placing a cotton ball beneath gauze wrapped around my arm. "The doctor also called in a prescription to your pharmacy for some anti-nausea and anti-dizziness meds."

On our way out of the room, I glance back at the wheelchair they used to roll me in. I never thought I'd need to use one of those. But I couldn't walk straight. Or keep my head up. Wow, I was a disaster this morning.

Yet now, after the replenishment from that IV, I almost feel like nothing ever happened.

The drive back home is short, which is surprising, because on the way to Urgent Care, it felt like a million years. I go to my room, fearful a mess of vomit is waiting for me there, but everything is spotless. My parents must've called the cleaners even though it's not Monday or Thursday. The bed is even made with fresh sheets.

I brace myself to read the texts, more nervous to see Ellie's messages than I was about a needle piercing my skin earlier. The first, at 9:15.

ELLIE:

Hey, are you on your way?

She'd waited a half hour before sending the next at 9:45.

ELLIE:

Is everything okay?

Then a final message at 11:00.

ELLIE:

I guess we're not going . . .

What do I even say? First things first. My hand is shaking so much that autocorrect has to do some heavy lifting with this message.

JACKSON:

I'm so sorry for this morning. Something came up.

That sounds flaky. I'm tempted to just call and explain, but I don't even know if she *does* phone calls. That doesn't seem like the right move.

JACKSON:

I had to go to Urgent Care.

Her response comes quickly now.

ELLIE:

Are you okay??

JACKSON:

Yeah, I'm fine now.

Should I offer to still meet up with her today? I sit down on the bed, getting ready to send another text, and exhaustion hits. Hard.

JACKSON:

Sorry, I'll explain more on Monday.

Even though I still need to eat something, I toss my phone to the side and crawl under the blankets, immediately falling fast asleep.

CHAPTER NINETEEN

Ellie

YIKES, JACKSON HAD to go to the doctor. I feel bad about how much I was building him up to be some sort of villain in my head. Of course he didn't stand me up. He wouldn't do that.

Maybe he twisted an ankle or stepped on a nail or something painful. I'm curious to know what happened, but we can perhaps leave out any of the grisly details. I really can't do blood. Or needles. I was young when I got my CI, and it turned out fine, but I still have nightmares if I think too hard about it—surgery on your head isn't exactly a fun time.

Jackson doesn't want to explain more now anyway, so I won't press.

I'm not sure what to do with myself for the rest of today. It's almost six, and I've pretty much just sat around worried and waiting, even after resigning myself to the fact that the Sign Museum wasn't going to happen.

I get another text, but it's not from Jackson.

SHAY:

> Heeeeeeeeeeeeeeeeey, throwing together a little group chat for us all

She's included me in a message with her, Izzy, and Alex. We start making plans for another hang at the Coffee Garden tomorrow afternoon. I'm glad to have something else to look forward to this weekend, since today was all over the place. It's been a while since I was added to a group chat. I'm so glad they want to hang out with me again.

Time to get cozy and decompress from every emotion I've experienced these past ten hours. I change into sweats and undo my braids. My hearing aid and cochlear implant processor go in a case on my bedside table. Scooping Cheese up, I hold him close as I get in bed. *"We're staying in today,"* I sign to him. He's easily mesmerized by my fingers. *"You like that? I know you do. You're so silly,"* I sign, my thumb and pinkie outstretched and twisted in front of my nose. *"Silly."*

Then he reaches out to nip at my extended finger.

"Cheese," I say sternly. Yet, having made his point, he curls up beside me, content. We sit here scrolling through videos together for a couple hours, until my mom comes barging through the bedroom door.

"What?" I ask.

Of course, I can't hear what she's saying, but she continues to talk, even as she sees me move to put my cochlear receiver back on. Couldn't she wait a second for me to at least have one-sided assistance for this conversation?

"I've been shouting for you. Dinner has been ready for fifteen minutes."

I motion with my phone. "Like I've told you before, you can text me."

"Why weren't you—" She continues saying something else as she walks over to my beside table and hands me the hearing aid.

I take it but keep it in my hand. "Because I'm just relaxing here."

"What if I'd been shouting because there was a fire?"

"I *think* the cat would have alerted me to any real danger . . ." I point up to the regular alarm on the ceiling. "Or, you know, they make some with flashing lights."

Mom crosses her arms, her voice matter-of-fact. "Unless you're sleeping, you need to be wearing these. I shouldn't have to keep reminding you."

"Oh, so I should wear them in the shower?"

"Enough of that. You know what I mean. Now get yourself downstairs." She stands there, pointing at the door. I wait for her to leave first, but she doesn't budge.

I roll my eyes. "You can go."

"Downstairs. Now," she insists.

Cheese is still beside me, so I gently nudge him away. He was cozy and is annoyed to be moved. *Me too, buddy.* I slide my hearing aid back into my ear and hurry out of the room, not giving my mom another glance.

Am I not allowed to be comfortable at home? This should be the one place I can relax and not deal with all the bullshit hearing expectations of the world. But I can't do that when I have to fight to exist as I am within my own family.

On Monday, Jackson's waiting for me at our lunch spot. His eyes are wide and puppy-dog apologetic. There's nothing visibly wrong with him—no arm in a cast or foot in a boot.

"I'm so sorry. Wait," he says, then signs, "*I'm sorry.*"

"Are you doing all right?" I slide my books to the edge of the table and take a seat, pulling out my lunch bag. I still have no sense of the severity of his doctor visit. "What happened?"

"It was just another weird medical thing," he says, skirting around the details. But he makes a stumped face. "I seem to be having a lot of those lately."

"Really, like what?" I'm being nosy. But he looks perfectly fine, so I can't fight this curiosity. I know it's not right of me to make any assumptions like this. Kind of ableist, actually. I hate when people look at me and do the same. Yet, after Cody, I'm having a hard time taking things at face value. "But you don't have to share if you don't want to."

"They said it was vertigo." Jackson fidgets with his fingers. "I got really sick, and then when I was back home, I just completely crashed for the rest of the weekend."

"Oof, that does sound like a rough morning. And that's happened before?"

"No, never."

"You said this was another weird medical thing. What else was there?"

"Just the leg thing that cost us the state game," he says, but that doesn't jog my memory. "I thought I mentioned it before."

I shake my head. "I might not have heard, sorry. What happened?"

"Something with my feet, and I fell." Jackson opens his lunch bag, avoiding the question. "Just all sorts of weird, unrelated things. My body hates me, I guess. I probably need more rest."

"That's annoying." I flip through my folder, clearing out a handout advertising a college fair that happened yesterday. Jackson reaches for it and groans as he reads. "You missed that, too?" I ask.

"I was supposed to talk with a recruiter there . . ." Frustrated, he crumples up the paper, tossing it into the nearby recycling bin. "Crap. Ellie, I totally forgot that it was this weekend. I can't believe I forgot."

"Well, don't worry about the extra credit," I say, holding up the history test I got back today with a large B+ scrawled across the top. "Turns out I don't need it as much as I thought, so no worries."

"It is a cool museum, though." Jackson relaxes and takes a bite of his sandwich. "Maybe we can get to it some other time. I'd say this weekend, but it's that big football game."

"A Friday-night game?" This is feeling like a flimsy excuse not to go out. Jackson's never expressed any interest in the football team before.

"Did you not get your spot on the—" he says, continuing with something I don't catch.

"Spot for what?"

"On the bus," he repeats. "*B-u-s,*" he signs.

I appreciate the clarification, but that wasn't my question here. I scrunch up my face, confused. "And why would we need to take a bus? Where exactly is the game?"

"It's a couple hours away. But it's more of an event," he explains. "For some old tradition, there's always one away game that the school rents buses for and everyone books hotel rooms to make a night out of it. It's about the parties and less about the football. My cousin already got a room to share."

"Interesting."

I don't really care about football. Cody played at Brandview, and I went to almost all his games. Do I really want to take a bus and root for a school I don't care about and a bunch of players I don't know?

"Do you want to come?" Jackson asks.

I'd be happy to never sit through another football game again. But I should at least entertain the idea. "Are there still rooms available?"

"I'm not sure. You could always just crash with us."

Hmm, and share a hotel room? With Jackson . . . and his cousin. What's the vibe here?

I'm trying to be cautious, not ready to jump into something and get my heart broken again. And a weekend away somewhere feels like the catalyst to really jump-start something . . . which is kind of exciting? In a very, *very* nerve-racking way.

"Okay, I'll think about it."

Jackson's face drops at my disinterest. "Yeah, but also we could maybe just do something else on the next weekend or—"

I shrug, trying to seem indifferent, but seeing his disappointment might just convince me. "It seems like it could be fun. At least it'd get me out of the house for a night."

"Exactly," he says with a grin. "It'd be a fun time, I promise."

CHAPTER TWENTY

Jackson

WEDNESDAY NIGHT, MY cousin Anthony makes the thirty-minute drive to come over for a free homecooked dinner. He didn't always have a car with him on campus, but now that he does, he's here whenever my mom makes her classic eggplant parmesan, which is obviously much better than anything he can get at the University of Cincinnati dining hall.

He's offered to take me driving before, and I'd never really considered it. But tonight, I hit him with a request across the dinner table. "Do you want to teach me how to drive?" I blurt out, surprising everyone, even me.

"Oh, now you want to learn?" Anthony laughs, then looks at my parents. "No one else wanted to be stuck in the car while he's behind the wheel?"

"I didn't know you were thinking about that," my mom says. "Do you think *now* is the right time, with everything—"

"Now seems fine," I say. I've tried the exercises, rolling my body and head around in specific movements to right the ear crystals, but nothing seems to happen. Regardless, I haven't gotten that dizzy again and seem normal enough, although I *do* keep bumping into all sorts of things. The little bruises on my body are multiplying.

"About time," my dad interrupts, not wanting to discuss the Urgent Care visit in front of someone else, even if they are family. He sets his utensils down on his empty plate and wipes his mouth with the napkin from his lap. "I can take you out on the road, too."

"Right," I say, scrambling for an excuse since I'd much rather have my cousin for a teacher. "It's just that Anthony's car is smaller, probably easier to start with."

After we finish eating, while the sun is lowering in the sky but not yet set, Anthony asks me, "Want to do a quick loop around the block? See what we're working with?"

"Sure," I say, standing from the table and trying to hide my nervousness. "Might as well jump on in . . ."

I help Mom load the plates into the dishwasher, then meet my cousin on the driveway. He tosses me his keys, which land a little harder than I would've liked against my fingers.

It's weird getting into the driver's side of Anthony's car. There's some religious medal dangling from his rearview mirror.

"Oh, one of the aunts will gift you one once you get your own car, for sure," Anthony says. "Easy enough to just hang it up."

"Yeah, I get that." But still, even though I'm set on getting my license, I don't think driving is going to be for me. I want to go to college in a city with a good transit system. I'm just doing this to have options.

As I start backing out of the driveway, my cousin says, "So, you've never shown interest in your license before. But let me guess: Now there's a girl?"

"You and Darius, man," I say. "Not everything has to do with re-lationships. Maybe I want to do this for myself. Get it sorted before college."

"Okay, okay."

There are a few cars parked along the curb, but none driving opposite me as I go slower than slow down the winding neighbor-hood road and brake about ten feet too soon for the stop sign. "But yeah . . . there is someone."

"I knew it."

"She mentioned something about it being good to learn," I explain, squinting ahead at the road. I don't like how dark it's suddenly getting. My field of vision doesn't seem to stretch as far to the right as it nor-mally would. "Even if I don't actually plan to ever get a car."

Anthony is chill, not nervous at all about being driven by someone whose only experience is from video games. "That makes sense."

"Best to get it over with."

"Then don't be begging to borrow my car all the time," he teases. "I'm a great cousin, but not that great."

Trying to go a smidge faster than ten miles per hour, I round a turn a little too tightly, feeling woozy all of a sudden. "Eh, I think this is enough for now."

"We've barely started?" Anthony looks around, trying to under-stand why I wouldn't want to continue. "At least do a second lap or something. There's no cars out."

"That's all right," I say, trying not to let on how nauseated I'm feeling and resetting our course back toward home. "Just hit me up the next time you're free."

CHAPTER TWENTY-ONE

Ellie

TECHNICALLY, I SPEND the week deciding whether or not to go to the football game, even though my mind is mostly made up. If it were anything other than a football game, I would've said yes, no hesitation. So I'm not going to let any hang-ups with Cody stop me from having a good time with Jackson. During study hall Friday, I let Jackson know I'm good to tag along.

But, in all my indecision, I haven't packed anything yet. It's going to be a tight turnaround racing home to get my things after school since the bus leaves from Amber High at 4:30.

Dad is back from work a little earlier than usual and watching something on TV when I stop by after classes are done. Rushing up to my room, I quickly throw some pajamas, clothes for tomorrow, and toiletries into a tote bag. I'm halfway down the stairs when I decide to change out of the outfit I've worn all day. A skirt doesn't really scream "football game." I'd rather wear something comfy. It's probably going to be cold all night, too, so I opt for jeans and a sweatshirt.

Then I check the time on my phone. *Shit.*

I include the socks I just finished knitting for Jackson in my bag. I debated myself on color for ages before settling on gold.

There's seventeen minutes until the bus leaves. I live fifteen minutes away.

"I'm going to a school thing!" I shout, racing back down the stairs. "I'll be back tomorrow."

With a confused look on his face, my dad meets me at the front door. "You're going to what?"

"The hotel with the football-game thing," I say, which doesn't seem to clarify it for him yet. "The tradition. I'm sure Madison went last year."

He scratches his head but nods slowly, still out of the loop. "That kind of rings a bell. Did you ask your mom?"

"I just decided to go today."

"Oh, I see . . ."

I step around him to slide my shoes on. Should I have asked permission? Since I've been living back home, we haven't really specified any rules. "And I need to hurry. The bus leaves, like, now."

"Um." Dad seems unsure but doesn't stop my leaving. Maybe he's relieved I'm finally partaking in Amber activities. He offers a feeble "have fun" as I race down the drive to my car. I throw my bag in the passenger seat and hit the road.

Four nineteen. I curse, getting stuck at a long red light at the second-to-last intersection before the school. I'm so close. Another minute ticks by. I reach for my phone to text Jackson, but the light turns green, so I keep my hands on the wheel and eyes on the road. I'm almost there.

They can't expect everyone to be exactly on time, can they? There's no chance I'm the only one who had to stop home first and is running a little bit late.

Picturing Jackson waiting outside the school for me, I squeeze through a yellow light and take a deep breath. *Four twenty-five.* I might make it there *right* on time.

Finding a quick parking spot, I grab my phone and notice several missed calls from my mom. I guess Dad told her I left for the night. Do they really think I'm going to answer this?

ELLIE:

What do you need? I've told you before,
I don't do phone calls.

If you need me, just text.

But then my mom calls again. They'll never learn.

CHAPTER TWENTY-TWO

Jackson

MY DUFFEL BAG is on the ground at my feet. Darius and I are standing next to the bus that's boarding in front of Amber High. I rub my hands together, then slide them in my jacket pockets. I'd brought my stuff with me to school today, but Ellie mentioned something about having to stop at home. And now she's still not back here . . .

I'm swaying a bit and could really use a seat, but we're about to be sitting on a bus for two hours, so it doesn't make sense to wait down on the curb or something. Just in case, I packed the anti-dizziness and anti-nausea meds. I haven't taken either yet today. They don't seem to work, only make me sleepy, which would put a damper on tonight's festivities.

"Are you sure she's coming?" Darius asks as he shifts his bag to the opposite shoulder.

I stare into the parking lot, not seeing any cars arriving. Maybe she changed her mind. "It's okay; you can get on the bus."

He checks his phone. "We do leave in three minutes."

"Right."

I blink a few times, staring off into the distance at a red car, trying to discern why my right eye seems funny. Cupping a hand over it and then my left eye, nothing really seems different, but something I can't place seems off. Like there's a darkness encroaching around the periphery. It might be time to get another exam and see if I need glasses. Especially after how difficult it was to see driving in the dark the other night.

Darius continues to wait beside me. "I haven't really asked, but how have things been going with the new girl? Ellie, I mean. How do you even, like, talk to her?"

Most of the time Ellie and I have spent together has been on our own. Traipsing through the woods during the 5K. Eating lunch in the hallway outside the teachers' lounge. Even our desks in study hall are off in the corner alone. But outside of our own little bubble, it's like we're from totally different worlds. I can't really imagine bringing her to chill with the soccer guys or her taking me to hang out with friends from her old school.

Yes, Ellie and I have made communication work, but how does it go when other people are around? Maybe that's why she didn't want to come.

"Well, I—" I look up and see Ellie rushing across the parking lot toward us. "You made it!" I say as Ellie joins us.

She's changed out of the skirt she was wearing earlier today at school into jeans and an oversized dark green sweatshirt. Instead of the clips she usually uses to hold her hair back, there's two small braids tucked behind her ears and devices. The setting sunlight casts a glow behind her, almost straight out of a movie. She looks beautiful.

"So are you two gonna share a bed or . . . ?" Ellie asks with a smirk, staring at me and Darius.

My eyes go wide. I really hadn't thought about the logistics of sharing the room. I figured we'd all just go to the game, hit up the after-parties, and then crash back in the room, exhausted and not overly concerned with any of this. But now the side-glare I'm getting from my cousin says that I'm not the one he wants to share a bed with tonight.

"I'll take the couch," I offer, as the obvious solution.

"You can have the room, maybe," Darius discreetly whispers to me with a shrug. He hurries ahead onto the bus. From the windows, I see him take a seat next to Jess, the girls' soccer team captain he's been seeing lately.

"Woo!" Jess cheers, along with a couple other girls sitting nearby, eager to get this show on the road.

About a third of the senior class is here, as well as a handful of juniors. It's going to be tight on the bus, probably with a couple people having to squeeze three to a seat. It's not limited to just the upper classes, but since it's an overnight without too much supervision, that's usually how it shakes out.

I gesture for Ellie to climb onto the bus ahead of me. As the last one to board, I'm not rushed up the steps. Yet I wobble and grab the rail, ignoring a suspicious look from the driver, who definitely thinks I pregamed or something.

Ellie grabs us an empty row in the front, right behind the teacher chaperones, since the back of the bus is already full. The driver closes the doors, and there's a smattering of hoots and cheers as we drive off. I take a deep breath to steady myself, but I'm already dreading all the potholes and winding roads we'll hit along the way.

"I'm glad you decided to come with," I say to Ellie, but she tilts her head. I try something else. "This should be a fun trip."

She shakes her head. "I'm sorry; it's impossible to hear you right now."

"Oh, right." Between the roar of the bus on the highway and the chatter of everyone behind us, that doesn't surprise me. "That's fine. I kind of need a nap anyway."

Ellie's watching my lips carefully. "Nap?"

I shrug. "Long day."

She furrows her brow but nods, probably regretting her decision to come. She looks out the window, hitting ignore on an incoming call, then typing out a long message. After sending it, she turns her phone over.

I close my eyes, but that doesn't really help with the movement. I put my elbows on my duffel bag that's in my lap and rest my face in the palm of my hand. We could text or something, to avoid talking over all the noise, but I don't think I could handle looking at a screen right now. I'm not a fun person to be around these days.

And on that miserable note, I fight to fall asleep, hoping it'll pass by the time this long drive is over.

Later, a warm hand gently taps my knee, waking me up. Ellie's peering at me. I immediately stretch out and sit upright.

"You actually fell asleep," she says, pointing toward my chin. "And kind of drooled a bit."

I turn my head toward the aisle and wipe it away with the back of my hand. It's gotten dark outside.

"Are we here?" I ask groggily. It's quieter. We must be off the highway, at least.

"They just made some sort of announcement, so I think so."

Sure enough, we pull into a hotel parking lot. This place is supposed to only be a ten-minute walk to the Buckeye Jr. Sports Complex, where the game is played.

We are the first ones off the bus, and thus, at the front of the check-in line inside the lobby. It's a bare-bones setup here, with only a few chairs in the lobby across from the elevators. There's a plate of cookies sitting on the counter, but they vanish as soon as the rest of the bus starts filing in.

"Excuse me!" Darius hurries past others to join Ellie and me since the room is under his name.

"And me, and me, and me!" Jess says as the crowd swells to cut her off from the path Darius just made. She makes it to the counter beside him to check in for her reservation, as well.

My cousin hands me the spare room key and his bag so he and Jess can hurry up to join some of the soccer guys before heading over to the stadium.

Ellie and I aren't in any rush in the hotel room. I hope none of this comes across as presumptuous of me. There are the standard two queen-sized beds, one of which I throw Darius's bag on.

"You can take that one," I offer, motioning for Ellie to claim the other, while I put my duffel on the table and take on the couch. "This has to pull out somehow," I say to myself, taking the cushions off the top, and, sure enough, there's the handle. This should be a quick motion.

Nope, it's stuck.

I try again, this time placing my foot at the edge of the couch frame. No dice. And, embarrassingly, this seems to have knocked the wind out of me a little bit.

"Having trouble?" Ellie asks, watching over my shoulder. "Let me help."

She leans forward and places a hand beside mine. With a nod, we pull it together, giving a solid attempt. But it still won't budge. I lose my footing, taking an extra step or two back, and steady myself against the bed.

"Careful." She takes a seat beside me on the mattress. "The couch just beat you in a fight."

"I'll just sleep on the cushions," I say with a sigh. "That'd probably be more comfortable anyway."

"No, I'm the one crashing. I don't want to take your bed." Ellie lies back, her feet dangling over the edge of the mattress. "Except for a few minutes right now. How much longer until the game?"

"Um." I search my memory. "It's at 7:15." But she doesn't hear me, so I lean back beside her and repeat where she can see me. She rolls to her side, staring at my lips closely.

It's tantalizing, watching her watch me like this. Her dark eyes wide and attentive. Her wide-necked sweatshirt has slid down on one side, revealing her shoulder and bra strap. Her mouth is slightly open, about to say something.

"This is weird," she says slowly, biting her lip.

I glance away toward the wall. She's the one who lay down on the bed first. I'm just following her lead. "What do you mean?"

"This school tradition," she says after a moment. Was that a pivot? She rambles on. "Like, it's not even a rivalry match-up or anything?"

I pinch a nail into my thumb to reorientate myself. "Nah, student government just picks one of the out-of-district tournament games and plans the trip."

She shakes her head at the absurdity of it and shifts how she's sitting. It just happens to position her another inch closer to me. "Do you even know what school they're playing?"

"They?" I ask, teasing her. "It's your school, too."

Ellie rolls her eyes and shoves my shoulder. "Don't remind me."

Do we *have* to go to the game?

Because I'm quite comfortable right here at the moment. Sure, it'd be better to kick off our shoes and chill here, but I don't want to do anything that would ruin the moment.

"I don't really know," I say, running a hand back through my hair and answering her question. "Heights something. Powell Heights? Yeah, I think that's it."

"Huh." Ellie recoils with a distant look on her face. She jumps out of bed and paces the room.

I sit up reluctantly. And slowly because there's the looming threat of a dizzy sensation. Not strong enough to make me sick. At least, not yet. I try to ignore it. "What's wrong?"

"Nah, nothing." She's cagey, not looking directly at me while she skirts around the topic. "I just think I might know some people on the team."

"Like from your old school?"

"Yeah." She heads over to the restroom. "Give me a second, and we can head over." When she's back out, she loops on a small crossbody bag. "Ready when you are."

"Okay." I use the toilet as well and wash my face in the sink. I'm not sure it helps me feel any better. If anything, bending my head forward makes things worse.

Will the world ever feel still again? I might be cursed to live slightly off-kilter for the rest of my life. That would really suck.

Ellie and I walk side by side over to the stadium on the narrow sidewalk along the mostly quiet road. The streetlamps are already shining bright above us. Our hands accidentally knock once, and she immediately pulls hers back. Did she think I was trying to hold it? I wasn't, but this is a very confusing reaction after how close we just were in that hotel room.

I really don't understand her.

There's already a huge crowd at the game swelling the small concourse. Ellie and I follow many folks to the concessions line first, then up the steps into the stadium seating area, where we take our place in the student section. Everyone's screaming over the marching band to make themselves heard.

Beyond the sidelines, there are cheerleaders doing their thing before kickoff. The golden Amber High players warm up on the field opposite the dark blue Powell Heights team.

I'm dreading having to stand the entire game.

"How about we sit while we eat," I suggest, although parents are the only ones who are seated at these events. Our seats are toward the back anyway, with the most die-hard fans up closer to the rail.

She nods in agreement, not as riled up as everyone around us.

On any other night, I'd scarf down all four of these chicken tenders with no problem. But I'm feeling queasy. "Do you want some?" I ask Ellie, but she isn't looking, so I hold out a piece toward her, which she gratefully accepts, having only gotten nachos for herself. But she munches it slowly, staring down at the field.

Soon, the game starts. We stand and half-heartedly participate in the wave, which zips back and forth across this narrow student section. It's clear Ellie and I aren't really into the spirit of the event. I watch the twelve minutes on the clock slowly creeping down. And this is just the first of four quarters. The bleachers are getting rowdy.

"I'm going to run to the restroom," Ellie says, stepping away suddenly. "I'll take the trash."

"Okay, I'll be here," I say, immediately taking a seat as soon as she bounds down the steps.

Yeah, it's going to be a long night.

CHAPTER TWENTY-THREE

Ellie

I CAN'T WATCH Cody play all night.

My ex is here. Right there on the freaking field.

His last name is strewn across the back of his jersey. Fischer, 48. That's basically the only distinguishing feature I can see of his right now since he's got his football helmet on. Fischer is common enough, but paired with his freaking *lucky number*, there's no doubt in my mind that's Cody.

I haven't had enough time to prepare to be in the same space as him again.

I rush down the bleachers and head back to the concourse, where I dump the trash into a garbage bin near the concession stands. I need to clear my head. Jackson's been kind of out of it tonight. Swaying and staring off into the distance, not seeming to focus on the game, nor as talkative as usual, which might be why he hasn't noticed how distracted I am.

Cody goes to Powell Heights. He looks at home with his team. They're all buddy-buddy even though he doesn't hear a single thing they're saying. When they come together in the huddle, there's an interpreter for him. Apparently, Cody's taught his teammates a few signs as well, but from what I can see, it's mostly swear words.

What are the odds that his school would be playing Amber? I was shocked when Jackson mentioned the name, but I didn't think it would affect me this much to see my ex.

My breath catches, and my heart aches. I was so angry I tried to fast-track mourning my breakup. And I might've been successful if this hadn't happened. With Cody right there in person, I remember how easy it used to be to take his hand, to curl up against his chest, to feel his lips press a kiss against my forehead. I knew one day I'd see him again. The Deaf community can be so small it's almost a given that we'd cross paths at some point. But so soon after we broke up? The miles between us were supposed to be a barrier. He's here, of all places?

I stand along the wall, checking my phone. For healthy boundaries, I'd muted Cody's socials ages ago. If I hadn't, maybe I would've gotten more of a heads-up about tonight. His profile has a lot of football photos. Too many, really. Like, it's basically *all* football stuff.

There's a link to some article about Cody being PHHS's new Deaf football star. It's super wordy about how the team has been amazingly accommodating for him, in a real pat-yourself-on-the-back kind of way. Some nice inspiration porn. Cody's probably lapping all that attention right up. He was popular at Brandview, but at Powell Heights he gets to be *unique*.

It's not fair. At his new school, he gets to stand out in a good way. Whereas without the PR that comes with being an athlete, I was just immediately considered a freak at mine.

Someone taps my arm, and I put my phone away immediately. But it's not Jackson.

Worse.

It's Cody's mom.

"*Ellie!*" the tall woman signs, warm and pleasant as always. She pulls me in for a tight hug, but as she leans back, her eyes are narrowed. With one hand still on my shoulder, she asks, "*What are you doing here? For Cody?*"

"*Cody's here?*" I feign shock. "*My new school, A-m-b-e-r, is playing.*"

"*Oh-I-see,*" she signs, clearly relieved I'm not stalking her son. Which I'm not. In person, at least. I don't think she caught a glimpse of my screen. "*I need to get back, but it's such a great surprise to see you. Come say hi after the game. I'm sure Cody would love to say hello, too.*"

"*Great to see you!*" I sign, not committing to anything else, but she's already rushing off. It's strange having such a brief interaction with someone I considered a mother for so many years.

It's only the start of the second quarter, but the crowds on Amber's side have begun to clear. Their team is down by *a lot*, and there's parties to be had at the hotel.

Jackson taps my arm. "Should we head out?" he asks, his eyes drooping and enthusiasm lacking.

But I want to stay to the end and see if I can wave for Cody's attention. I would feel weird leaving without at least signing a quick hello, especially with his mom knowing I'm at the game. I'm not avoiding him or anything, though I guess I don't need to seek him out, either. What's the right move?

"Let's just wait," I tell Jackson. "I don't really feel like going to a party yet. We can sit for the rest of the game, though."

Grateful to rest again, Jackson immediately plops down on the bench and doesn't ask any questions about why I want to stay. Why is he so tired after napping the entire way here on the bus? Will he still want to go to any of the hotel parties?

Eventually, the game ends, and PHHS celebrates their victory. Cody takes off his helmet, revealing that he's grown his hair out several inches. I always told him how good that would look, but he never took my advice until now. Figures.

"Ready to go?" Jackson gestures toward the bleacher steps.

I lead the way but pause at the rail, looking down toward the field. Cody's team is migrating over to greet their families and friends. I think he's looking this way, so I wave, but he doesn't see me yet. Something compels me to wait.

Jackson asks something ending in "there?"

"Someone from my old school," I say, assuming that's what his question was.

I wave again, and Cody finally notices me. He doesn't look surprised. He must've recognized that they were playing the school I go to now.

"*Nice win,*" I sign across the crowds.

"*What are you doing here?*" Cody signs back, shoulders raised in confusion.

"*You played my new school.*"

"*Right.*" He nods. Okay. Did he not remember Amber is where I go now? Why is he so indifferent to the fact that I'm here right now?

Before I can sign something else, a girl runs down the bleachers, onto the field, and into Cody's arms. He holds her in a hug, and I see from the back that she's wearing his spare jersey. The matching 48. The "you look so cute in my lucky number" jersey. The girlfriend-of-a-football-player outfit. When they finally pull apart, she cups his cheeks and gives him a passionate kiss.

Oh.

Relax, he didn't win the freaking Super Bowl.

After making out in front of everyone, Cody looks back up at me with a shrug.

My blood boils. I don't know what I expected. "*Okay, then.*" I grit my teeth.

"*Stop, Ellie,*" Cody signs. The girl stands at his side, so impressed with his signing, clearly having no idea what he's saying to me. "*Get over it. We were only together because you clung to me and everyone expected us to be.*"

Only because he never let me hang out with anyone else. *Agh, I could scream!* Out of the corner of my eye, I notice his parents watching our exchange. That's what happens when you sign across a public space like this. But I don't censor my response.

"*Okay, asshole.*" My hands fly. He's stooping low. Like I'm right back in it and he's dumping me all over again. *Get over it*—I'm so tired of letting him dictate my emotions. "*You're not that great. Always so full of yourself.*"

I feel Jackson standing beside me, watching curiously. Has he pieced together that we just spent the last hour watching my ex play?

Cody had broken up with me so jarringly, but maybe I should have seen the signs along the way. Had I been looking back at things with rose-colored glasses? Was our time together really that bad? Brandview was small. There weren't many options when it came to dating. But I know for a fact he chose me as much as I chose him.

Honestly, all things considered, he was a pathetic choice.

"*Sorry you can't find someone else,*" Cody signs, glaring up at me.

"*Or maybe I just take my time.*" I tilt my head forward incredulously. He didn't realize how good he had it. I'm a catch. I'll make Cody regret those words. He really thinks I've just been sitting around pining after him? I'm *not* losing this breakup.

Jackson looks down at the field, then back at me. "Everything okay?" he asks.

I step forward and take hold of his open jacket. "Hey." I press even closer, looking up into his brown eyes. "Can you kiss me?"

He twitches, shocked, eyes darting toward the field, but without giving it another thought, he leans into me as I pull him closer.

Our lips meet. A simple peck might have sufficed, but Jackson hasn't backed away. So I don't, either. I reach my arms around his neck, feeling a flutter of delight as he, in turn, wraps his around my waist.

Jackson certainly didn't shy away from me this time.

For a moment, I forget the jealousy and anger that initiated this. Jackson is the first guy I've ever kissed who *isn't* Cody. And it's different. It's *better*. I'm not kissing to go through the motions or to act like how a couple is supposed to act, which was always the case with Cody. How hadn't I seen this yet?

I'm actually drawn to Jackson. At Brandview, Cody and I were kind of inevitable. At Amber, no one would expect me and Jackson to be together. We're nothing alike.

Yet it works.

I shiver as Jackson raises a hand to graze my cheek. I pull him even closer, standing on my toes. He sways, but I hold on to him.

Almost inadvertently, I pull my head back for a second to peek a glance down the field, unable to resist the satisfaction I'd have seeing Cody standing there in shock.

I hardly locate my ex before leaning back into Jackson again, but his eyes are now open. He steps back and can't let go of me fast enough. He dips his head and latches onto the rail, gripping it tight. He noticed me looking toward the football players. While we were kissing. *Shit.*

"I—" How do I fix this?

Cody waves his arms for my attention. *"Wow, really nice. Sucks to be him."*

"Nice?" Jackson asks, having recognized one of the signs Cody just used. The color drains from his face. "So that's—" He looks from me to Cody. "Of course," he mutters through gritted teeth, rushing away down the aisle, turning into the stadium concourse.

I run around the corner after Jackson. I've really screwed this up. And for what?

CHAPTER TWENTY-FOUR

Jackson

I CAN'T IGNORE the dizzy sensation anymore. It's violently taking over me.

I don't know exactly what makes it escalate from an off-kilter feeling to an inability to stand. Maybe it's from moving too fast. I keep walking but stumble, having to catch myself on the rough concourse wall. Leaning back, I slide to the filthy ground, unable to coax my body to move any farther.

I'm sick, tired, and decidedly *used*.

Everything needs to stop.

Is that why Ellie came this weekend? All because her ex was on the other team? If only I knew what she was signing furiously across the field. She kissed me just to get back at him. Is that all this has been? Am I just some distraction to her?

I take a deep breath and close my eyes. Okay, if I stay perfectly still, maybe this will all go away. But my head still sways ever so slightly, side to side, and I can't stop it.

I shouldn't have come on this trip. I could be home in bed right now, and none of this would've happened. This was supposed to be a way to make it up to Ellie for missing last weekend, but I guess she wasn't really that bothered by it after all.

Her kiss took me by surprise since neither one of us had seemed to be enjoying the evening. But I didn't want to question it. Ellie's lips were so warm and soft. Inviting. Eager. Kissing her initially seemed like everything I'd hoped it would be.

But it wasn't real.

At least, not for her.

"Jackson?"

Ellie's nearby. Her voice is soft, cautious. She crouches down beside me. I don't acknowledge her presence.

Why is this freaking happening again?

She's speaking. "I'm sorry. I didn't mean to—"

I turn to the other side and cough, interrupting her. It takes everything in me to keep the chicken tenders down.

"Are you okay?"

"Mm-hmm," I mumble, unwilling to unclench every muscle in my body. "I just need a moment." By now she probably realizes that I'm not just sitting here to be dramatic about her and her ex. I couldn't care less about that kiss anymore. I need to get out of here. Back to the hotel.

"Can you get up?" Ellie offers a hand. With no other choice, I accept but waver on my feet. She wraps an arm around me. "Do you need to see a doctor?"

I try to shake my head. A mistake. This is awful.

"Jackson, I think—"

"No." I close my eyes, trying to steady myself. "This is what happened Saturday," I say. Or, at least, I try to say. It may come out more like, "Tbhib what happened." I really can't be sure.

"Jackson . . ." She's concerned. Are my lips not shaping the words correctly, either?

I do my best to enunciate. "Vertigo. The doctor said."

"What are you doing?" another voice calls toward us. Someone older. Someone from school. A teacher?

"He's not feeling well," Ellie explains, practically holding me upright.

"Have you been drinking?" he asks.

"Drunk? No," she says sharply. "Smell his freaking breath. He's not."

The teacher steps forward and sniffs. This feels much worse than being inebriated. I do my best to stand up straight. And not vomit on him. "Really," I say, trying to stick to short words and enunciate. "I'm fine. Some vertigo. Basically nothing." To sound more convincing, I manage to string a full sentence together. "I just need to go back to the hotel. Now."

Ellie wraps an arm around my back and guides me a step away. I guess we can leave. We hurry off without further question. But once we've exited the stadium, I lose momentum.

"Slow," I croak out. Clutching her tight, I close my eyes for the rest of the walk back to the hotel.

We take the elevator.

Why are there so many people in this hallway? Why is it so long? It's like it stretched out by a mile while we were gone.

The door. The key is in my wallet.

Ellie is reaching a hand into my pocket.

Wait, I'm mad at her.

We're in the room, and I let go, following the wall toward the bed. But I don't want to lie down. Down is bad. Down is dizzy. Yet I can't stand, either.

Sit. I need to sit. I slump to the floor.

And hurl.

Ellie slides the empty ice bucket into my lap right in time.

Nice of her.

But she's the worst.

Vomit, again.

Ellie asking something. I can't answer.

Then I remember.

"Mm—"

"What was that?"

"Mmmedicine." I raise a shaky finger toward where I think my bag is sitting.

I close my eyes.

Ellie reappears with two orange bottles. Reads the labels. Hands me a pill from each.

And water.

Both. I hope they'll stay down.

"Just a m-minute."

We sit.

It's been some time.

How long?

Ellie's still here.

Is this medicine even doing anything?

Maybe if I close my eyes again.

And stay very.

Still.

CHAPTER TWENTY-FIVE

Ellie

JACKSON HAS BEEN frozen in place for fifteen minutes. He's clutching his arms wrapped around his knees, both resting his chin and keeping his head upright, with his eyes squeezed shut. I can't figure out how to adjust the temperature in this room, so I gently draped a blanket over his shoulders. I don't know if that helped, but he didn't shrug it off.

I'm not even sure how we made it back to the hotel. I ducked my head beneath Jackson's arm and led the way, his legs moving enough to manage some of his own weight despite having his head drooped over my shoulder. We left the stadium with a burst of energy. He was in a rush, trying to cover as much distance as he could, until he could only manage a snail's pace. Then the fifth-floor hallway was party central, which made it nearly impossible to get to our room unnoticed.

I sit beside him, leaning against the bedframe, watching him closely. I keep trying to reassure myself that he'll be fine. He said this is what happened last weekend and had medicine that he could take, which is the only reassurance I have right now that he's okay to stay here.

Whatever's going on, he needs to go to the doctor again.

He was slurring his words. He was very dizzy. But he said he was fine, right?

It's getting late. If he isn't doing better in the next five minutes, I'm finding help.

I watch his chest rise and fall. Slow, steady breaths. Carefully reaching forward, I brush a strand of hair away from his eyes. He flinches at my touch.

"I'm so sorry, Jackson," I whisper.

I really, really hope it's not my fault that this happened.

He'd been quiet most of the game. He was eager to sit down and wanted to go back to the hotel. But I made us stay later. And then I kissed him.

He must be so mad at me right now. He doesn't even seem to want me here. But there's no way I'm leaving him alone like this.

My stomach rumbles. I need something more to eat than the concessions we had earlier, and Jackson must, too, considering how empty his stomach is right now. Except I don't really have an appetite. Even though I'd bagged up the vomit, it's still sitting by the door. With a very strong scent.

Okay, screw five minutes. I need to find a chaperone. How long is this supposed to last? Isn't vertigo usually a symptom of something else?

As I stand up, Jackson finally stirs.

He reaches to rub his hands down his cheeks and leans back slowly. Cautiously.

"You're alive." I kneel, joining him on the floor again and searching his face for any sign of something going on still. He's pale and exhausted. But groggily alert and becoming more aware by the second. "Oh, thank god."

"I'm . . . starving, actually." He reaches an arm to the bed but must not have the strength. I move forward to offer my assistance, which he reluctantly accepts. "Ugh. I really want to brush my teeth."

"I'm sure."

"And get changed."

Grabbing both of his hands, I help Jackson up. Our arms break apart once I'm standing before him, so I place my hands on his chest. He's warm to the touch. I try to help slide his jacket off, but he narrows his eyes and gives the smallest head shake.

"I can do this by myself," he says.

I can practically taste the disdain. So, yeah. He remembers that he's mad at me. And I get it. What happened at the game wasn't my best look.

Hoping this will change how he feels, I reach into my bag for the socks. "I brought these for you. That I knit, that you asked for. I thought it'd be good to give them to you this weekend . . ."

Will he understand that I meant for this weekend to be about us? That I had no idea my ex would be here? That I wanted to kiss him, admittedly under better circumstances?

He takes the socks but leaves them on the bed as he walks to the bathroom.

"Do you want me to order something to eat?" I ask, reaching for my phone and holding it out. I don't have anything else to offer him right now.

Jackson waves his hand back as if to say "whatever." Right, I should've known that's how that would go.

I order a plain cheese pizza and some sodas. By the time the order arrives twenty minutes later, Jackson is still in the bathroom. Which is unfortunate because the driver is calling me.

"Hello?" I answer the call, but it's gibberish on the other end. "Sorry, I can't hear you. Are you here with the pizza?" More gibberish. "Um, wait a second. I'll just come down to the lobby." More gibberish, with obvious attitude. I hang up.

"Jackson?" I knock on the bathroom door, but I'm unable to hear if he says anything. "Jackson, are you okay in there?" Trying the handle, I find it's unlocked.

Opening the door a crack, I immediately feel steam. I didn't realize he was taking a shower. Jackson has just stepped out and is standing there, towel wrapped around his waist, glaring at me.

Whoops.

"You couldn't just *wait* a second," he says, eyes narrowed and unfazed by my shock. "I was coming to the door because I know you couldn't hear me."

Water drips down his arms to the floor. He clutches the towel but doesn't cower away or seem uncomfortable about the fact that he's standing in front of me essentially naked. I dart my eyes away to the clothes piled up on the countertop next to his toothbrush and toothpaste. It all feels very domestic, and it's not lost on me that, if I'd done things differently and not messed everything up, this night could have gone in a very different direction.

I'm seeing Jackson in a completely new light. I took for granted the easy familiarity between us. Right now, we might as well be strangers.

"Um, I'm going to grab the pizza."

"Okay." He nods toward me. "Can you go already?"

Despite the heat, the atmosphere is frigid in here.

I turn on my heel and pull the door shut behind me. Rushing out of the hotel room, I remember to bring the bag of vomit to throw away, but it's not until I'm riding the elevator back up with the pizza from the very annoyed driver that I realize I didn't grab the key card.

Knocking once, I wait, trying to be patient this time. Jackson hasn't opened the door yet. He might be getting dressed. But did he hear me knock? Should I do it again? Remembering the glare he gave me as I broke into the bathroom, I decide to wait.

A few seconds later, Jackson pulls the door open wide, stepping away as I let myself back into the room.

He's in a long-sleeved gray shirt and athletic shorts, with his hair partially towel-dried and brushed back. He reaches out for the pizza, so I hand him the box, and he takes a seat on the bed, propped up against the headboard. I stand there, unsure if I should grab a slice and go to the couch.

Jackson rolls his eyes but says, "It's okay; just sit here."

I climb onto the bed beside him, careful to move slowly so as not to shake the mattress. He's not wearing the socks I made him, nor are they anywhere on the bed anymore. It wouldn't surprise me if they're in the trash. We each finish a slice in silence. That seems to be all he wants right now, but I eat a second piece. "Are you doing all right?"

He takes a deep sigh. "Better now."

"That's good." I want to tell him how worried I was, but I also don't want to add to any stress he may be under. "But, please, can you make an appointment to see another doctor? I think this is something you need to get checked out more."

"They didn't really do anything about it last time."

"Sometimes there's dizziness that accompanies certain types of hearing loss," I suggest, thinking of Ménière's disease. "Maybe it's like that."

"No"—*something*—"different." Jackson's eyes dart away. Then he mumbles about "you would" and "if I was." Is he trying to say that he thinks I'd like him better if he was also deaf? What have I done to make him think that would be some sort of requirement?

Desperate to explain and apologize, I reach out to touch his arm. "I'm really sorry about how—"

"I don't want to talk about *that*." Jackson slides under the blankets and lies back.

"Oh, I didn't know . . ."

He closes his eyes. I'm sure he's exhausted, but this is him blatantly ignoring me now.

"It wasn't like that," I say softly. "But I *do* like you and really liked that kiss and wish I hadn't been so messed up by my ex that I ruined the moment."

Jackson doesn't move. He might be asleep now.

I slide off the mattress and put the pizza box on the dresser, then step into the bathroom to get ready for bed. There's a spare blanket in the little front closet, and I take an extra pillow from his cousin's abandoned bed. I could probably sleep there, but I wouldn't want to take Darius's spot if he does end up coming back. Plus, this uncomfortable couch is all that I deserve tonight.

Before I turn off the light, something sticking out of Jackson's bag catches my eye. The golden pair of knit socks.

CHAPTER TWENTY-SIX

Jackson

I'M READY TO forget this terrible trip ever happened.

After last night, I don't say a word to Ellie all morning. I'm glad for her help getting back to the hotel, but I'm still pissed about what happened at the football game. We leave the room together, but then she stops for a cup of coffee, so I go ahead to the bus outside, where my cousin is already waiting with some of the soccer guys.

"How was the room?" Darius asks, winking. "I struck out, but we saw the two of you looking very cozy, so I crashed with some of the guys."

It's hard to pay attention to what he's saying. The dizziness is really lasting this time, more than ever before. I need to hold on to something or sit down. This bus ride home is going to be miserable.

For many reasons.

"Actually, it was—" I'm about to explain to Darius what happened when Liam steps forward from the back of the group.

"Yeah," Liam taunts. "Figures the only girl you could get is the one who doesn't hear the shit you say."

"What are you talking about?" I ask.

But then I remember Ellie helping me back to the room. And the key card in my pocket. How could the guys think that that looked like any sort of fun? I was moving like a zombie. I must not have been vomiting yet.

Oh, I threw up so much. Ellie stuck around to take care of it all. She really didn't have to do that. I probably should've tried talking to her more last night, but I was so exhausted and still angry about the game.

Her ex was there. And that's why she kissed me.

It certainly didn't feel like that was the only reason why she kissed me. I'm not imagining that, right? It was a good kiss. It could have been a great one under any other circumstances. But then I went and got sick, so we couldn't even have a proper fight about it.

We're not going to be able to talk about it on the bus, either. So now what? Do we just forget it ever happened?

Liam's still trying to get a rise out of me. "Can deaf people even have sex?" he taunts me. "But I'll bet you found a way to make her scream." He motions in a very disgusting, suggestive way, managing to mock both ASL and Ellie in one go. This needs to stop.

I look over my shoulder and see Ellie coming this way with her eyes welling up, but she brushes right past us. She's tough. I never thought I'd see anything that could break her. But she also had a rough night.

"Did I get that right?" Liam shouts, still waving his arms around nonsensically. Ellie removes her hearing aid and cochlear implant receiver, shoving them in her pocket as she climbs on the bus. "So you can hear!" he yells after her.

"Back off, Liam," I say, going after Ellie.

"Hey, man." He gives an indifferent laugh. "I'm just asking questions."

I need to pace myself climbing the stairs. I clench the side bar. It's only a few steps. One at a time. *Don't vomit.*

"Okay," Liam calls after me, before making a big pronouncement to the guys he's standing with. "Here's Grandpa, holding on to the rail for dear life, and he thinks he's gonna come back to the team?"

My phone slides out of my right hand, bouncing off a step, and cracks on the pavement. Ignoring the laughter behind me, I carefully step back down to pick it up. The screen is shattered. Great.

I find Ellie a few rows from the front, clutching her bag and looking out the window. She doesn't move when I sit down beside her. A single tear slides down her cheek.

Everyone else is boarding the bus now. Fortunately, behind the lines and discoloration, my phone still works, so I send her a text.

JACKSON:

Ignore him. Liam's the worst.

I hear her phone vibrating in her pocket. She doesn't move to grab it until I gently nudge her. She reads the message and types back one word.

ELLIE:

Sure.

Does she understand that I was just as offended by Liam as she was? I send another text.

JACKSON:

This wasn't a good time.

She shakes her head as she types her response.

ELLIE:

No, it wasn't.

But she turns and leans into me, resting her head on my shoulder. I sit straight and close my eyes.

Let's just get home.

CHAPTER TWENTY-SEVEN

Ellie

IT'S A LONG drive back to Amber. Jackson dozed off quickly into the drive, and I wish I were tired enough to do the same.

What's it going to be like in the spring when Jackson officially starts back up with soccer again? If Jackson decides he's done hanging out with me after this terrible trip, he'll probably go running right back to the team. He'll return to sitting with them every day at lunch. There's always been a time limit to our relationship. He's using me to get through the offseason, and I'm using him until I can leave Amber. I guess that's all this has ever been.

Except Jackson's here right now. Asleep on my arm. He's upset with me but still chose to sit by my side. How do I make things right?

Back in the school parking lot, Jackson hesitates as we are about to leave. I'm dying to talk about last night, but he simply says, "I don't want to throw up in an EasyRide right now."

"I can take you," I offer without hesitation.

He's unsure. "Can you—" he says, then something about "my cousin?"

Darius is over there with Liam and the others, probably planning to keep the weekend outing going. "He's with some of the soccer guys," I say.

"Ugh, Darius usually hangs out with the better guys on the team, not those assholes." Jackson groans, then gives me an apologetic look. "I promise they're not all as bad as Liam—I'm not sure how much you heard of what Liam was saying . . ." His words trail off as he closes his eyes and scratches his forehead. "I had nothing to do with that. They were just trying to get a rise out of me."

It's not the first time I've come across gross, ignorant behavior like that. I know Jackson wasn't a part of it, so I don't want to deal with that right now. "Really, just let me drive you home. It's the least I can do."

"Okay," he mutters. He trails behind me to my little old sedan and grimaces as he lowers himself into the passenger seat.

"What?"

Jackson doesn't answer—maybe he didn't actually say anything—but he reaches out a hand for my phone to enter his address. It's the complete opposite direction from where I live, so I'll be getting home later than I expected.

As we pull out of the school parking lot, I'm sure Jackson says something this time.

"What was that?" I ask, turning to face him.

"Watch the road!"

I stare ahead. "I didn't veer at all; *relax.*"

Whatever it is that he said, I'll never know, which is beyond irritating. He doesn't try talking again for the rest of the twenty-minute drive.

There's a giant fountain at the front of his neighborhood. The huge houses are spaced far apart, and each one seems to have three- or four-car garages. The sprawling front lawns are bright green. Many properties have gates that require keycodes to access.

Dang, Jackson lives in the *rich* part of town. If I'd had to guess, I would've assumed his family was well-off, but this is next level.

"You can just park here," Jackson says as we approach the gate to his house. As soon as I stop the car, he pushes the door open.

"Wait," I say, jumping out to follow him before he goes through the walkway entrance. "Can I just . . ."

"What now, *Ellie*?" Jackson turns slowly. There's so much exasperation in the way he says my name. If only the ground could swallow me whole.

I wring my fingers together. "I know none of this went as we might've hoped. But thanks for inviting me."

He shrugs, avoiding my eyes.

"Maybe some other time we could—"

Without letting me finish, Jackson answers, "Maybe." He walks away.

I beat myself up over it the entire drive home. Why did the game have to be against Cody's school? Why did I have to look down at the field? Why did Jackson have to notice me doing that?

My mom must've heard me park the car on the street in front of our house because she's waiting for me at the door, arms crossed. She mutters something.

"What?" I ask, not really caring.

Louder, she repeats, "You are *not* allowed to take off for an entire night."

"It was a school thing." Seriously, why is she so mad about this? "I told Dad I was going."

This doesn't appease her at all. "Right, you *told* him and left. But you should've asked us beforehand."

"We got it all cleared up over text. I'm back now." I roll my eyes and continue toward my bedroom, but she stands between me and the stairs.

"While you live here, you need our permission."

I don't care about this. Why are they trying to act like I'm a little kid? Just because I'm living at home now doesn't mean we've gone back in time.

I walk around her up to my room, where I turn and shout a parting shot down to her before closing the door. "I haven't needed your permission for a long time. You can't expect me to follow rules you've never put in place. You thought I was plenty responsible when I went away to school. Since I've been home, the only thing you've done is hold me back."

CHAPTER TWENTY-EIGHT

Jackson

WAKING UP SUNDAY morning, I still feel like shit. Somehow worse than I felt yesterday. The metaphorical truck didn't just hit me. It smashed me into the pavement.

Mom lets me sleep in but comes to check on me each hour with offerings I didn't ask for. "Jackson, are you feeling all right? Here's a glass of ice water." "Actually, I thought some orange juice would do you good." "Dried mango, since you've missed breakfast and now it's lunchtime." Until finally, it's two o'clock and she thinks I need to move. "Let's go sit down on the couch, okay?"

I literally drag my legs out of bed, thumping heavily down the stairs as I clutch the railing. The dizziness won't quit, and I'm certain now that something weird is going on with my right eye. I can see out of it, but also, I can't. There's a pressure behind it, and my vision is dark and hazy. What the hell is causing that?

Mom fluffs a pillow on the couch, brings me a new glass of ice water, and places the untouched mango in my lap. I put something on TV but give up after feeling the strain in my eyes. Instead, I scroll through my phone, which is still shattered. I can't ignore the tingling in my fingers as I swipe through Instagram, dreading everyone's photos from yesterday. I'd rather forget all about last night, so I give up on looking at this, as well.

I grab an ice cube from my glass of water and press it against my eye, hoping to dull the pain.

As much as I hate sitting here doing *absolutely* nothing, my dad hates watching me sink farther into the couch.

"Come on; what's that going to do?" he asks, clapping his hands like a football coach trying to rally the team out of the huddle. "Get some fresh air. You'll only feel worse sitting around."

"I don't know." I'd love to get up and move, really. But that doesn't seem in the realm of possibility right now.

My dad pulls out his phone and sends a text. To me—and all thirty-seven members of our extended family group chat.

DAD:

Darius. Come over and practice with Jackson.

Dad has the chat on mute, so his phone doesn't blow up with responses the way mine does.

ANTHONY:

Dannnng, what about me? Ahh I see, he's got time to dribble but no time to drive.

UNCLE CONNOR:

Cousins helping cousins

AUNT DONNA:

Jackson, I heard you were finally going to get your license. So proud of you!

MOM:

He is!!

ROSA:

Any cousins going to help me and Dan finish painting the baby's room?

AUNT MARY MARIE:

How wonderful!!! Praying all goes well!!!

DARIUS:

Yes sir, on the way.

Dad claps again, waiting for me to stand. "Come on, go get dressed. I told your cousin to come over. I'll get the net out in the backyard."

"I *know*," I say, holding up my phone, which is still buzzing as more family members chime in.

"When did you break that?" Dad takes my phone and frowns at the screen. "Didn't we just upgrade?"

Mom steps in for the save. "You were going to run to the store soon anyway, so you can take it for him next week. And, Jackson, I threw some of your clothes in the dryer, and they should be ready."

Taking a deep breath, I hoist myself from the couch, ignoring that now familiar tingle, an uncomfortable combination of itch and tickle across my feet, and slowly march to the laundry room. At least I don't have to go back upstairs. I search for my things in the dryer and somehow manage to drop both my shirt and joggers to the ground on the way to the first-floor bathroom, where I get changed.

Darius must have hopped in the car as soon as he got the text, because he pulls up to our house a few minutes later, right as Dad comes inside the back door, with the soccer net now in place out on the lawn behind him.

"You really didn't need to come over," I say, leaning on the door for support as I open it for my cousin.

He steps in, waving hello to my parents. "Yo, when Uncle Roberto actually uses the group chat, and for the sole purpose of summoning you, you don't say no. I've seen the movies—family is everything."

"That's not what it's for?" my dad asks, face stoic, though he's clearly amused with his own antics. He pats my back as Darius and I head outside, but even the light touch to my shoulder has me staggering beneath the motion, almost knocked over. "All right, son, you can shake this off. Go run around and get out of your head."

The worst part is that it is a gorgeous sixty-degree day. I take a cautious step off the patio onto the grass, stretching my arms out wide and admittedly feeling a little better taking in the sunshine. Darius jogs over to the net and picks up the soccer ball, which needs some air. It's been a while since I used it.

Darius runs to the shed to fill up the ball, then tosses it my way. I pass it back to him—an easy, weak kick.

"So you didn't party with us Friday," Darius calls out after running to stand in the goal. He tosses the ball back to me. "Are you going to avoid the team forever? If it's 'cause you're dating Ellie, you know I can say something to the guys and—"

"That's complicated right now."

I pass the ball between my feet but struggle to maintain my balance. Why is this so difficult? Since I haven't attempted to score, Darius jogs back to me so we don't have to shout across the lawn.

He says, "Sorry, I shouldn't have brought her up in front of Liam. He'll make a joke out of anything. I was like, *yikes*, when she noticed him doing that shit."

"Yeah, that wasn't cool."

I'm not sure how much of that Ellie heard or saw. And hopefully she didn't think I'd said anything to Liam. Why would I? It's not like we even hooked up or like I would say anything to the guys if we had. The night was just a huge embarrassment for me.

I bend down to pick up the soccer ball. *Oof, not a good idea.* My vision flickers. I spread my fingers wide, holding the ball tight against my chest, trying to stabilize myself.

"But I don't know how much I'm going to be hanging with her anymore," I say.

"Did something happen?" Darius would usually tease me more, but he's been uncertain how to act around me lately.

Shrugging it off, I point toward the goal. "Okay, I think I'm ready now."

Darius runs back into place. I toss the ball out in front of me, ready to kick. But my legs don't move.

They've gone fully numb. I'm so startled that it takes another moment to realize that I've lost feeling in my right arm. It's significantly worse than the tingling I've been putting up with for a while now.

Darius runs over to me. "Dude, what's up?"

"I, um." Part of my face feels strange now, too. Warm, numb maybe. Talking feels funny. I have to force the words out. "I think thomthing issss wrong."

He runs inside for my parents while I stay stuck in the grass, my head spinning. I need the world to stop turning. I shut my eyes tight, watching the red behind my eyelids swirl and swirl. I try to walk toward the house. But my legs give out beneath me.

I trip over nothing.

Dad sprints over to catch me before my head can hit the ground. Mom gasps loudly, and Darius mutters something nervously under his breath.

"We're going to the hospital," Dad says softly as he carries me to the car. "We're going now. We're going."

Mom buckles me into the back seat and holds me upright as Dad pulls the car out of the driveway. I brave a small glance to see Darius standing on the drive apprehensively before squeezing my eyes shut again and rolling my head onto my mom's shoulder.

Am I dying?

CHAPTER TWENTY-NINE

Ellie

WITHOUT TELLING ANYONE at all this time, I leave the house on Sunday to hang out with Shay, Izzy, and Alex again. We've got the Coffee Garden all to ourselves this afternoon. Even though October is still around the corner, the shop is decked with ceramic ghosts and jack-o'-lanterns.

"*We never made it to Oktoberfest this year,*" Shay signs, disappointed.

"*That already happened?*" Izzy shakes her head. "*I forgot it's in September.*"

"*I should have mentioned it.*" Alex scrolls through something on her phone and signs one-handed. "*It was a lot of fun last time. I'm adding it to my calendar for next year right now.*"

They sign about making plans, but I'm not paying attention. I'm still caught up thinking about yesterday. Maybe I should text Jackson.

Shay nudges me. "*What's going on with you?*"

I take a deep breath, knowing my story is dramatic. "*I ran into my ex.*"

All three of them wince in response and drop what they were doing.

"*From Brandview?*" Shay asks. "*Where did you see him?*"

"*The football game.*" I pull up the article about Cody on my phone again. It's just as self-serving as I remembered. I hand it over to her, making a sour face. "*He's their special player now. Thinks he's the shit.*"

"*Is he the only Deaf there?*" Izzy asks.

"*Probably getting a bunch of hearing girls because they think he's all quiet and mysterious,*" Shay signs.

"*I don't know if he's the only one, but with the hearing girls, yeah, that seems like it.*" I'm really worked up recounting all of this. "*I mean, this girl was kissing him, then just watching us have an argument in sign and looking like*"—I angle my shoulders to role-shift and sign from the girl's perspective—"*'Oh, how cool.'*"

"*Ridiculous,*" Izzy signs.

"*This is that guy who dumped you over FaceTime?*" Alex asks.

I scrunch my nose. "*The very same.*"

"*Wait, who did you go to the football game with?*" Shay asks. "*Not the guy you ran off with at the 5K?*"

Holding the back of my hand up to my face to sign my frustration, I make my eyes go wide. "*And I messed that up now.*" I don't want to go into the specifics. "*Plus, when I got home from the trip, my parents were the worst, as always. I really, really hate living at home again.*"

Shay purses her lips in contemplation. "*Do you want to move out?*"

"*Absolutely.*" I shake my head. I've dreamt of moving out ever since I got back and had to make myself at home in my sister's room. "*But I have nowhere else to go.*"

"*We were just talking about renting a place near ACC.*" Alex looks toward Izzy. "*And you and I would share a room?*"

"*Right.*" Izzy nods, reaching for her phone to find pictures. "*It's a three-bedroom house.*"

"*Yeah, we need someone for the last room,*" Shay signs to me. "*I didn't realize you needed a place.*" She turns for unanimous approval from the others. "*It's yours if you want it!*"

I could move out. I don't have to live at my parents' to finish out the year at Amber. This would make life so much easier.

"*Yes.*" I don't need to consider it a minute longer. "*One hundred percent yes.*"

"*Deaf house!*" Alex adds a flourish of applause.

Izzy shows us the rental listing for a cute little house less than a mile from the community college. It has super outdated appliances, a splintering porch, and a small backyard with patchy, browned grass. To me, it's perfect.

But I hesitate when Shay shows me the monthly rent. "*It would be split cost?*"

"*Yeah.*" Shay nods. "*You can have a roommate for your room if you want. Since Izzy and Alex will have the main bedroom with their bathroom, you and I would share the hallway bathroom. I'm fine with another person sharing that bathroom, too.*"

"*Okay-okay.*" Even though I have absolutely no idea who I could possibly room with. Or how big of a fit my parents will throw when they find out I want to move. They only just got me back home, but it's their fault that I want to leave. "*When do you need to know?*"

"*The owner said we can tour next week,*" Izzy signs with a shrug. "*And if we like it, sign the lease a few days later.*"

All right, so not much time to find a job and a roommate. Or at least a job that pays well.

"*I'll figure it out, for sure.*" I take a sip of coffee, the plan already taking shape in my head, though I'm not sure how quickly it could all come together. I try not to seem too emotional when I share my gratitude. "*I'm so lucky to have found you all.*"

Izzy waves her hands toward the others excitedly, as if recalling something. "*I was just saying the other day how you fit into the group so easily.*"

"Oh!" I exclaim, remembering a very important question. "*Could I bring Cheese to the house?*"

Shay furrows her brow. "*Yeah, you can eat cheese?*"

"*I mean,*" I sign, poking two fingers into my opposite palm, "*my cat.*"

"*Cat!*" Alex signs enthusiastically. "*You're not allergic, right?*" she asks Shay, who smiles and shakes her head.

"*I think we can have pets,*" Izzy signs. "*I'd love to have a cat there.*"

"*Perfect.*" I'm not sure how Cheese would do with a move, but I'm sure he'd be happier there with me than alone at my parents' place.

Ha, my *parents' place*. That's how quickly I've given up on referring to that house as my home.

$$\searrow\diagup$$

I'm the first one at our lunch spot outside the teachers' lounge on Monday. Usually, Jackson beats me here. I wait to open my lunch.

How will this go? There's a chance he shows up and pretends like nothing happened. That this weekend changed nothing. Even though everything is different now.

That kiss *wasn't* nothing.

I don't want to have a whole discussion about my ex, because I'm closing that chapter. If anything, maybe Cody was an excuse for me to kiss Jackson. It was the wrong place, the wrong time, and to-tally skewed logic, but that's it. I wanted to kiss Jackson. And seeing my ex kissing someone made me want to kiss the new person in *my* life, right?

Ugh, I need to pull myself together. That's not an explanation Jackson's going to be a fan of. It all looks bad no matter how I try to frame it.

Now it's halfway through the period, and Jackson hasn't shown up. I dig into my lunch but don't feel like eating. Is he avoiding me? Is he back in the cafeteria? He'll have to be in study hall, though.

Except he isn't there, either. Okay, so he probably wasn't avoiding me, then. I stretch my arms out on the desk, looking around, unsure what to do now. I hope Jackson is okay.

CHAPTER THIRTY

Jackson

YESTERDAY, THE DOCTOR and nurses in the emergency room took my vitals, did a lot of bloodwork, asked a ton of questions, and set me up with an IV. The CT scan came back negative, which was a relief because we could rule out a stroke. Or a tumor. Or a whole host of other scary-sounding things.

But that didn't answer why I can't feel half my body. I was moved out of the ER and admitted to another floor of the hospital for a longer stay.

I spend much of Monday lying in the bed with my parents hovering nearby. It's clear I'm not leaving here anytime soon. I couldn't walk out even if I wanted to. They're going to do an MRI as soon as it's available because whatever this is seems to be in my head.

Because everything's pointing to something wrong with my brain.

An old lady with a walker paces back and forth down the hallway, getting in some exercise. She smiles at me each time she passes my door.

I don't want to interact with anyone. I want to be home. I won't be here long. I'm only eighteen.

This can't be what comes next. I have to be able to play soccer again. Or go to college. Or have a serious girlfriend. Or get my freaking driver's license. Or be able to live on my own.

I'm not ready for this. Whatever this is.

My parents take turns staying with me. Mom is at home gathering some things, so when Dad gets a call that he needs to swing by the office because there's a problem at his company's factory, he has to leave me alone for a few until she gets back.

"Your mom is minutes away, and I'll be right back," he says on his way out the door, then pauses at the doorway. "I'm sorry."

The word is loaded. It's more than an apology about having to check in on the business. It makes me uncomfortable because I don't think my father has ever apologized to me like this before. I scrunch my shoulders down, lowering half my face beneath the thin sheet draped over me.

"It's okay," I say.

Moments after he leaves, Mom rushes in with a tote full to the brim. "Phone chargers, underwear, a couple outfits if they let you out of that gown, some books . . ." She continues listing everything she brought, but I notice the golden knit socks in the bag, as well. "You meant these, right?" she asks, following my gaze. Before I can say anything, she's slipping them on my feet. My toes must be frigid, because she gives them a squeeze. Everything is still so numb.

"What time is it?" I ask.

"Just after four," she says, looking at her fitness-tracking watch.

"Can you send a text for me?"

"Sure." She reaches for my phone, wincing at the cracked screen again. "I need to get this fixed for you so it's not broken when you—when . . ." She's stuck because we still don't know how long I'll be here.

"Um, to Ellie. She's probably one of the last people I texted," I say, knowing full well she is likely *the* latest one. "Can you say something like, 'Hey, I'm not going to be in school for a little while'?"

My mom types for a minute. "Okay, sent." She stares at me, eyes welling up. "Maybe I can meet this Ellie soon."

CHAPTER THIRTY-ONE

Ellie

WHEN I GET home from school, I get a text from Jackson saying he won't be at school for a while. But he hasn't acknowledged my response asking how he's doing, so I'm left to spiral about where he might be. I hate that the last time I saw him was after that terrible football game.

As soon as I walk inside the house, I go straight to my room. Too many problems to worry about. Time to figure out how I'm going to find a roommate or money for rent.

At Brandview, Kayla and I were assigned to the same dorm since her original roommate left the year I started. We were pretty good together. We had none of the arguments that most roommates have. I'm not sure I'd call us close friends, especially since we haven't been in touch since leaving. Well, I haven't really been in touch with anyone because they were all better friends with Cody, apparently.

I should check in to see how Kayla's doing.

ELLIE:

> Heeeeeeey, long time no see! So weird
> we're not in our dorm right now.

Kayla replies instantly with a link to video chat.

KAYLA:

> I miss it so much!!! Are you around?
> Can we sign please?

This is going much better than I would've thought, which makes me sad I hadn't thought to reach out to her sooner. I join the video from my laptop.

"*Hi, hello!*" Kayla signs, cheery despite our questionable internet connection threatening to lag the video and disrupt our signing. "*Can you see me okay?*"

"*Yes, how are you?*" I try to match her enthusiasm, but that's always been difficult.

"*Fine, you know.*"

There's clearly more to it than she's willing to say, so I break the ice first. "*Being back home sucks, seriously.*"

Her hands explode again, ready to pile on. "*It's really not good! I'm still so sad about it.*"

"*I'm so sorry. But glad to know it's not just me having a rough time.*"

Kayla's phone lights up on the table beside her, but she ignores it after a quick glance. "*Have you seen anyone from Brandview since?*"

"*Funny you say that.*" Cheese walks in front of me, waving his fluffy black tail and blocking the camera. I nudge him away but appreciate when he turns back around and curls up at my side. "*Actually, I just saw Cody.*"

Kayla makes a disappointed face. "*I thought you broke up?*"

"*Yeah, we're definitely broken up.*" I hold my hands out. Totally done.

"*Good; he was always a dick.*"

"*Wait, really?*" I didn't realize Kayla had such a strong opinion about Cody. She never made that known before.

She nods and takes a sip from her water glass. "*He was always picking on me before you got to Brandview. Like the kind of cruelty people excuse because they say that teasing just means a boy likes you.*"

That would've been a long time ago. Cody had kind of been like that to me before we got together, so I understand what she's saying. Being a jerk to someone is not the right way to express your emotions no matter what. I only wish I'd known not to mistake interest for affection.

"*I'm so sorry,*" I sign. "*I didn't know.*"

"*Yeah. Then, when you two got together, he kept you for himself. We never got to hang out, you and I.*" Kayla shakes her head, then laughs. "*I was kind of surprised when you texted.*"

"*Looking back, I realized I didn't make many friends there. I want to say because of Cody, but I have to take some of the blame myself. I don't know, I was, like, stuck on just him.*" I poke two fingers against my throat. Then I reach out my arms and make a pushing motion to the side to reset and sign a new topic. "*Where are you at? Aren't you near C-i-n-c-y, too?*"

"*Yes, same. I think we might be like thirty minutes apart.*"

"*Ooh, that's perfect.*" Maybe we could still get to know each other better, even after Brandview.

Kayla lowers her eyebrows in question. "*For-for?*"

Will she even want to move out? No idea. But I'll plant the idea and hope for the best. I hadn't realized it was possible before Shay mentioned the house, so maybe when faced with the possibility, Kayla will be eager.

"*Would you want to be roommates again?*" I ask.

She leans back, intrigued. "*Oh, we could?*"

"*Yeah, I made some friends who go to Amber Community College, and they're gonna rent a house.*" I smile wide, saving the best for last. "*All Deaf.*"

"*Wow, I miss that.*" Kayla hasn't answered the question yet, but I can see her eyes light up at the idea. "*That's why I wanted to hop on video. I never get to sign anymore.*"

"*Do you use an interpreter at school?*"

"*No, my parents didn't request one.*" Kayla shakes her head. "*Totally dependent on my implants. It's whatever; I just have to manage to finish out this year.*"

"*I understand. Hey, even if you can't move into the house with me, I'd love to hang out soon.*"

"*Yeah, let's hang out! And I'm interested in the house, for sure. What's the rent?*"

We go over the details and plans for jobs and breaking the news to our parents. Izzy mentioned working at the ACC library last I hung out with them. She mostly reshelves books, which sounds ideal, so I asked her to see if they were hiring soon. I tell Kayla my plan, then we continue to chat for another two hours about our families, new schools, and more.

"*Yeah, I'm in,*" Kayla signs at the end of our call. "*I'll let you know how it goes asking my parents.*"

My cheeks are exhausted from grinning. I'm so glad we reconnected.

And when we hang up, I find a text from Izzy with the link to a library job listing. Perfect timing.

CHAPTER THIRTY-TWO

Jackson

IN THE EVENING, a nurse comes to roll me over for an MRI to get imaging of both my brain and my spine. We enter an area of the hospital where a sign says NO METAL BEYOND THIS POINT and go into another smaller hallway where the exam room is located. The door is open, waiting for us. I can hear the *whoosh* of the machine before I see it: a giant circular white device with a concave center. The tube where I'll be spending the next hour or two.

Since I'm still struggling with my legs and arm, the nurse helps me transfer onto the long slab table, placing a warm blanket over my hospital gown as I lie back. *How am I supposed to fit in this circle?* I didn't really think I was claustrophobic, but now I'm doubting myself. We overshoot where my head needs to go, so she slides me farther down. I squeeze my eyes shut.

"Oof, dizzy?" the nurse asks. "Are you going to be able to lie like this for the exam?"

"Mm-hmm." *We'll see, I guess.*

She tucks my arms at my sides and unfolds the blanket up toward my chin. The MRI technician takes over from there, raising the table off the ground, wedging foam behind my neck, and inserting plugs into both of my ears.

I think I'm about to go in the machine when she lifts some sort of cage up and locks it into place around my head. I start to panic.

"You're all right," the tech says in a somewhat soothing tone.

I try to calm myself. "I just wasn't expecting that part."

"Did they give you any antianxiety meds before this?"

"I didn't realize that was an option."

"Will you be okay to continue?"

Do I have a choice in any of this? "Yeah," I lie.

My eyes are wide open as I'm slid into the machine, watching the light of the exam room slide out of view. My arms brush against the sides of the tube. I thought I'd maybe be able to peek out to the room, but other than a little bit of my legs, all I can see is the cage on my head and the machine I'm inside. This is already terrible.

And then I find out why she gave me earplugs.

This machine is *so* loud. My eardrums could burst. If I didn't have any hearing loss, I certainly could develop some now.

Knock. Knock.

How long does this go on? Sometimes there are brief pauses, then a different tone of knocking begins again. Almost like the sound effects of an old video game. My back is stiff. There's a small itch at my nose that I'm dying to scratch. I take slow, steady breaths, aware of my chest rising and falling. Does that count as moving?

Eventually, the technician's voice comes through the speaker. "I'm taking you out to inject the contrast agent now. And then, after that, it'll only be about ten more minutes or so."

"Okay," I say quietly. Does this mean another needle in my arm?

It does. I wince my way through it.

Back into the machine I go. I close my eyes as I slide in. But once inside, I open my eyes and discover that I can stare down at my feet . . .

Knock. Knock. Knock. Knock. Knock.

. . . and the golden knit socks.

CHAPTER THIRTY-THREE

Ellie

THE DAY AFTER catching up with Kayla, I've been packing my things back into the two suitcases I used to take stuff back and forth to Brandview. It's quick because a lot of things are going straight into the donation pile due to the association they have in my mind with Cody. Unfortunately, a lot of my favorite outfits now leave a bad taste in my mouth. I'm not too upset about it, though. It's like I'm getting an actual fresh start now—this time of my own accord.

I'm deciding where and when I go.

I haven't told my parents yet. There's no perfect time to be like, "Hey, Mom and Dad, goodbye." I've generally been avoiding them, so the opportunity hasn't presented itself. It doesn't matter how that conversation ends up going, because my mind is totally made up.

It's still a tricky task figuring out how I'm going to pay rent. The library job Izzy sent me would be the perfect fit. Except, there was one requirement I don't meet. It's only open to ACC students.

I think there are some classes taught here at Amber High that count for college credit through ACC. Does that come with a student ID? I guess I need to stop by Ms. Lily's office.

Why can't *anything* ever be simple? There are always so many little hurdles to clear before accomplishing a big goal.

The next day at school, I go see the guidance counselor during study hall, requesting that Kim come along to interpret for me. If Jackson were here, he'd probably know all the logistics of these class credits, but I have to figure it out without him.

Ms. Lily waves me into her office. She's wearing a dress with a very busy pattern that seems to match the bowl of candy on her desk. Her doorway is down the hall from where I've been eating lunch, the spot feeling significantly lonelier without Jackson, and anytime Ms. Lily walks by, she gives me a pitying look, which hasn't exactly made me want to stop by for a chat. Now she quickly positions the second chair to the side of her desk for my interpreter to sit on.

"Ellie Egan, am I glad to see you again!" Ms. Lily says, and Kim relays, matching the enthusiasm.

"*Hi, yes, nice to see you,*" I sign.

"*Happy. Here.*" She's clearly practiced, waiting eagerly for this day. "*You!*"

Nodding, I push ahead with the topic at hand. "*I want to know how to sign up for one of the college credit classes through ACC.*"

Ms. Lily turns from me to watch Kim as she finishes speaking, then scrunches up her face, unsure. She types something on her computer. "I'm not sure there's anything you'd be eligible for at this time. Is there something in particular you're interested in taking? Do you know what you're planning to major in?"

What do other students usually take? Probably some math or science requirements. Either way, I don't know what I want to study in college yet. I might as well just be honest about why I'm asking.

"I'm trying to get a job in their library, but you need to have a student ID. Since I'm going there next fall anyway, I wanted to see if there was a way to start earlier."

Ms. Lily moves the mouse around to conduct another search on her computer. "Your algebra grades are decent. There's a chance we could switch you over to the ACC credit course after the semester break if you passed a placement test. Would you like me to ask the instructor if we could try that?"

"Yes, please!" I've never been this excited to cram for a math test in my entire life. But my plan is working. *"When could I do that?"*

"I'll send you an email once I know if we can arrange it."

"Thank you. Would I get student registration, like, right away so I can apply for the job?"

"Yes, if it all goes well, I think you'd be able to get set up with that soon."

After leaving the guidance counselor's office, Kim sticks with me for the rest of the period since there's only a few minutes left before my next class. She takes the seat in study hall where Jackson usually is.

"Where's your friend?" she asks. She's not usually one to make any personal small talk, unlike Pamela.

"Out sick."

"Sorry about that. I hope he's better soon."

"Me too."

I send a text, unsure if he's been getting my messages.

ELLIE:

Hope things are going all right.

If he were here, I'd be gushing over my plan. Things are in motion. If all goes well, I'll not only be able to move into the house, but I'll be officially enrolled at ACC, cementing my plans for the fall. Kayla hasn't confirmed yet, but I hope she'll be on board and we can split costs. This could really work.

CHAPTER THIRTY-FOUR

Jackson

I ADJUST THE hospital bed so that I can sit upright. I'm not sure how long the MRI results are supposed to take, but we've been waiting most of the day. I don't bother looking at my phone. Mom and Dad trade off turns between the more-comfortable tan sofa and the chair in the corner. They're trying to act calm so they don't stress me out any more than I already am, waiting for what's sure to be life-changing news.

I test my sensations, poking my numb arm and wiggling my toes. Everything feels off. And my eye. My freaking eye, where my vision is wonky and I feel like I got punched in the socket. What's making all this happen?

Finally, the attending doctor comes back. My parents lean forward anxiously. I turn my head to look but can't bring myself to make eye contact with the physician as she tells me, "The MRI results do indicate demyelination. We've got a neurologist coming by early tomorrow morning to review with you further."

What on earth does demyelination *mean?*

Mom jumps into action. "Is it on his portal? Can we review the results ourselves?"

"Yes, it should be up there soon if it isn't already."

After fielding a few more logistics questions from my parents, the doctor leaves, and my mom whips open her laptop. "What's your password?" she asks me.

I'm still trying to wrap my head around what just happened. "For what?"

"The health portal. Since you're eighteen, I can't access your information through my account anymore."

"I've never used a portal or made a login." Why couldn't this have all happened when I was seventeen and my parents could do everything for me?

Mom figures out a way to set up my account anyway.

I turn to my dad and ask, "Can you google—"

He holds up his phone, where he's already been scrolling through the results for *demyelination*. Demyelinating diseases. They play a part in several chronic conditions. Neurological problems. Autoimmune diseases. What does any of this mean?

Still, no one has answered the question at the front of my mind. *Am I dying or what?*

Despite me half-heartedly telling my parents they don't have to, they spend another night here with me. Those chairs do *not* look comfortable. *Whew.* In truth, I'm not sure I could handle being here by myself, but being in a hospital, it feels like I'm not supposed to let on how scared I am.

As promised, first thing in the morning, a neurologist comes to my room. He's got a trim beard, wire-framed glasses, and a pen tucked behind his ear. "Hello, Jackson Messina?"

"Yes," I croak, having not spoken yet today. I clear my throat.

The doctor greets my mom and dad, then, presumably pressed for time, he gets right down to business. On a tablet, he pulls up the results from my MRI. "The images show white lesions on the brain and spinal cord." He turns toward my parents. "This is indicative of . . ." He continues on, and I know this is all important to understand, but I space out, unable to compute the magnitude of the information. *Lesions on my brain and spinal cord?*

I tune back in to catch the most important part: the diagnosis.

"Multiple sclerosis," the neurologist says.

The type of thing that happens to other people. The type of people my parents' charities raise money for. MS . . . It might've even been the disease Amber High's 5K was supporting. Never in my wildest imagination did I ever think something like that could happen to me.

My mom takes notes, which I'll need to consult later, as the neurologist continues. "We'll schedule a regular neurology appointment to do a full diagnostic workup and go over what options are available to you."

"Um," I say, voice shaking, "what exactly is happening?"

"Your immune system is targeting your nerves. It thinks the coating around them is something that needs to be destroyed, which results in damage that interferes with the communication between your brain and your body. The impact of this disease varies greatly from person to person because different nerves can be damaged. Does that make sense?"

I nod, but I don't understand it at all. *What does any of this mean for me?*

Does the dizziness go away? Will I regain feeling in my body?

Does it get better? Or will it all get a lot worse?

"While the disease can continually advance, usually it does the most progressing during periods of relapse," the neurologist explains. "Treatment would function as a means to hopefully have fewer relapses."

"Okay." I still don't fully understand.

"Fortunately, the more we learn about MS, the earlier we're able to discern and make this diagnosis, which hopefully bodes well for patients in the long term."

I guess that's what I just went through. "Will it, I don't know, go away, then?"

The neurologist pauses before saying gently, "At this time, there's still no cure."

Huh. This is it.

Mom shifts in her chair, taking a long, deep breath. "Will he be paralyzed?"

At the same time, Dad throws in a heavy-hitting question of his own. "Will this impact Jackson's life expectancy?"

We're really getting to the meat of it. I guess they've heard of people with this disease before. Maybe it's better that I'm in the dark here.

"It's certainly not what it used to be. With the new treatments available, we can keep this disease at bay, doing our best to prevent loss of functionality. Like I said, we'll get you set up with an appointment at our MS center, where we'll do a full examination and go over treatment options with you in greater depth."

"What can we do about it now?" I speak up for the first time.

"*Now*, Jackson," he says, giving a small smile, "if you want, we can tackle your active lesions with a course of IV steroids. That should help you feel better sooner rather than having to wait for your current symptoms to run their course."

"And that's different from the treatments you mentioned?" my mom asks, still scribbling frantically. The neurologist rattles off the long scientific names for a bunch of treatment options. Eyes wide, Mom catches the administration of each. "So basically pills, injection, or infusion?"

"Yes, there are now a lot of disease-modifying therapies—DMTs—to choose from."

"What are the side effects?" Mom presses, while Dad gives me a half grin that's likely meant to be encouraging.

"Well," the neurologist continues, "as part of the examination, we'll first need to do additional bloodwork to make sure he's eligible to take certain DMTs and isn't at high risk for something like PML, which is a rare brain infection. Once we've gathered all this information, then he'll be able to choose a treatment option."

"Is there a holistic approach? Or a specific diet that could help?" Mom asks, though I know she won't like the answer. Yoga can't fix everything.

"In my professional opinion, I recommend getting started on a DMT as soon as possible. With something like this, every day counts. Diet is something that certainly can help how well a patient feels on a day-to-day basis, but food does not cause this disease, nor can we reliably expect it to cure it."

But all I see my mom scribble down on her notes is *diet certainly helps*.

"Do you have any questions for me, Jackson?" the doctor asks. "I know this is a lot, and I promise we'll go through things more closely at our later appointment. For now, let's focus on getting you back home."

I'm sitting up quietly, letting one of the most important discussions of my life go on basically without me. If anything, I have *too many* questions. The only one at the tip of my tongue, however, is "Will I be able to play soccer again?"

The neurologist looks at me, his expression softening. "I typically advise patients to do their best to stay active. You may find yourself needing to make adjustments when it comes to heat management and fatigue."

"All right." But what exactly does that entail? "I'm just tired of being lazy. Even before this got this bad, I hated not being able to do anything because of the dizziness."

"Please remember you do need rest. It's not being lazy. Your body is hard at work recovering and taking care of itself. The best thing you can do is not actively fight against that process."

"Okay."

Mom writes *rest* in her notes and underlines it three times. She's never going to let me leave the house again, is she?

"There's a lot to know about the disease and what we have left to learn. I'm sure you'll google to learn more," the doctor suggests, but then side-eyes my mom. "Within reason. I recommend the MS Society to find reliable resources."

"Okay," I say again.

The neurologist says his goodbyes and flags down the nurse to get things in motion for the multiday steroid course. My parents and I sit in silence, processing everything. We don't really know anyone with MS. Mom and Dad take health seriously, so I'm hoping this doesn't come as too much of a disappointment to them. But that's something to stress about another day. Right now, I'm just feeling a bit . . . relieved?

Rather than being swallowed up by fear or anxiety, I feel light. Because I have answers now. Even if there's still a lot unknown about

MS, now I generally have an understanding of what's going on with my body.

Something Ellie once said comes back to my mind. *Anyone can become disabled at any time.*

She was right. I'd originally doubted how straightforwardly she'd said it, but now I'm also finding comfort in her clarity. I didn't do anything to cause this. It's not some personal failing of mine. It's just . . . anytime. And I'm anyone.

My mom is already several web pages deep into the internet rabbit hole. "I just don't know if we should risk those side effects," she says of the treatment options. "That brain infection, I know they say it's rare, but—"

"The doctor hasn't even officially discussed treatments yet." Dad puts a stop to this. "Jackson's got to stop this relapse first, and then all those other preliminary examinations, and then we can worry about what treatment he'll choose."

"What used to happen to people before the injectments?" I ask, annoyed that I'm still stumbling over words. My brain is smashing two different ideas together at once. "I mean treatments, like injections. It doesn't fix it, just manages it?"

"Well," my dad says slowly, "the disease progressed. And then"—he pauses, his voice lowering to almost a whisper—"they died."

That word hangs heavy in the air.

"Maybe they just didn't eat correctly, then," Mom says after a while, still not willing to trust the medications yet.

Dad shakes his head. "Do you really think they didn't try anything they could?"

I know I will.

CHAPTER THIRTY-FIVE

Ellie

THAT WEEKEND, MY parents both leave together to go pick up Madison for fall break. It's not lost on me that only my dad drove to bring me home from Brandview. They'd gotten into a routine over the years of Mom driving me there and Dad bringing me back. That didn't change for the final ride. But Madison's been away for like two months and it's a whole production to go get her.

While they're gone, I use the time to clear off Madison's bed, which I've been using to arrange and pack my things. The closet is still stuffed with her belongings, so I shove my suitcases along the wall and hope it doesn't look too obvious that I'm getting ready to take them somewhere.

By the time my parents get back from Indiana with my sister, Madison has already told them all about her time at college, so no one bothers to recap for me when we sit down for dinner.

"How about these?" my dad says, holding up a crispy potato slice. "Better or worse?"

"Oh, no offense, Mom, but—" Madison gushes something about the "chef at Kappa," wearing her new IU sweatshirt. "The sisters invite me over all the time. They're so great."

"How fun—your kind of sisters," I mutter, but everyone ignores me. I stab a salty wedge with my fork, cramming the entire thing in my mouth.

"I can't wait until rush in January. The house is—" she says, and then something about "huge windows in almost all the rooms." Madison throws her arms out wide and dramatically. She says something about "natural light!"

"And did you know that—" Mom jumps in, totally absorbed with everything Madison has to say. "Because you know the curtains—" Something, something, something. Get me out of here.

"I know, right!" Madison exclaims.

"What do you think?" Dad asks me.

Now all three of them are staring at me, waiting for a response. "I think . . . that I haven't been paying attention to anything you're talking about."

Mom looks irritated, while Dad is disappointed. Madison makes a face and keeps talking. "Anyway—" She turns her back toward me as she entertains our parents. "And then I will—" She continues on and on.

Even if I were trying to follow along, I would be mishearing all sorts of things. Earlier, I thought they'd gone on a tangent about "crackers" until I realized what Madison had actually said was "jackets." Not sure how I got that from *that*. It's hard to understand when I can only pick up the most familiar-sounding parts.

I'm about to slip away from the table when Madison acknowledges me directly. "I heard you've been hanging out with Jackson Messina?"

I give a side-eye stare, not liking where this is headed. Did Mom and Dad tell her that he was here? "Yeah . . . How do you know that?"

"I heard from my friend Ashley, who actually just got elected vice president for student government. Good for her." Madison takes another bite of dinner. "What's going on with you and Jackson?"

Dad nods eagerly. "We've met him. He was very nice."

"You weren't cut out for long distance with that other guy?" Madison pauses to recollect his name, never mind that I dated him for five years. "Cody, right?"

"No, I'm not dating Cody anymore."

"And you're going out with Jackson?" Madison presses, grinning like she's ready to tell that Ashley girl all about it. "I can see that; he always did love a project." Wow, she really went there.

"Madison!" Even my mom realizes this is offensive.

"No, I don't mean it like *that*," Madison insists. "Just that he'd be all over helping out with a new student, you know?"

"Right, yeah," I say, standing up. "It was a total charity thing."

"Come on, that's not what I'm saying. I'm joking around."

"I know," I concede. Even though her idea of a joke isn't funny to me. "It's not really anything anyway."

"That's unfortunate. I think you guys could be good together." She nods sincerely. "I mean that. He's cute and sweet, and you deserve someone nice."

"He is nice," I say, regretting how badly I screwed everything up with Jackson.

I know he said he'd be out of school for a while, but I assumed that meant a day or two, not the entire week. I'm concerned but hope this means he's getting everything checked out. I keep meaning to text more, but I can never find the right words to say.

As I leave the dinner table, my family resumes their easy conversation, going back to the good old days when it was only my parents and their preferred daughter at home.

Cheese trails behind me up to the bedroom I'm once again sharing with Madison for the weekend. But this time, I get to keep the good bed. "It's you and me, buddy," I say, scooping him up for a hug. "And soon, we're going to be out of here."

On Monday, Ms. Lily arranges for me to take the algebra placement test the next morning. Talk about no time to prep. But I think I do all right. By Wednesday, I'm back at her office again, waiting in the hallway with Pamela, who has caught the attention of some freshman from the ASL club and is answering their questions about how she became an interpreter. I understand that occasionally Kim needs to take some time off, but that means I get stuck with Pamela for a full day, and that's much more than I can handle.

The student before me leaves Ms. Lily's office. I go inside without bothering to stop Pamela's conversation and ask her to join me.

"Hi, Ellie," Ms. Lily says, then looks past me. "Is your interpreter here?"

I point out the door and smirk as she goes to fetch Pamela, who rushes inside. *"You could have told me it was time."*

"I didn't want to interrupt you," I sign back with a shrug.

"Okay, now that we're all ready," Ms. Lily says, and Pamela interprets. "I wanted to share the good news in person."

It better be good news. I swear, if I spent all Monday night brushing up on algebra, as well as having to show up to school at seven for a Tuesday morning test, it better have been worthwhile.

"You passed the placement!" Ms. Lily congratulates me with ASL applause.

"*I'm so excited!*" This is a tremendous relief.

I needed this piece of the puzzle to fit because I didn't have any sort of backup plan. Everything about moving out was really hinging on the success of passing a math test. Who would've thought?

"We'll get you set up to transfer into the college credit course next semester." She reaches across the desk to hand me a piece of paper. There's a long link that I'm going to have to type out to get to a website. Maybe this would've been better as an email. "Here's some information on how to officially register, and that will make you eligible for the student ID card for job purposes, as well."

"Thank you, thank you," I say and sign while rushing out the door, then spend the rest of study hall on my laptop getting the registration and student portal all set up, as well as applying for the ACC library job.

Once I submit my application, I tab back to my inbox to look at the email that's been there for a few days: the lease for the house. It's waiting for signatures. When I get the job, I will sign that—there's no going back. I send a text to my future roomies.

> **ELLIE:**
>
> I THINK I'M ACTUALLY GOING TO BE ABLE TO MOVE IN! JUST APPLIED FOR THE JOB!

The group chat lights up, and Izzy replies right away.

> **IZZY:**
>
> I'm with my boss right now and gonna tell him to look at your application asap!!!

I'm buzzing with excitement. Last night, I'd gone with my friends to tour the house, but I was trying not to get my hopes up in case everything fell through. I've really got my heart set on it.

The room that would be mine is on the ground floor. The walls are painted blue. There's a tiny little closet and creaky old floors. Still, I sent Kayla photos, and we both drooled over the possibility of it being our new home. She hasn't sorted everything out with her parents yet, either, but I've got a good feeling.

CHAPTER THIRTY-SIX

Jackson

THE FIVE-DAY COURSE of IV steroids brings my hospital stay to over a week. It's playing with my mood. Up, down. Happy, sad. Energetic, tired. Glad my parents are with me, annoyed they haven't left my side. But the steroids do seem to be curtailing this flare-up, as I regain sensation in my limbs and the numbness fades.

Now I'm the one walking back and forth in the hallway, gratefully clutching the cane they gave me. I haven't seen my old lady neighbor in a few days—hopefully she's back home and well. I don't know what she was in for, and I don't want to consider the alternative.

Finally, I'm cleared to go. I'll get to sleep in my own bed again. And leave here in one piece. I've been taking everything one day at a time, but now that this part of the saga is over, emotions hit hard. I'm not going home the same. I'm going home someone diagnosed with MS.

Back at the house, my parents and I sit around the table for dinner, out of things to chat about. I push a pile of peas around my plate with the third fork I've used this evening. My right hand couldn't manage to keep hold of the other two, so I guess I'm a lefty for tonight. My grip isn't totally back yet. And there's still a bit of ongoing tingling, which I can sometimes forget, yet other times it's all I can think about.

"When do I have to go back to school?" I ask.

"Not until next semester," Mom says, and I jolt in surprise. "I've already got you excused for an academic leave of absence for health reasons."

"That's a good idea." There's no way I would've been able to catch up at this point. Yet a sinking feeling nags at me. Another negative added to a huge pile of disappointing things I'm dealing with right now. Everything I did in high school was to prepare for college, and I'm not sure an incomplete semester looks great on a transcript.

But feeling the weight of the diagnosis, I don't even see the point now. Am I still supposed to go study business and spend every remaining day of my life at a plastics company? Likely without any extra stamina to pour my spare time into something like CrossFit the way my dad does.

It all seems bleak. I've lost any enthusiasm for that path. Whether my parents like it or not, MS is going to have me making some changes to my plans.

"You're always so positive," Mom says, completely unaware of how I'm feeling. "I'm inspired by how well you're taking this diagnosis. I know it's hard."

No, what was hard was pretending I didn't hear my mom stifling her tears while curled up on the hospital couch each night. She seems more upset than I am. It's probably more difficult watching this happen to me. I'm just here, taking everything one step at a time.

Over the course of the next few weeks, as my parents feel assured enough by my slow recovery, Dad returns to work and Mom picks back up her usual routine, leaving me with a lot of time to sit alone with everything that's happened. And it eats away at me.

I've got more questions than answers. No one knows what my future is going to look like. No one can guarantee that I won't end up in a wheelchair. No one can assure me that my body won't give out on me and create limitations I might not know how to tackle. No one knows anything with absolute certainty.

You know who might understand this better than I do right now? Ellie. She'd know something about disabilities and diagnoses and have all the right things to say. For the first time in what feels like ages, I send her a text, feeling a skip of guilt as I scroll past the couple unanswered messages she'd sent while I've been gone this past month.

JACKSON:

> Hey, any chance you could come over for a visit soon?
> Maybe after school Friday?

It's a school day. But she replies about a half hour later during a passing period.

ELLIE:

> How have you been??? I've been thinking about you all the time. Sorry, I have a shift that day. Does Saturday work?? I could drive over whenever. Anytime.

She started a new job? Or did she always have one? No, she would've mentioned that before. So much has changed in so little time.

JACKSON:

> Okay cool, let me know if you need the address again

ELLIE:

I think I've got it. I hope you're doing okay.

I'm a little nervous for her to see me like this, since I'm still so slow and sluggish and tripping over words, not to mention using a cane.

But my desire for her company outweighs all that anxiety. I've got a couple more days to pull myself together—emotionally, at least.

CHAPTER THIRTY-SEVEN

Ellie

WEDNESDAY AFTER SCHOOL is my first shift at the ACC library. It's a straightforward job, and it really helps that Izzy is the one training me. Along with Alex and Shay, she's also given me a tour of ACC, and it already feels more like my school than Amber does, mainly because the three of them are there.

After work, I stop by the Deaf house to drop off a few more small bags of stuff. Only Kayla and I haven't moved in yet. I've been drawing out the process over several days, making sure to bring things with Cheese's scent on them so that he'll be comfortable.

In the living room, Shay unrolls a large Deaf pride poster with splashes of bright colors and ASL iconography, and hangs it above the fireplace.

"That's cool," Alex signs. *"Where'd you get it?"*

"Do you remember E-t-h-a-n?" Shay motions a time way back. *"At that party we went to in N-Y-C. Short, wild hair."*

Izzy remembers. *"Right! The guy who works at that summer camp near Chicago?"*

"Yes! I followed him on IG, and he shared this website with a lot of different posters and T-shirts for sale."

I put my old Brandview nameplate on the inside of my bedroom door. Will Kayla bring hers, too? It'll be just like old times. This blue bedroom is so empty, but with two of us living here, I'm sure we'll make use of every little bit of space.

Kayla managed to figure everything out on her end, too, and will be moving in next week. She told her parents, and surprisingly they were okay with it as long as she comes home for dinner after school most nights. I can't imagine my parents reacting that well to the news, which is why I'm waiting until the last possible minute to tell them.

Friday night, after my second library shift, I finalize my move into the Deaf house. I can't wait to tell Jackson about this tomorrow. I've been worried about how Cheese will do, but he's settling in just fine, exploring the mostly empty rooms in search of bugs to toy with.

Shay, Izzy, and Alex get back from a trip to Ikea. They borrowed Shay's cousin's pickup truck to haul the boxes. I asked them to pick me up the cheapest bedframe and mattress they could find, which is going to eat up most of my first paycheck—when I finally get paid in another week—but it's all *mine*. Even if all my furniture's unassembled.

"Building night!" Shay signs as we drop the boxes off in my room.

Alex carries in a tall, rolled-up rug that's puzzle-patterned with neon colors. She unfolds it and uses some of the boxes to flatten the ends. *"Rugs are expensive, dang. This is the best thing I've ever thrifted. No one spill anything on this!"*

There are a lot more pieces to this bed than I would have expected. Cheese watches from his little cat tree in the corner as I spend a full hour assembling the frame, turning that little wrench tool so many times that my wrist hurts. When I'm finally done, it's such a relief to stack all the trash in our recycling pile and put clean sheets on my mattress. This is starting to look like a real bedroom.

I grab my phone from my backpack to see there's no messages from my parents. They must not have made it home yet. I also realize that I forgot my laptop charger. I guess I need to face them eventually. They'd be worried if I wasn't home tonight, so this confrontation was going to happen no matter what. Might as well get it over with.

"Hey, I'm running back to my parents' real quick," I sign to the others, who are out in the living room unboxing the couch parts.

"Good luck!" they all sign.

"I'm going to need it!"

When I drive back over, I get home before my parents, but as I climb the stairs, I notice the headlights of their car illuminating the driveway. Shit, I was really hoping to have more time to collect my thoughts. I grab my laptop charger so I can be ready to make my exit.

When they walk in and Mom sees me, she comes in hot, ready to lecture me. "You can't just wander off at all hours. While you live here—"

"I *don't* live here," I interrupt her, feeling bold.

"What are you talking about?" she shouts.

Ideally, this would've been a civil conversation—the way Kayla had discussed the move with her folks. Arranging dinner plans to keep in touch, talking about the pros and cons. Real mature stuff. This is *not* that.

"I moved out," I say casually. "All my stuff is gone. I even took Cheese." I hold up the laptop charger in my hand. "I just came back for *this*."

Her reaction has a range of emotions. Confusion and anger all mixed into one. "Eleanor, what are you talking about?"

"I moved into a house with some friends."

"You can't just move out!" Mom is beside herself. "You can't! Didn't we have a whole talk about you needing to ask permission to go anywhere?"

Dad rushes over to her side. "Where are you living? Did you sign a lease? How are you planning on paying for that and the car?"

"A house near ACC. Yes, I signed a lease, and I got a job at the library."

He lets out a defeated sigh, realizing it's better to meet me where I'm at. "Okay."

"Okay?" my mom yells. "How is this okay?"

"I don't know what else you want me to do," he says. "She's been independent her whole life. She is eighteen. She seems to have it figured out."

"So?" my mom asks, folding her arms and digging in her heels.

"I moved out at eighteen." He shrugs. "But *you* are finishing school," he says to me. "If we let you do this."

"Whatever, yeah, I'm finishing school." To prove I've thought this through, I add, "I also signed up for an ACC class for college credit."

Dad nods solemnly, then continues, "And you'll visit home."

I shrug. It was never my intention to cut them out entirely, but I wasn't exactly planning on rushing home for Sunday dinners, either. "Sure, I mean, I'm staying in town."

"In town!" Mom echoes my own words at a significantly elevated volume. This isn't productive. I knew telling them I moved out wasn't going to go smoothly, which is why I avoided it until the last possible moment. "Why are you doing this?"

I sigh and manage to stay calm. "Because this has never been a welcoming home to me. I just needed you to realize that I'm Deaf, and things should've been a little different. It's not that hard. We didn't have to reach this point."

My parents sit in the silence. Maybe, for the first time ever, my words are getting through to them.

"I'm not leaving forever. I'll be around. But I need to do this." With that, I turn around and leave. And no one chases after me.

When I get in the car, I look back at the house and notice the front door is closed. I can't see my parents inside through the window. They just let me go. Isn't that what I wanted? I thought I'd be more excited about this. To have my freedom back. But I just feel . . . down.

I get to the Deaf house, where Shay, Izzy, and Alex have finished assembling the couch. It's a small two-seater, but we all cram together onto it. Even Cheese jumps on my lap. Already this house feels more like a home than anywhere I've ever lived.

Shay notices me wipe away a tear and signs, "*I'm sure it wasn't easy.*"

"*I wanted this.*" I shake my head. "*Still, it was harder than I thought it would be.*"

I click the button on the intercom outside Jackson's house. A garbled voice erupts from the speaker, and the gate slowly opens into the driveway. I'm guessing that was Jackson? I pull forward slowly, parking as close to the exit as I can.

Jackson's standing at the front door, leaning against the frame, waiting for me.

He usually carries himself tall and confidently, so it's concerning to see him slouching. His cheeks are puffy, and to be honest, *weak* is the first word that comes to mind when I see him—like he's really been through it. Somehow less steady on his feet than before, which is really saying something because he was already always tripping all over the place.

I want to pull him into a hug and squeeze him tight. But when I get out of the car, unsure how we are with things, I lead with "I'm kind of surprised you go to Amber High." I'm still unable to get over his rich neighborhood and figure he wouldn't want me opening with some blunt observational comment about his appearance.

"What do you mean?" Jackson fidgets with the end of his shirt. "I know I've been out for a while—"

I gesture around to his ridiculously large home and chuckle awkwardly. "Your parents didn't want to send you to a private school?"

"Nah, I'd rather go close by." He looks like he hadn't considered this before.

"I come bearing gifts," I say, holding out my latest knit project: a navy beanie with a white stripe around the base. "Well, gift. A hat. I need to keep my hands busy when I'm anxious, and I had a lot of study hall time to worry about you, so."

"Thanks, Ellie," he says, accepting it. "Come in."

Stepping inside a void with minimalist white-and-gold decor, I find the floors immaculate. "Should I take my shoes off?" It's safe to say I'm more used to friends' houses where there's piles of sneakers by the doors, but my scuffed-up boots would look sad and out of place sitting here in Jackson's pristine foyer.

Walking with a narrow black cane he was hiding behind him when I arrived, Jackson pulls open the large hallway closet and points to an empty spot on a shoe rack. How long has he been using a mobility aid?

With his free hand, he slides the beanie on, though it's not quite centered. I reach up and adjust it for him, my hands grazing against his forehead.

"Cozy," he says, avoiding my eyes.

"It looks great."

As I'm putting my shoes away and my jacket on a hanger, his parents walk over to us, eyeing me curiously. Someone must have already said something, because they're staring at me with expectant looks. His mother is whisper thin, in perfectly fitted athleisure, and sporting freshly painted nails, while his father loosens his tie, perhaps having recently come home from a long day lording over his plastics empire.

"Oh, hi, I'm Ellie," I say. Jackson's mom is taken aback. I'm suddenly self-conscious of my Deaf accent.

"We didn't realize—" his father says in a quiet, low tone, barely attempting to disguise the frown he gives his son. I don't need to hear the words to know what he said. I can tell they're glad to see Jackson invited someone over, but they're surprised to see it's me.

They didn't know I'm Deaf. Didn't think to mention that, Jackson? I know he's had a lot going on, but we'd have avoided this awkwardness if he'd prepared them with something like, "Hey, my friend Ellie is coming over, and, by the way, she's Deaf."

His mother grins and says something I'm sure was meant to be apologetic, but I can't hear her *at all*. Not in the slightest. It's like watching the TV on mute, but she doesn't even move her lips enough for me to try to read them.

They're soft speakers.

The kind of family that keeps the volume low. That doesn't project across the dinner table or shout to each other from different rooms. That somehow gets *even quieter* when it's bedtime. I hope they're not the type that gets annoyed with Grandma when they have to speak up for her to hear them.

Their smiles could be entirely genuine, but I'm walking on eggshells trying to keep up with the conversation.

"Yeah, I invited her over," Jackson says.

His voice booms and echoes across the spacious entryway. So loud and clear. Finally I can understand someone. I could kiss him.

You know, if he wants that.

With the end of his cane, Jackson guides me toward a nearby door. "Let's go down to the basement. After you."

He walks slowly behind me, and his mom must say something else.

"Just leave it alone," Jackson quips. "I'm tired of knocking into everything."

I hurry down the stairs, eager for it to be just the two of us. Though only taking one step at a time, Jackson clearly feels the same way.

There's a whole bar built down here, and a pool table, which would be fun to play, but I'm sure Jackson would prefer the couch, so I take a seat there as he lowers himself beside me with a sigh.

"They don't want me relying on the cane. They seem to think my body won't work to get better if I use it," he says, rolling his eyes.

"Is it because you're still dizzy?" I ask him. "Like at the hotel?"

"Not like *that*, exactly, anymore." He rests the cane along the side of the couch and leans back into the cushions, taking off the hat.

"You went to a doctor?"

"Yeah. It's gotten better, fortunately," he says, speaking plainly, but it doesn't escape my notice that his eyes start to well up. "Though my legs and arm are still kind of lingering with weirdness. Yet my vision is clearer."

"Do you want to talk about all of that?" It does sound like *a lot*. I glance down at his knees—bare beneath his athletic shorts despite the cold weather—and notice several small purple marks.

"Yes." He pauses, wringing his fingers together. "But not yet. It's been consuming my life, honestly." He mumbles a bit about "the hospital" before saying, "I'd love to talk about something else first."

"I get it." I bite my lip. "I guess *anything* probably wouldn't really include the last time we saw each other, either."

"No, it wouldn't." To my relief, he smiles. "When you drove me home, though, I was trying to tell you that I was starting driving lessons."

"Whoa, really?" I scooch closer on the couch so that our legs are pressed together.

"Yep, but that's on hold, maybe forever." He frowns and looks off to the side, then turns back to me a moment later. "Anyway, what's new with you?"

"I moved out."

I lay it out there casually, knowing the reaction it'll get. If we'd been able to chat about this during lunch, would he have been encouraging? Or tried to talk some sense into me?

"Whoa." His jaw drops.

"Big things happening over here, too," I joke.

"You did what?"

"You know my friend Shay, the teacher from the ASL club?" I wait until he nods. "Well, she and a couple friends from ACC were renting a house and asked if I wanted to join."

"When did you move?"

"Yesterday after work, technically."

"Damn, I miss a few lunches and you move houses."

"More than a few," I say quietly.

"You didn't want to stay at home anymore?" He asks something else ending with "okay with that?"

"My parents?" I ask for clarification. "There was too much butting heads. And, in any case, I'm used to being on my own."

"I understand." While my mom and dad have been distant, his seem *too* present.

I give a reassuring smile. "There's a lot to catch up on. It's been ages since you've been at school."

"I didn't expect to be gone so long. The semester is more than half-way over." He looks down at the ground. "It all feels like a lifetime ago. So much has changed."

"But I . . ." A lot is different, but how do I make it clear to him that my feelings haven't changed at all? If anything, seeing him again is creating a whole tidal wave of emotions. I reach for his hand. "I really hope not *everything* has changed, because when we—"

Jackson turns toward the stairwell like he's heard something.

"Ellie." He shakes his head slowly, almost nostalgic, like he can't believe he's about to say this. He laces his fingers with mine. "I wanted to kiss you. Just not how that all went down."

He's so direct about it. My heart races. I'm desperate to say more. "Okay, and—"

But he pulls his hand away and stands, steadying himself with the cane. Don't tell me the moment has passed. "We should go check upstairs. My mom's—" He continues with something I can't catch.

"Got a page?" I ask, sure that's incorrect.

He slowly turns and repeats to clarify, "Been on a rampage."

"How so?"

"I don't know. She really wants to—" He tucks the cane beneath his arm and uses air quotes as he says, "'Beat this disease naturally.' She keeps attacking the pantry. Whenever she reads a new article suggesting some other food is terrible to eat."

"Huh." I try to match his annoyed expression, but I'm really stuck at the word *disease*. So he did get a diagnosis? Will he tell me more?

"You can go first if you want." He gestures to the stairs, then slides the hat back on to free his hands. "I need to take my time."

"That's okay; I don't mind." I hope he won't feel like he needs to go fast if I'm behind him.

He must not, because he still goes slowly, holding the railing and cane. It doesn't seem like he needs to be that cautious, but I guess, at this point, the last thing he'd want is an injury on top of whatever else is going on.

We round the corner to the kitchen, where his mother is absolutely tearing through the already mostly empty walk-in pantry, clearing out the latest round of food she must have deemed unhealthy. It's not even super junky stuff that she's set out on the counter, since I assume anything of that category was swiftly eliminated a few rounds ago. It's simple things like crackers and boxes of organic mac and cheese. Why is she getting rid of those?

Oh. Anything processed.

Leaning against the counter, Jackson protests. "Ugh, I said not my kettle chips. Mom, I told you we don't need to—"

She must be angry, because she speaks up, loud and clear. "Jackson, just let me do this." His mom dives back into the pantry; it seems like nothing is safe. She also piles up fruit on the counter, which really confuses me. Soon there'll be nothing left to eat.

"You can't get rid of these." Jackson puts the carton of strawberries back in the fridge.

"What if they have too much sugar, though . . ."

"They're anti-inflammatory, which is what I'm supposed to eat a ton of. All the diet tips you've been finding contradict each other. Can I eat cheese or not? Eggs, yes or no? Meat, every meal or never?"

"Well, it's—" His mom tries to justify herself, but Jackson continues.

"Come on, changing what we eat now isn't going to make a difference; we've already been eating healthy for years." He turns back to me, rolling his eyes. I read his expression easily. I've been there. Jackson needs a break.

"*Want food?*" I sign, hoping he'll understand. Raising my eyebrows to ask the yes or no question, "*Fast food?*"

"*E-a-t,*" he spells out, his hand shaky. I nod. Relief washes over him. "*Yes, please.*"

CHAPTER THIRTY-EIGHT

Jackson

I KNOW THEY'RE concerned, but I'm so tired of my parents right now. Ellie could've suggested anything in the world, and I would've been down to leave for that. She was signing something about food, but I'm not sure what other word she was saying with it. It doesn't matter. That was all I needed to know.

At the door, I waver, unsure whether I should bring the cane, though I'm still not reliably walking in a straight line without it. Ellie notices my hesitation. "Yeah," she says. "Bring it!"

As we walk down the driveway, I know it's the right choice. I don't want to attract any attention, but I need the stability. So I can be surer of myself.

"I've spent too much time with my parents lately," I say, but Ellie has climbed into the car and isn't looking. "Or all by myself."

"What was that?" she asks me to repeat when we're both seated.

"I've been stuck with my parents at home since the hospital. I'm basically a hostage."

"And I'm basically a runaway." She gives me a mischievous grin.

"What a pair we make." I smile. "It is really good to see you." But I'm not ready to talk about feelings, so I quickly segue to "So, how about chili?"

"Sure thing. Is there a Starlight near here?" She searches on her maps app to pull up an address to one of the franchise locations and hits the gas.

When we walk inside the bright blue fast-food chain with a painted night sky dotting the ceiling, I'm hyperalert, searching for anyone staring at me as I move with the cane. We get in line to place our order. It's busy since it's a Saturday night, but I eye an empty table in the corner.

When it's our turn to order, Ellie goes first, and I immediately follow so it'll all be on the same bill. She shakes her head, but I wave my hand. "You're driving me around. I got this." Gesturing back toward the spot I noticed earlier, I suggest, "Wanna grab that table?"

I meet her there with the order number, realizing I'm not stepping with the leg opposite my cane. This is still taking a while to understand how to best use it, especially because my dominant hand is weak right now. I switch the stick to the other side, and it seems to go a little more naturally.

Some kids at a nearby table are laughing about something. Is it me? Or are they looking at me now because I looked at them first?

Our food arrives quickly. Staring down at my cheese-covered bowl of chili, I realize my appetite may not be what I thought it would be. Eating a couple crackers on their own first, I try to coax my stomach into cooperating.

"My parents haven't been that great, either," Ellie says, trying to start up a conversation and probably wanting me to delve deeper into what's going on.

A sip of soda is what finally convinces my stomach to let me take a bite. The food really hits the spot, especially because it's the exact opposite of what I'm supposed to be eating these days. After taking another spoonful, I say, "My parents are stressed. And I get that. But they seem so concerned about their own fears that they haven't even asked about mine."

"Oh, I *get* that." Ellie nods encouragingly.

I scrunch up my lips, trying to bring levity to what's an unavoidably serious statement. "Well, it's MS."

She tilts her head, uncertain. She must not have heard me. "What?"

"*M-S*," I sign, not wanting to voice it again.

"No, I heard that. It's just that you have a look on your face."

"It was the first time I've said it out loud." It doesn't roll off the tongue easily because it isn't simple to say. It's kind of a heavy thing to drop on someone. "You're the first person I've told. I mean, my parents have shared it with everyone they know, but I personally haven't told anyone."

I realize I didn't even say "I have MS," just that "it's MS," adding a layer of distance to the whole situation. Like it's something external happening and not a real condition creating lesions in my brain and on my spinal cord. I hope Ellie doesn't ask too much about it, because I don't think I'd know enough of the answers yet. It's like I'll need a whole medical degree just to confidently understand what's going on with my own body.

I'm not ready for this lifelong thing. Stuck to me forever, for better or for worse. In sickness and in health. So far, as I understand it, there's no guarantee how I'll feel waking up on any given morning.

Or what my ability will be. What I *do* know is that I want to tackle this disease. With the best treatments possible, regardless of what my parents think.

Ellie's tilting her head. "Thank you for telling me." She squints apologetically. "I'm afraid I don't really know what it is, though."

"That makes two of us." I skirt around the question implied, ending up on a tangent. "All the answers I have come with more qu-questions," I say, tripping over the word yet carrying on anyway. "I'm mostly relieved. But also anxious."

"I'm sure. I'm glad you got some answers, though." She is trying to be patient and takes a sip of her soda, but she can't wait any longer. "I'm sorry, but what exactly is MS?"

"Um, well." *Questions. Great. Okay, I can do this.* Everything the doctor tried to explain to me comes to mind at once but all out of order. "I'm toward the end of a relapse now. Then hopefully I'll be in remission and kind of, I don't know, be normal-ish? But bad symptoms could happen again at any time, except there's these treatments that can try to prevent that. Though the treatments have some *scary* potential side effects that I'm just choosing to ignore because that's too much to wrap my head around."

"Is it always vertigo?" Ellie asks, trying to follow along with my rambling.

"I went to the hospital 'cause I went numb all over and couldn't't really walk. It's like fatigue, vision loss, pain, numbness," I say, listing off the seemingly never-ending symptoms. "Tingling, spasms—um, I don't know. And brain problems, not thinking as straightforward as I used to. And probably more stuff that I'm forgetting right now. Yeah, vertigo can be one of them."

"Wow." Her face scrunches up with concern. She's receptive, open to whatever I have to say. "Has that all been going on for a while?"

I didn't realize how much I needed someone who wanted to listen. The words come pouring out.

I tell her about the time in class when the answer just disappeared from my head. About the soccer match, after my leg had been numb for quite some time. About how the muscles in my legs sometimes twitch so bad I'm kicking at night and unable to fall asleep. About how the vision in my right eye is only now clearing up, the pain behind it subsiding.

"What causes it?"

"I don't think they know exactly." I clear my throat. "Which is why there isn't a cure for it yet."

"Oh." Ellie is really concerned, and I can tell she's holding back an *I'm sorry*, which I really appreciate that she doesn't say. "That sucks."

I laugh, relieving the tension. I'm glad she understands I need acknowledgment, not apologies. "Yeah." I gesture playing a little sympathy violin for myself. "It sure does."

"Did your doctor explain this all to you?"

"Kind of. I need to go to another appointment soon. He basically told me to google it."

"Seriously?"

"There's just a lot to cover, I guess. But there's also this MS Society thing." I'm not sure what else to say. I've pretty much put it all out on the table. "But, yeah, so that's what's been going on."

With a deep breath, she takes it all in, nodding several times. "Are you going to come back to school soon?"

"This semester is a wash. I'm just going to have to start back up in January."

"That makes sense." Staring down at her food, she adds, "I'll miss you."

We finish our meals and, after spending an hour at Starlight, climb back into the car. It's dark outside. My fingers are frozen, so I rub my hands together, waiting for the heat to warm us up. But I'm not ready to go home yet. Neither is she.

Ellie reaches over to touch my arm. "I'm glad you're okay, all things considered. You'd been gone so long I was beginning to worry you might never come back."

I take hold of her hand and, this time, don't let go. It feels right—the two of us here together. Comfortable, as if no time has passed and no drama has gotten in the way. Absently playing with her fingers, I ask, "Have you still been eating near the teachers' lounge?"

"All by myself. They must think I've scared you away."

She needs me to reassure her that she hasn't. Honestly, the football incident hasn't been at the top of my mind. With everything that's been going on, it feels kind of silly. I like her, and she likes me. We don't need to play these games anymore. Her wide eyes are watching my every move.

"Nah, I don't think you're that scary," I say teasingly. "Anymore."

She laughs and I smile, maybe a little wider than I intended, not exactly playing it cool. This whole diagnosis journey has been rough on my self-esteem. I know I'm different now than I was a few weeks ago. But despite that, Ellie is still here.

"Well, since you've been gone, I've needed your advice on all sorts of things," she says. "It's too late for the whole moving-out situation, but you can still help me pick a good spot for my tattoo."

"Oh, you're full of surprises today. Getting a tattoo now?"

"Don't tell me you dislike them." She gives a playful, challenging look. "I've been thinking I should save up to get one to commemorate all the big changes this year."

"It depends. What are you thinking of getting?"

"Obviously the Amber High Hornet, like, right on my cheek."

I burst out laughing. "Sure, you go first, and I'll get a matching one."

"Okay, but actually, something for Deaf pride. Like a colorful ASL I-love-you hand," she says, holding up the iconic sign with her two fingers folded in toward her palm. Then she brushes her hair back, resting her fingers at a spot behind her ear. "Somewhere like here."

I lean forward, even though there isn't anything to see yet, and am immediately taken in by how her hair smells fresh, like coconut. "That would look nice there," I say as she turns to watch my lips, so close our noses almost touch.

Another vehicle parks beside us in the parking lot, and the guys stare into our car before they walk into the Starlight Chili. This isn't the best place to hang out, and Ellie might have somewhere else we could go.

"Um, so your new place show," I say, my brain forming the sentence out of order. I start again. "Can I see your new place?"

Ellie nods eagerly. "Yes, let's go."

Suppressing a chili burp that would ruin the mood, I help myself to the pack of mints in her cup holder. Ellie holds out a hand to request one for herself. *So this is how we both see the night going . . .*

She drives us through winding hills to a nearby quiet neighborhood with several small houses all close together. There's plenty of kids' toys scattered on driveways, and a stray cat climbs onto a nearby porch. Ellie parks on the street and leads me up to the single-story home, smiling to herself as she unlocks the door. The inside is dimly lit, and what it lacks in furniture, it makes up for in charm. Her friends are crowded together in the kitchen, making dinner. I can tell they're intrigued by my presence.

"Hey, I'm Jackson," I say, a little shy, not wanting to botch this introduction. "*J-a-c-k-s-o-n,*" I spell out in sign, slowly to not mess it up, grateful that my hand is cooperating with me.

Shay signs something that Ellie voices. "She says she remembers you."

"Yes, hello again," I say, buying myself time to put together the signs. "*Again, hello.*"

"Shay, Izzy, and Alex." Ellie points with each introduction, then signs a question to them. "Oh, they said Kayla's in the room."

"*Want food?*" Izzy gestures to the plastic box of leftovers that Alex is about to pack away in the fridge.

"We just ate," I say, copying the sign I just saw for food.

"I'll give him the house tour," Ellie says and signs, reaching for my hand. I leave the cane propped against the counter and hold on to her instead. As we walk down the hallway toward the bedrooms, something brushes up against my leg, and Ellie leans down to pick it up.

"Meet Cheese." She holds a large black cat out toward me. He dangles there, apparently comfortable, with his eyes fixed on me. I stabilize myself along the wall while offering my other hand for him to sniff. "Aww, he likes you!" she shouts, and the cat isn't startled by the loud exclamation in the slightest. He's used to Ellie's volume.

I don't really know how to read a cat's expressions, and as soon as she puts him down, he races away, but I'm glad he seemed unbothered by me. "He's cute. When you said Cheese, I thought it might've been an orange cat."

"If only he was named based on color." She lets out a theatrical sigh. "He's a stinker."

There's a hammering noise coming from the open doorway nearest us. Ellie leads the way and introduces me to her roommate Kayla, who is assembling a small dresser.

"Are you planning to decorate?" I ask Ellie, pointing to the bare blue walls.

"I want to do a whole string of photos." She motions toward the corner and down the side of the wall above her bed. "But I don't have many to put up yet." Ellie signs something to Kayla, then leads me back out into the hall. "The others should have just left for a night class. We can hang out in the living room."

"Okay, yeah, I could sit down."

Ellie grabs my hand again. She keeps holding it as we take a seat on the stiff couch. "Are you doing all right?"

"Yeah." The way my heart is racing definitely distracts from any of the lingering dizziness, fatigue, or twitches.

"I'm really glad you texted me."

"You were kind of the only person I wanted to see."

"Really?" She leans beside me, resting her chin on my arm as she looks up at me. "I wanted to text more while you were gone, but I wasn't sure where we—"

"We're good now," I reassure her, not wanting to belabor it. My life has been miserable these past few weeks. I can't remember the last time I was as happy as I am sitting here with her. "But just to be sure, that ex of yours . . ."

"Is completely out of the picture," she says, her face suddenly serious. "I promise."

"That's a relief."

"Yeah?" Ellie puts her arms around me in a tight hug, which causes her hearing aid to squeal when it brushes against my shoulder. "Whoops." She bends her knees to sit back on her legs.

Her face is inches away from my own, and I know two things. The first is that she doesn't want to be the one to initiate a kiss again. The second is that she really wants me to kiss her right now.

"You don't happen to have a vomit bag or anything?" I scrunch up my face, feigning concern.

"Oh!" She jumps to her feet.

I burst out laughing and draw her back to the couch, pulling her onto my lap. "I'm just kidding. I don't think I'll need one tonight."

I take a deep breath, hoping I didn't just jinx myself. "As long as I don't have to run anywhere."

Ellie narrows her eyes, smiling as she shakes her head and closes the distance between us. "We can stay right here."

"Good because . . ." I trace my fingers down her back. "I want to kiss you . . ."

Her breath is minty and inviting. I lean forward to meet her warm lips, slowly. It's the opposite of last time, when I seized the opportunity and met her frantically, unsure of how fleeting the moment would be. Ellie runs a hand through my hair, planting a soft kiss on my neck, and my cheek, before returning to my lips.

Now we have all the time in the world.

CHAPTER THIRTY-NINE

Ellie

LIVING AT THE Deaf house has been going great. It's almost like being back in the Brandview dorms. However, there's no dining hall or maintenance crew, so we've had to figure out meals, take the trash out, and cut the grass regularly. After a few spats that luckily didn't fully explode into arguments, Shay got a calendar for the fridge so we all have assigned chores and don't run into any more issues.

I'm working on homework and eating some chips at the kitchen table Wednesday night when the doorbell light flashes. Izzy and Alex are on the couch in the living room, and we all stare each other down, waiting to see who will get up to answer it. Since I'm closest, I shrug and get up from the wobbly dining set, taking my dish to the sink before opening the front door.

There's no one there.

But there's a small brown package with my name written on it in Sharpie. There's no postage or address. Clearly, someone just dropped it off.

"*This is weird.*" I hold up the box. "*It's some random package for me.*"

My roommates jump up to inspect it as well. It's in decent condition and not super heavy or anything like that.

Izzy hesitates. "*Is that safe to open?*"

"*Do you recognize the handwriting?*" Alex asks.

Hmm. Actually, looking closely at it, I know exactly who this package is from. I roll my eyes and tear open the box. Inside is the little lamp I used to keep by my bed at my parents' place, as well as a hastily scribbled note that says *I thought you might be missing this, Mom.*

"*That's nice, I guess.*" Izzy shrugs.

"*She could've waited to say hi, though.*" I shake my head. "*Right?*"

Alex laughs. "*How fast she must have driven off. Sorry, that's not funny.*"

My mom racing down the driveway back to her car is an image I won't get out of my mind soon. I know I left things on a bad note, but now that I'm not under their roof anymore, I can be the bigger person. If she'd stuck around, I could've shown her the place.

We could work toward having some sort of healthy—or at least not toxic—relationship. If I stayed at that house, we would've continued to fight to the point of no return. Maybe I need to tell them that more clearly.

Jackson seems to be doing better lately. He's not up for taking an EasyRide yet, so I always go pick him up and bring him back to my house.

Often, his mom steps outside to send him away with snacks like bags of mixed nuts or strawberries since Jackson insisted on retaining control of his diet. She hasn't bothered trying to talk to me much since our first meeting. Did she realize I couldn't hear a single thing she said? There's really a lack of effort on both of our parts here, and I'm not inclined to make any changes to that.

As annoyed as I am with my parents, I'd rather see them than Jackson's parents—but it's his mom and dad who I see the most these days. Though they're a bit cold to me, I know that they're grappling with their son being newly disabled, probably wanting to disguise and rectify that as best they can, but he's dating someone so obviously disabled that they don't know what to do about it.

Some people who grow up Deaf, especially from Deaf families, don't consider themselves disabled. Yet I don't mind the label. I *am* disabled. I want to pursue advocacy for the community as a whole. Despite what people may think, disability isn't a bad thing; it's not an offensive word or something that needs to be skirted around. It's straight to the point.

That being said, I don't know disability the way Jackson is experiencing it now. I've never temporarily lost a sense that I was used to having my entire life. I've never been hit with taxing fatigue that makes it tremendously difficult to get around. I've never lost feeling in my hands or feet or had any sort of mobility problems.

Also, Jackson doesn't have any community of his own yet. He's facing pressures to push through things and "overcome" his disability. That can take a tremendous mental toll.

Trying to be more informed, I googled multiple sclerosis, which was a scary space of a lot of doom, despair, and unknowns. I stumbled upon many articles about "dating with MS" and people being afraid to share their diagnosis. It really pained me to learn that often partners in committed relationships will end things because they don't want to deal with their loved one's disease.

I'm doing my best to not let any of this weigh on me. To go into this relationship with the excitement it deserves and to let Jackson, not Google, tell me what he needs. And knowing firsthand how family can make things difficult, I'll be sure to be pleasant around his parents, not to add any drama there, either.

Which is why it really, *really* pains me to admit to myself that sometimes I miss Cody's Deaf family and how easy they all were to hang out with.

CHAPTER FORTY

Jackson

EACH DAY, MY vision gets clearer. The pain subsides. The dizziness wanes.

Unfortunately, some things stick around. Extreme fatigue. Muscle twitches. Little shocks in my arms. A vibrating sensation up my spine. Irritating, yes—but considering where I was a few weeks ago, I'll take it. Even though it's taxing, I never take walking for granted now.

Mom drives me to all my follow-up appointments, and boy, there are a lot of those. More bloodwork, more MRIs, and a bunch of different examination tests of my speed and function, such as walking down a hallway or putting pegs into a board. Finally, it is time to decide on my treatment.

"I'll go with the infusions," I tell the neurologist, who then turns me over to the MS coordinator to get logistics arranged.

"We've got an infusion center here that you can come to," the nurse says. "I'll go ahead and schedule the first appointment for you. Does Tuesday, November twenty-first, work?"

"I think so," I say, knowing there's nothing else on my calendar right now.

"Yes," Mom answers for me.

"Lots of patients look forward to the appointments since they get a burst of energy for a while afterward. In fact, at the end of each month, you'll probably be looking forward to the next infusion."

"Interesting. Yeah, I'm hoping it can help with some of this fatigue."

We're quiet in the car after the visit, my mom knowing better by now than to voice any doubts about the treatment I've chosen. There are potential risks to the infusions, but not the guaranteed gamble I would be taking by not doing any treatment at all. For me, this is the choice I need to make. So hopefully the odds are in my favor when it comes to avoiding side effects.

Mom drops me off at school to get the next semester arranged with Ms. Lily. "I can wait and drive you home after," she offers.

"That's okay. I think I'm good to get a ride myself."

My mom looks unsure. She might not actually leave.

It's unsettling—being back at Amber while the semester is beginning to wind down. What test would I have been studying for? What has everyone been up to? Things move a mile a minute at high school, so much so that missing a single class could set someone back, and I've missed several weeks. Which is exactly why there was no point in me returning until January. But right now, in this moment, part of me feels the urge to turn back and never return at all.

That's just fear. I'll get past it.

I climb out of the car with my cane and doubt going into the building with it for a moment, but I've already walked across the parking lot with it. There's no turning back now. I'm not sure how my legs will hold up for such a long stretch.

Yet, stepping into the school, I regret bringing my cane here. Have any of my classmates ever seen someone our age using a walking stick before? Crutches, for sure. But a cane? I don't think so.

I want to stash it in my locker. But the bell rings, and I'm having a difficult time keeping up with everyone rushing through the halls. I hold the cane up by my side and keep walking, steadying myself against the wall whenever there's an odd break between lockers. Still, I basically just bump into a lot of people who give me salty looks.

Including Liam.

I brace myself for a taunt that never comes. Instead, there's a flash of disgust on his face. Maybe even pity. Then, as he shuts his locker door, he calls out to no one in particular, "Look who's back from rehab."

Speeding down the hall to get away from the stares, I'm relieved the vertigo seems to have truly subsided now. The world feels steadier by the day, but still, I don't want to risk it, especially not here.

By the time I get to the guidance counselor's office, I'm taxed and very much relying on the cane to help keep my balance. Ms. Lily's door is open, and she looks up at me expectantly. "Jackson, welcome. Please take a seat."

I sit on the chair, grateful to be off my feet. My muscles are dancing in my thighs and glutes. *Twitch, twitch, twitch.*

"Glad to see you seem to be doing okay," Ms. Lily says, clicking something on her computer—probably my file. "Are you eager to get back to school next semester?"

"Sure, yeah. It's strange to take this much time off." I tap my foot, trying to distract myself from the symptoms.

Ms. Lily slides a printout across the desk to me. "I've worked out your schedule, and because you took extra classes, you've already completed certain minimum credits that colleges need, so you won't need to retake some courses. After this spring, you'll just need to take three courses next summer to be fully caught up on our requirements."

"And that will make up for everything?"

"Correct. And don't worry; you'll still be able to walk with your class at graduation." She must question her word choice as her eyes drift to the cane that I've propped up against the chair. "We mail out diplomas months later anyway, once all the coursework is officially graded, so you'll just get that once all your credits are completed."

"That makes sense."

"Now for the bad news." She winces as she looks down at the giant calendar spread out on her desk. "Unfortunately, it is November third already, and it says here that, for the schools you're targeting, the early decision deadline was the first."

College.

What university to go to consumed my thoughts the last two years, but it has almost completely been wiped from my mind. So I missed the first deadline. And regular decision is due in the new year, which is right around the corner. In a single heartbeat, I've gone from being eager to have more back on my plate to absolutely *drowning*.

"Um, I haven't . . . well, I haven't asked for recommendation of letters," I say, clearing my throat and correcting myself. "Letters of rec. Or looked to see what any of the essays would be. Because, you know, I think if . . ." I trail off, having not completed the thought but looking at Ms. Lily expectantly for help.

With pity in her eyes, she suggests, "Maybe you could take a gap year. Use the time to get better and refreshed—to start strong with new plans."

She must not know I'm dealing with something *incurable* here.

Can I even go to college? I don't want to study business and sit in an office all day. MS has changed a lot about my future, including that I need to make the most of life. I'm not putting limitations on myself; it's the opposite. If I'm going to have limited energy, I need to find something that feels incredibly worthwhile to do.

I need time to figure out what's next for me. It's for the best that I missed all the deadlines—something I never would've been able to see the bright side in several months ago. Still, I leave the meeting a mix of determined and overwhelmed. Both ready to take on the future and also to collapse in bed for several hours.

I planned on trying to see Ellie while here, but not now. As expected, Mom is waiting in the parking lot, and I tumble into the passenger seat without saying a word.

Then I feel the twitching in my legs again. Or maybe it never stopped? Am I only aware of it when I'm not moving?

Twitch, twitch, twitch.

I hang around at home all afternoon, waiting for Ellie to be done with classes for the day. After spending a few minutes researching online, trying to reconfigure my entire life to no avail, I close my laptop and take a nap, realizing my brain was too fatigued to do much of anything. When I wake up, I'm even more tired than I was before I went to sleep, so I take a second nap. After that I'm finally a bit refreshed and eager to eat. I also decide to do something that will turn my mood around, so I plan an outing for Ellie and me tonight.

It will be a movie night, because sedentary is the way to go at the moment, with open captions on the screen so that Ellie can enjoy it, too. We've been watching shows at her place with the closed captions on, and honestly, I don't mind it. It's helpful for scenes where there's too much noise and very quiet dialogue.

I search all the movie theaters in our area, and almost none of them have any open-caption showings. One spot does, but only for a time on Wednesday at 2:00 p.m. Absurd.

I've just got to get on the phone to figure this out, I guess. No one answers at the first place I try, but I finally get ahold of someone at the Walnut Theater.

"Hey," I say, "I see you're playing *Hidden Spies* tonight. Can we make one of those showtimes have open captions?"

"Uh," the worker says on the other end. "Let me get my manager."

Very obnoxious hold music blares in my ears until another voice chimes on. "So, we do have closed caption glasses that we offer."

"No, I want them on the screen." It shouldn't be that difficult to have them the way they are when you turn them on the TV at home. I don't want Ellie to have to wear something uncomfortable.

"We can't do that."

"Seriously? Why not?"

"It's not an open-caption showing."

"I understand that." I grit my teeth. "How can we make it one? Can we pay or something?"

"You can rent out a theater."

"The entire theater?"

"Yeah. Hmm, there's a 4:37 spot that you could reserve."

"Tonight?" I ask.

"Yeah."

"And how much does that cost?"

"Uh, for *Hidden Spies*, you said? The run time would bring it to three hundred twenty-seven dollars with tax."

That's one expensive date. "Fine, I'll book it."

"Sure," the manager says, indifferent. "We need the card for a deposit."

"One second." I dig my credit card from my wallet. My parents let me spend within reason, and while this feels like price gouging for an accessible experience, it probably won't raise too many red flags on the bank statement. If they ask, I'll just say that Mom can stop buying organic strawberries for a few weeks to offset the cost. I read the manager the number. "And email me the confirmation, please."

I really hope Ellie is still able to hang out tonight.

JACKSON:

> Hey, you're free after school, right? Not a question, actually. Please say you're available tonight!!!

She replies during class.

ELLIE:

> Yeah, definitely! What's up? Are you coming over?

JACKSON:

> It's a surprise. I'll come meet you at Amber so we can drive over together.

A little while later, I get an EasyRide back to Amber. This time, I insist to my mom that I go alone to regain some independence. Still, she watches from the door as the car pulls away from the house.

I meet Ellie in the parking lot, and when we hop into her car, she leans over to kiss my cheek. "Where are we going?"

I share the directions to her phone. We arrive at the old ornate Walnut Theater and head inside. Ellie reaches for my hand, but she's next to the cane. Without missing a beat, she dances around to the other side, running her fingers across my back before lacing them around my other hand.

I show the email confirmation at the ticket counter, and they tell us to wait right there. Ellie gives me a confused look, but I just hold up a finger to say it's okay.

The manager walks over. "You're all set for theater nine."

It's all the way at the end of the hall, and where the movie title is usually lit up, it just says PRIVATE EVENT.

Ellie raises one eyebrow, getting suspicious. "What's this?"

I shrug. "You'll see."

It's completely empty inside, and the trailers are already wrapping up. There are no captions on those, however, so I really hope they have this all ready to go for us.

"Where do you want to sit?" I gesture.

"All this," Ellie says, waving her arms around, "is just for us?"

"Yeah . . ." I panic, wondering if this was a bad decision.

But she immediately gets giddy. "Okay, let me see what seats are best," she says, taking off up the stairs, then racing down through each row, before plopping down in the middle of the theater. "How's this?"

"I don't know," I say, smiling as I climb the single step and walk along the railing to our spot. "You didn't run through the super-close ones."

She leans back, catching her breath, pretending to observe the seats in front of us. "Nah, I think we're good here."

The screen goes dark, and the opening score for *Hidden Spies* begins to play. And fortunately, everything is set up correctly, since there's a caption bar describing the music at the lower third of the screen.

Already having a good time, Ellie lights up with delight. In disbelief, she points to the screen. "What?"

I lean toward her, speaking loud over the movie speakers. "Can you believe we had to get the whole place to ourselves just to get some decent captions?"

"Oh, you didn't!" She laughs to herself.

"Is this oka—"

Ellie pulls my face forward for a kiss. *I'll take that as a yes.*

A character starts to speak, so I lean back. "You're missing the captions!"

She smiles, sitting back and reaching for my hand.

The movie is fine enough, both dramatic and hilarious, and I'm happy that Ellie gets to experience all the jokes. She bursts out laughing and even heckles the characters since there's no one around to bother. "What did you *think* would happen in that tunnel? Seriously!"

Nevertheless, some of the action scenes are a bit too much for my brain to handle, so I cover my eyes with our joined hands—planting a kiss on hers before setting them back down to continue watching.

Presumably, there's a joke to be made about a matinee showing where I've got a cane and she's got hearing aids, but for the first time in a long time, I actually feel my age again. I'm eighteen, on a date to the movies, and everything is, well, normal.

I squeeze Ellie's hand, never wanting this night to end.

After the *Hidden Spies* credits roll, Ellie drives us over to the Deaf house. I leave my cane in the car and walk slowly to the door, regaining confidence in my stability.

"You seem to be getting the hang of things again," she says, squeezing my hand.

The pessimistic part of me wants to say something like "for now," because who knows what could happen down the line, but I don't let negative thinking interrupt our great night. I *am* feeling sort of like a person again tonight. I know that might not be the most glowing status, but it's been a long time since I've felt even somewhat *okay.*

Shay, Izzy, and Alex are squeezed together on the small couch, watching something on a laptop, in fits of laughter. Kayla is cooking at the stove but rushes between the kitchen and living room so she doesn't miss what's happening.

"*Hello.*" I wave, still eager to make a good impression on her roommates.

Ellie doesn't miss a beat. "He rented out a whole theater for an open-caption showing!" she says and signs. "I would've texted, but it was early, and you all had work or class."

"We can all go together next time," I offer. "*Again all,*" I add in sign. Hanging out here, I've been improving my ASL, but admittedly, Ellie and I don't spend much time chatting when I come over.

Ellie practically squeals, leading me by the hand to her room while her roommates break into laughter behind us. I can only imagine what they're signing to each other right now, but I'm sure it's hilarious.

We kick our shoes off, locking the door behind us. Ellie puts her arms around me, drawing me in for a kiss and guiding me toward her bed. When I'm lying against the pillow, she climbs on the mattress and wraps her legs around my waist. We've been taking things slow, on account of the symptoms I'd been managing until now, but Ellie changes that with one motion, dipping back to pull her shirt off.

She flings it to the floor.

That bra she's wearing really looks amazing on her. She quickly puts her hair up and stares me down expectantly. I reach up to tuck a loose strand of hair behind her ear, careful to not cause her hearing aid to whistle. She wraps a hand around my arm and plants a soft kiss on my wrist.

Ellie bends forward, reaching a hand up my shirt, feeling my racing heartbeat. I help her tug my tee over my head. This all feels so right.

Then why do I feel like I need to *not* be touched right now?

I reach up to kiss her, trying to fight off whatever this interference is, but I tense up and turn away, ending the moment before it's really gotten started.

Ellie narrows her eyes, leaning back and giving me space. "Are you okay? If this was too much, I—"

"No, it's not." I curse myself. "It's just . . ."

I don't know how to explain what I'm feeling right now. It's like my broken brain isn't sending any of the right signals. I want to keep kissing her. I *really* want to. But my legs, my hands, my lips, my *everything* isn't functioning as I want them to. I'm freezing up and getting too inside my head.

Why won't my body let me enjoy this?

Ellie mentions carefully, "I did see some articles how guys—"

"Shit." I don't even know what she saw, but I'm embarrassed as hell. Depression? Disfunction? Clearly nothing that makes me look great.

I'm filled with adrenaline, but my body has frozen. I don't recognize my life anymore.

"Jackson, it's okay, really." Ellie curls up beside me. Her cat jumps up on the bed. Has he been in the room the whole time? She shoos him away.

I stare down at our shirts together on the floor. I will my body to want to take action, to kiss her again, to keep advancing things, but I'm just stuck here.

My eyes water. That would really be icing on the cake. I'm absolutely falling apart. Too much for anyone to deal with.

"Jackson." Ellie brings a hand to my cheek. "Tell me what's going on."

"I just—I don't want to bother you with all this."

"What?" she asks. I turn away, but she guides my head back. "I just didn't hear you," she explains. "Please."

"I don't have the same control over mownody." I sit even taller, punctuating my words. "Over. My. Own. Body. To other people, I look *fine*. Yet I feel anything but. And sure, I'm better now than I was a few weeks ago, but for how long? Everyone expects me to be normal. Meanwhile, I have no idea what's coming in the future. Will I wake up one day and not be able to move my legs ever again? I don't know. My brain and ability are just going to . . . keep slipping away from me."

I'm not sure how much of that Ellie has heard or read off my lips, but she pats my arm empathetically and lets me keep rambling on.

"I didn't think anything like this could ever happen to me. That would completely mess up my future in the most uncertain of ways. And this disease isn't something a lot of people know about, like getting in a car crash or having cancer. You get what I'm saying? Why couldn't this be something that people understood better?"

I regret not having my shirt on now to wipe away a tear that breaks free. Ellie reaches up to dry my cheek with her hand.

"You're still *you*," she says. "And I'm sure it's going to take some time to process, but you're going to get a handle on this and become even *more* yourself. You will have an incredible future; it just might not look exactly how you originally thought."

"Yeah, I guess."

"Not on the same level at all, but I didn't expect to be at Amber. That's not what I wanted. But now I get to be here. With you." She traces a finger down my arm.

A smile fights its way across my face. "Yeah, I never expected I'd be here with you . . ." I widen my eyes to try to get them to stop watering. "But I'm crying all over your bed even though you look amazing in *just that* right now."

"Oh, this?" Ellie laughs, pulling her hands to the straps to playfully show off her bra. "You can see this again."

I blush from head to toe. "At least your roommates couldn't hear my whole sob story."

"Well, if Alex has her hearing aids in . . ." Ellie starts but notices my alarm. "Though she doesn't usually wear them at home; don't worry!"

"Ellie?" I say her name like a question because I want her to understand the gravity of the one I'm about to ask. Tracing a finger behind her ear, to the spot where she wants to get that tattoo, I ask, "I know you're so proud of your disability, but am I allowed to want a cure for mine?"

She takes a moment to gather her thoughts. "I think it depends on how you're approaching pride. Does it mean that you're proud that your body is fighting against you? No, I don't think it means that at all."

"Exactly, because this all *sucks*."

"Yes, it sucks. And you can acknowledge that. Don't pretend everything is perfect all the time."

"'Cause it's not. I'd do anything to ditch this diagnosis."

"But you're not lesser-than for having it. You know that, right?" Ellie considers what to say next. "Cures are a tricky thing. Like, I don't want a cure for my deafness. I don't want to live in a world where the desire is to eliminate all disabilities. But at the same time, I don't want people to have to live with pain or symptoms that could be improved."

"Exactly."

"We can go to the walks, and raise awareness, and fundraise, and petition for access, and so much more." She pauses. "Just don't put your life on hold waiting for something that may never come."

"Right." It's hard not to. And sometimes the detours seem unavoidable. This year was entirely interrupted. I didn't get to make a choice, but this is my life now.

"I think where pride comes in is that, through it all, you accept yourself as you are," Ellie says. "Which is a radical choice when you exist in a society that is actively working against you."

I nod, impressed. When she discusses all this, it's like a fire ignites within her. "Acceptance . . . I'm not sure if I'm quite there in the stages of grief yet." But what Ellie is saying makes sense. I can't just sit around being miserable. "I knew you'd be able to help make sense of it," I say.

"Disability advocacy is important to me. I talk about this stuff with my friends all the time."

"'I'm glad you were 'in the mood to educate me right now,'" I tease. "Do you remember saying that to me when we first met? I do *not* think you liked me then . . ."

"Well, you know, now you understand more about the concept of fatigue," she jokes, dragging out her words. "To be fair, I didn't really want to like *anyone* that first day. But I could already tell I had a soft spot for you."

"That's a relief."

"And then, after we got our lunch spot, part of me kept worrying you'd go running back to the soccer guys, and I wasn't ready for that."

"Yeah . . . soccer." This is something else I'm dreading figuring out. "I was never gonna, like, go pro. I thought I'd at least play through college, but after last season, I never got any scouting opportunities, especially since I didn't get to sign up for club this year. Hopefully I'll still get play time for Amber this spring . . ." I say, trailing off.

Ellie brushes my hair back, listening intently as I try to make sense of my thoughts.

"I have to find a way to keep moving. Put my energy into something I really care about and see where that leads me. But I don't know . . . what."

"And you will figure it out. It doesn't have to be right this second. Good things take time."

"True." I pull her toward me for a long, soft kiss, grateful for how comfortable and safe I feel talking with her. "Thank you, though. Seriously."

"Anytime."

CHAPTER FORTY-ONE

Ellie

MONDAY BEFORE THANKSGIVING, I'm making applesauce for our Friendsgiving at the Deaf house. My hands are still so sticky from slicing chunks of fruit that I don't grab my phone right away when it vibrates with a text.

MOM:

Are you coming Thursday?

Hmm, I'm not sure how to phrase my response. Large family gatherings are like the drama at the dinner table times ten. And right now, I don't think my parents are open to finding a solution for that yet.

ELLIE:

I've already got plans here for Thanksgiving, but maybe next year.

I brace myself for her anger, but I'm pleasantly surprised with the response I get.

MOM:

I'll drop off a spare Crock-Pot.

ELLIE:

Okay, I'm around until later.

I can't bring myself to say it, but maybe she'll understand that to mean she can ring the doorbell and stick around for a few minutes this time. We still haven't seen each other since I moved out, so I'm not sure if we can have a civil conversation.

After stashing the applesauce in the fridge, I get ready to go with my friends to the first-ever Deaf Night Out event hosted at our very own Coffee Garden. They usually close around six but are staying open late specifically for the event.

Shay led the charge on this one, getting the word out to folks all over the Cincy area with the help of a certain tall, handsome Xavier University student she met recently—a CODA eager to hang out and use the sign language he was raised with.

"Are we going to finally meet Arun tonight?" I ask.

"I've told you all it's not like that," she protests, a little too much, almost tripping over a Crock-Pot that's been placed on our stoop.

"Whoops!" I say, grabbing it and bringing it inside. So much for Mom stopping to say hi.

We hop into Izzy's car, with Alex up front beside her, and Kayla, myself, and Shay squished across the back. Even though we're the first to arrive to help set up, others start to flood in, and soon the place is packed. The owners of the Coffee Garden seem surprised but delighted by the turnout.

Shay's been running around making sure everything goes smoothly, so the next time I see her, she's giggling in a corner with the guy who could only be Arun. Sensing her nervous energy, I sign to Alex and

Izzy, "*Time to go help Shay be the one to find some love now, am I right?*" They push me toward her encouragingly.

I center myself and become party-Ellie, the confident girl I can only fully channel when the lights are dim and my hands are set free. "*Hey! Is that the famous man Shay has told me so much about?*" Shay looks more relieved than irritated. "*Nice to meet you,*" I sign.

Arun chuckles, sharing a glance with Shay that convinces me he's smitten. "*Let me guess—one of the roommates?*"

Giving Shay a side-hug, I sign, "*E-l-l-i-e.*"

"*A-r-u-n,*" he replies, even though I obviously already know that. "*I'm helping DJ.*"

"*Ooh, whatcha got on?*" I glance toward the playlist approvingly. "*Now, that! Is my favorite.*" I point to the next song, and he skips to that track.

Holding out my phone, I record the three of us enthusiastically signing along to the song, before slipping away so that it's just the two of them left dancing together. My work here is done.

I post the video and stroll back over to find a seat with Kayla. She's with a few former Brandview students who were different years than us. I hadn't realized how many others would be in the area. Even after getting Shay and Arun together, we need to make this event a regular occurrence.

My phone lights up with a text from Jackson.

JACKSON:

> You look very cute tonight. I hope you're having fun!

Flattered, I smile. I was hoping he'd see the video.

ELLIE:

> It's great, wish you could've come with.
> Definitely next time!

JACKSON:

I should bring an interpreter or something
so I don't slow you down with friends.

ELLIE:

It's all fine, we'll figure it out!!

For anyone else, it might get annoying, but I don't mind making sure Jackson's in the loop. He's been learning sign; I'm sure he'll start getting the hang of things soon enough.

ELLIE:

I hope you're getting rest for
your appointment tomorrow!

CHAPTER FORTY-TWO

Jackson

TODAY IS MY first infusion.

After deciding upon treatment with my neurologist, it took a while for my insurance to approve it. They denied it at first, wanting to make me start on something less strong until it failed, a tactic that would cost me time I couldn't afford to waste, but fortunately, my doctor knew how to fight that and push through the preferred treatment. I'm nervous, but I've taken this seriously, done my research, and feel reassured knowing I'll be monitored with bloodwork and MRIs to make sure the treatment's effective at preventing more lesions. There's no use getting worked up over whether or not this is the right choice. Nothing to do but start the treatment.

The staff called ahead of my appointment to check in and give me reminders of what to expect. I wear comfortable clothes and drink plenty of water beforehand, hoping that I won't need to use the bathroom during the hour-long infusion.

Taking a seat in the chair, I lie back and pull a blanket over my legs. The nurse puts a pillow on my lap, and I rest my arm on it. *Look away. Deep breath. Pinch. Exhale.* The tube is taped and wrapped into place.

"All good?" the nurse asks.

"Yeah." I avoid looking down at my arm, though. It'll be best for me if I don't watch the fluid flowing.

Mom sits on a chair beside me, reading a book, while I watch a movie on my phone. The staff checks in regularly, but I'm doing all right. By the end of the hour, I'm sleepy, but they keep me for another hour for observation.

"How are you doing?" my mom asks, once my arm is disconnected and bandaged.

"All right." I smile and settle back into the chair, more relaxed now that the first infusion is over.

"You're braver than I am, that's for sure."

"If it's what it takes."

Stifling a yawn, I open YouTube and watch a short ASL video even though I don't have the energy to move my hands and practice. Admittedly, I've let my lessons slide more than I would like. It was one thing when it was just schoolwork getting in the way, but now I also have to somehow wrangle my brain and hands into cooperation. It's hard.

"You're still doing that?" Mom asks, nodding to the video. There's skepticism in her voice.

"Yeah."

"Don't you have a lot of other things to catch up on first?"

And there it is, what my mom is really trying to say. She doesn't think this is worth my time because she thinks Ellie won't be in the picture for long. My parents have been perfectly pleasant around

Ellie, but definitely nowhere near as welcoming or inviting as I know they can be.

"This is what's important to me," I say. "She is."

"Well, you know, once you're away at college—"

"I don't know when that will be."

Mom purses her lips. She returns to her book.

But I hate that my mom just touched on the insecurities I'm feeling, except not the way she's thinking. I don't think *I'm* good enough for Ellie.

Ellie was mesmerizing in that video last night. Hands flying, carefree smile, having the time of her life. I watched it several times while glued to the couch, crushed by heavy fatigue. Not just tired, but like my limbs were pressed down by hundred-pound weights I couldn't shrug off. There was no way I would've had the energy to dance with her even if I'd managed to get up and leave the house.

And then it hit me.

I want Ellie to go do anything and everything. She'll want to go out, and there'll be days when I can't. I shouldn't hold her back.

I won't let myself.

Never knowing how I'll feel when I wake up each morning can also lead to some surprises, because today is the first day in a long time that I truly feel like myself again. The treatment is already making a difference. I feel so shockingly myself again that I could almost forget how bad things had gotten.

It's the day before Thanksgiving, and my last neurology appointment of the year. Once it's established that the treatment is working well for me, I won't need to go as frequently. It's an early appointment—8:30 a.m.—but I'm up hours before.

Walking down into the kitchen, it dawns on me what I want to do. "I think I'll go for a jog," I announce to my mom as I grab a banana from the counter.

She's immediately torn with indecision. Would I be safest stuck here on the couch, or will getting my blood pumping be good for my brain? "I'll go with you," she finally says.

"Okay, yeah." I'd be lying if I said I wasn't a little bit nervous about what would happen if I tripped and fell out on the street on my own. A lot of confidence left to regain.

We get changed and laced up, then start with a warm-up walk around the block. I've never gone running with my mom before. Usually we wouldn't match pace, but as we pick up the speed this morning, I'm happy to take it easy. I won't be breaking my PR anytime soon, but damn, it feels good to be running again.

I'm back, baby!

It's not until I return to the kitchen, sipping on a green smoothie, that the fatigue creeps in. And when I take a seat on the couch, no surprise: *twitch, twitch, twitch.* This is how I live now.

On the way to the doctor, Mom reminds me of all the things she wants me to ask. "Remember, it depletes your immune response, so you need to be careful with infections now. And—"

"I know, Mom," I say, holding up the folded piece of paper she handed me before we got in the car. "I've got your list of questions."

At the neurologist's office, the nurse must think I seem more animated.

"You're looking well," she tells me as she takes my blood pressure. "Treatment can really boost you up."

My mom, sitting on the chair beside me, doesn't say anything. She might not like my decision, but it's just that—*my* decision.

Anything to keep this disease from progressing, I think again. The look on my face must have shifted from my previously lighthearted state.

"Am I remembering correctly you said you'd be going back to school soon?" the nurse asks. "I'm sure it's hard getting back into things. Have you given any thought to attending an MS support group meeting? They're a helpful community to have."

"Okay, maybe I will."

When we get home, I'm supposed to go hang out with Ellie, even though we didn't have solid plans. Not one to ghost, I send her a text.

JACKSON:

Hey, sorry, not feeling up for it today.

It's only partly a lie.

Physically, I feel all right. Mentally, I'm a wreck.

ELLIE:

Aww no worries.

I'm letting her down, but this won't be the only time I have to cancel on something. It'll happen again and again and again.

Because I'm hit with the realization that, even on one of my better days, I'm not sure I can be the person I want to be for Ellie.

CHAPTER FORTY-THREE

Ellie

AFTER HE CANCELED yesterday, I thought I might still get texts from Jackson, but he went quiet. Since today's Thanksgiving, he'll probably be busy with family. Does he know I'm totally open to low-key days? Yesterday I could've driven over to hang out at his house or something.

Shay waves through my open bedroom door. She has an apron on and looks delighted but frazzled. *"Come help with the turkey! We've got so much food to figure out."*

I finish doing my hair and makeup and join her in the kitchen.

It's my first holiday at the Deaf house, which feels easier than celebrating at home. No expectations. As a joke, we cut out hand-shape turkeys that we fold into letters, spelling our names and other funny words to decorate with. I text a picture to Jackson of one of our more juvenile ones. *P-o-o-p.* I cackle just sending it.

ELLIE:

> Totally super grown-up celebration over here.
> How's your day going?

Kayla drove back to her parents' yesterday, so it's Shay, Izzy, Alex, and me, which is still a few more people than this tiny kitchen can handle, but it's hectic and homey in the best possible way. Under different circumstances, having a big dinner celebration at the Deaf house would've been an amazing time.

But I'm getting a weird vibe about Jackson, so I'm in too much of a funk to enjoy it.

"*He still hasn't replied?*" Alex asks, signing one-handed as she stirs some chunky applesauce.

"*No,*" I sign. "*You don't think he's somehow jealous about the party? I felt bad he wasn't able to go.*"

"*You said he was really sweet about it.*"

"*Yeah, he was.*"

"*He's had a lot going on,*" Izzy signs, before reaching into the fridge for the bottle of cider. She opens it and fills Alex's glass. "*He's just overwhelmed by everything. I'm sure it's all fine.*"

"*The way Jackson looks at you, he so loves you,*" Alex chimes in. "*He rented an entire movie theater for you!*"

All I can think about, though, is how upset he was the other night. I think I helped, but I'm no expert by any means. Jackson probably needs to talk to someone who understands more about what he's going through.

I need him to know that I'm here no matter what.

CHAPTER FORTY-FOUR

Jackson

WE'RE HOSTING THANKSGIVING again this year. I have an hour to get myself together before the family comes over. There's no way I want to make small talk today, especially since it's the first gathering since my diagnosis, where I'll be expected to rehash everything to each individual relative. I'm fatigued and miserable, hiding in my room, and so far, my parents haven't told me to come downstairs. I'll stay here as long as I can.

I also keep berating myself for falling for Ellie. She made it clear from the beginning that she felt everything about being at Amber was temporary. Whether she realized it or not, that should include me, too.

But she's been so helpful.

On the other hand, to be honest, communication isn't flawless. How much is she really hearing when I talk? And I'm stuck at the bottom of a huge, difficult-to-scale mountain when it comes to trying to master ASL.

There, I said it. I can't do it. I've got so much of my own shit going on. And it's not like she ever expected me to become fluent. From the get-go, when I said I would learn, she gave an encouraging yet skeptical look, like she already knew I would disappoint her.

But with everything going on, I can't ever live up to her expectations, now can I?

Unfortunately, my troubling thoughts go both ways.

Ellie can't be expected to want to stay with someone like me, can she?

I don't know what my diagnosis has in store. If someone I was dating had this, would I be able to stick around? Didn't I used to make snap judgments whenever I saw someone using mobility aids or using the disabled parking spots? Wondering why they were using them—especially if, like me, by all appearances, they seemed "healthy."

"Jackson!" My mom knocks on my bedroom door but walks in without waiting for an answer. "Sweetie, you have to get dressed. Your dad is almost back from picking up Nonno."

"Okay."

But I don't move from my bed when she leaves. I reach for my phone to discover several texts from Ellie, even though I didn't respond earlier.

ELLIE:

> Hope I didn't lose you at the poop joke.
>
> I'm just gonna spam your texts cause I misssss you.
>
> You're busy with family today, but let me know if you want me to swing by later or tomorrow or whenever.
>
> I don't know if I added enough sugar to this applesauce, but everyone says it's fine. Yikes.

My head swirls, getting a terrible headache that's going to make today even more of a mess. I go wash my face, then put on the new sweater Mom got for me. It's itchy. Fitting, since I'm already feeling generally uncomfortable.

I finally tuck the cane away in my bedroom closet. I haven't been using it lately, so I'll go without it. Taking the stairs carefully, I greet everyone who has arrived, giving my elderly grandfather a hug first. Nonno slaps my back twice and gives an approving nod. "Strong. Healthy."

I quickly slip away toward the kitchen, hoping to snag a quick bite of something. My aunts are dashing around, taking foil off the dishes they prepared at home and helping my mom bake the hundreds of handmade raviolis they batched last weekend. Mom steps to another counter to quickly arrange a plate of appetizers, losing a battle against the tight lid of an olive jar.

I grab the jar to open it for her. I hold it in my right hand and twist the lid with my left, but nothing happens. I switch hands and hold the lid under the edge of my sweater. *Less grip strength . . .*

Before, this would've been incredibly easy, but I can't manage it now. Mom takes back the olives and, with considerably less strain, twists it open with a pop. "You loosened it for me," she offers.

"We both know that's not it."

I go sulk away on the living room couch. I barely have a moment of peace before Aunt Donna takes a seat beside me.

"So how are *we* doing?" she asks, like I'm a five-year-old who needs coaxing to talk. "I'm sure it was a shock. My friend Lana recently found she has it, too. It was bad right after she had her last kid." She puts a hand to her chin and chuckles. "Although, now that I think about it, it wasn't *that* recently, since her daughter might be about your age. Maybe I could introduce you."

I narrow my eyes skeptically. "To her daughter?"

"Oh, no, I meant Lana, if you have any questions. Though I could see if I could arrange an introduction to her daughter, as well . . . But I thought your mom said you had a little lady friend in your life already?"

"Well, I—"

"Yo, Jackson!" Darius walks in the front door, saving me from this conversation.

"I should go say hi," I say, excusing myself.

"Is Anthony here already?" Darius asks.

"Probably outside. He wanted to set up bocce."

"Sweet, let's go."

Anthony greets us in the yard, standing alongside his bundled-up girlfriend of three years, who's making her first Thanksgiving appearance, though she isn't as appreciative of the weather being in the fifties. A couple of our uncles are on the patio, hiding out from responsibilities they'd otherwise be tasked with inside.

He tosses me a heavy green ball, which slips through my grasp and lands on the ground with a *thunk*. Picking it up, I walk forward to retrieve the pair rather than attempt to catch one again.

"Sorry, man, forgot baseball wasn't your thing."

"It's not that." I don't correct him further because, if he's somehow the one person here who doesn't know yet, I'm not going to change that.

"No, yeah, your ma told us about his," the girlfriend says to Anthony in a hushed whisper, "diagnosis, remember?"

Well, then. She knows something really personal about me, and I can't even remember her name. It was somewhere in my brain before this whole MS shake-up, but I can't recall it for the life of me.

"I'm sorry, I forgot your name," I say apologetically.

"Clara," she says with a smile, grabbing the yellow set for herself. "Have you been doing all right?"

I shrug, looking up at the sky. "There's too much going on. But I guess I'm doing better."

"Did you invite Ellie today?" Darius asks.

"Ooh, Ellie?" Anthony asks, tagging onto this line of questioning. "You two can't possibly have been dating long enough to score a holiday ticket."

Anthony tosses the small white ball about ten feet away to start the game. As we take turns getting our own close to that, I tell them what's been going on.

"There's more of a culture divide than I thought," I explain. "And I thought it would all be fine because I *really* like her. But with everything changing so much, I'm not sure how I fit into her life anymore."

Thankfully, Clara understands the situation better than my cousins. "Has she told you any of this? Or is that just how you're feeling?"

I shake my head. "She has to be thinking it, right?"

Darius tosses a ball that knocks Anthony's away from the center. He smirks, then turns back to me, serious again. "Don't get all in your head about it. She would've said something if she didn't think it was going well."

"But would she?" I wince, half-heartedly lobbing out my first ball. "She didn't know what she was getting into when we started hanging out. What if the only thing stopping her from ending things is because she doesn't want to seem like a jerk? I'm here, already getting tired from standing for half a round of bocce, and she's going out to parties and having a great time without me."

Being with Ellie didn't use to feel like a risk, but trying to consider it all objectively, that's all I see. Maybe I need some time to focus on myself and adjust to my new way of life.

"Everything comes back to trust," Anthony says with a knowing look, like he's about to drop some wisdom. "Do you trust that the treatment you're starting will work? Do you trust you'll be at peace with yourself even if it doesn't?"

"I find therapy helps with big questions," Clara says, wrapping an arm around Anthony. He nudges her to finally take her turn, which she does without letting go.

Darius starts the next round, and the rest of us quickly make our final throws because we're being called in for the early dinner. The uncles all head inside. No surprise, Darius ends up winning.

"Like, whenever I end up going to college, what do I even study?" I say with a laugh, picking up the conversation where we left off. "Anyone here feel like taking over our grandfather's very not-boring company that Dad wants to hand down to me? You could be the next king of plastics."

"No way that's what he calls himself," Anthony says with a laugh.

"Nah, it's something that E—" I stop myself before I say Ellie's name.

"So you're not that into plastic, who would've guessed," Anthony says with a chuckle. "Well, I'd prefer to be nowhere nearby when you drop that bomb on Uncle Roberto."

I shake my head slowly. "A lot to figure out. A *lot*."

Especially when it comes to Ellie.

CHAPTER FORTY-FIVE

Ellie

I LEAVE MY phone in the bedroom as I help clean up after Thanksgiving dinner. It was a distraction to me all day, stealing my attention away from conversations with friends who were only doing their best to try to cheer me up. It can be difficult to multitask with a visual language, so by staring at my phone in anticipation, I was effectively choosing to not pay attention to the people right in front of me.

But they were patient with me, so as a thank-you, I volunteered to do the dishes. This *mountain* of plates and bowls and spoons and forks and knives and pots and pans, and when did our kitchen get this stocked? My fingers prune in the sudsy water.

I know Jackson needs rest time, but this feels more pointed than that. Why isn't he replying? Did I do something to upset him?

I scrub the dishes until my fingers are raw. Then I wipe down the stovetop and counters. Our kitchen has never been so clean.

Izzy, Shay, and Alex are scattered around the house, exhausted from the sheer amount of food consumed, so I go to my room and flop into bed. My phone lights up, so I yank it from the charger plugged into the wall.

Oh, thank god.

JACKSON:

Hey Ellie

He's still typing another message, so I wait. It's an excruciating few minutes.

JACKSON:

Sorry, I meant to respond earlier.

ELLIE:

Finally! How's it going, stranger?

JACKSON:

Um, not great, actually.

ELLIE:

What's wrong???

My heart races as he types.

JACKSON:

Ellie, I'm a mess.

I'm tired and depressed and worried and

The typing goes on even longer now. This feels familiar in the worst possible way.

ELLIE:

Jackson, I know you're going through a lot. It's okay, I promise. I'm here for you.

JACKSON:

I don't know how to do any of this.

I don't know how to be in a relationship right now.

I bite my lip and hold back tears. He wouldn't do this over text, would he?

ELLIE:

Does that mean

I stumble over what to write.

ELLIE:

That you want to break up?

Wait, don't answer that

But his text came in too quickly.

JACKSON:

Maybe?

I'm still racing to send more messages.

ELLIE:

Because I don't want to

But I understand if

I don't know what the right thing to say is.

JACKSON:

I don't, either.

Ellie, I like you. A lot.

I just don't know how to handle everything right now.

He's leaving the door open. I can't push him.

ELLIE:

I know, you're going through so much.

But even if you don't think we should, like, date right now, please let me be there for you any way I can be.

I like you so much and want to help with whatever. If you need me to sneak you some food or drive you somewhere so you can get a break from your parents or anything.

Honestly.

Please.

He takes a long time to send a response, but I grip my phone tightly the entire wait.

JACKSON:

I could use a ride to something Sunday morning. I think I'm going to give the support group meetings a try.

I can't type my response fast enough.

ELLIE:

I'm there.

CHAPTER FORTY-SIX

Jackson

I'M NERVOUS ABOUT my first MS support group meeting. But I'm looking forward to the company. I've been out of school so long it'll be nice to socialize and meet some new people. Especially those who understand what I've been going through.

Shortly after eleven, when it's time to leave, Mom walks into the living room, looking in her purse for her keys. I get up from the couch and shake my head. "Actually, Ellie is going to drive me," I say.

She falters. "Are you sure? It's nearby and no trouble for me."

I play the I'm-so-grateful card rather than admitting that I could use some space. "I really appreciate it, but your life's been disrupted having to take me everywhere. I'll call when it's over if you want to get me afterward."

I make my way to the front door and wait a minute for Ellie to drive up. I press the button to open the gate. She parks, and I glance back to make sure my mom isn't looking out the window.

"Hey," Ellie says as I open the car door, wringing her fingers together uncertainly.

"Hi." I get in, unsure what the boundaries are here, but I know I need to set them for myself. It's harder than I thought, seeing her in person. I think taking time apart will be a good thing, but I also want to hug her and forget everything. "Thanks for driving me."

"Anytime."

I fumble with the seat belt. Our fingers graze as she hands me her phone to plug in the address, and we take off.

We listen to some pop music and arrive at the hospital a few minutes later. It's much closer than I remember. She drives into the half loop at the entrance to drop me off.

Was this short ride together worth it? I couldn't bring myself to let go of Ellie completely, and knowing I'd be seeing her today made it easier to sleep at night. Yet it just served as a painful reminder that things are different between us now in a way that feels bigger than I can fix.

"Don't forget to give me five stars," she jokes. But her eyes are wide, loaded with questions. "Want me to stick around?"

Her question replays in my head. *Do I?* "Not right now," I say, realizing the double meaning in my words. "But thank you for getting me here."

The blare of an ambulance siren grows louder as it nears the other hospital entrance. "Well, you have my number." Ellie seems to blink back tears, and I feel awful.

I wish I could say more, but I just walk away into the hospital to find where the MS support group meeting is held. This November meeting got pushed to after Thanksgiving, so the nurse told me to expect a smaller crowd, which is a relief for my first visit. From the lobby,

I turn a corner to find a small conference room on the entry level, five floors below my neurologist's office. Except the door is still locked.

A few others arrive—a fairly diverse group of mostly women. I'm easily the youngest person here, though. But I guess we all have at least *one* thing in common.

Soon, a nurse opens the room from the inside. "Welcome!"

Letting the others go in ahead of me, I wait to follow suit, wondering how exactly this meeting's going to go. There's a lot of talking among the other attendees as they take a seat in the circle of folding chairs.

"Sit wherever you'd like! I usually wait a few extra minutes to start." The nurse goes to grab a few more chairs from the storage closet to accommodate everyone. She also brings out a large fan, plugging it into the wall and setting it to rotate. "I'm so sorry it's warm in here. Let me know if anyone needs an ice pack to keep cool."

Now that she's mentioned it, I do find my body is reacting to the temperature, even though I've already taken off my jacket. The usual suspects creep in, subdued but ever present—my right eye vision slightly fading and my feet tingling.

"Can I crack these open?" one woman asks, jumping up to reach for the windows along the wall.

"Sure, that'll help cool things down," the nurse says. "We can close them if it gets too chilly." She gives a big smile. "So, like I was saying, we've got a great group today. A mix of new and familiar faces. Maybe we start off going around the circle and making introductions?"

The woman to my right volunteers to go first. I start sweating, nervous I'll have to go next.

"Hi, all, I'm Emily." There's a smattering of hellos said back to her. "I was diagnosed almost ten years ago now. A real nasty flare-up likely brought on by the stress of planning my wedding. Made it through the ceremony! But spent what would've been my honeymoon in the hospital, oof!" she says with a sort of laughing-at-herself-type cheer. "Don't worry, we rescheduled and had a lovely time in Paris, but then all that walking tired me out. Lately, I've been doing all right but wrestling with a lot of chest tightness, as well as a very persistent phantom itch, gah!"

Many around the circle nod knowingly. There's some "nice to meet you" or "good to see you again" comments before all eyes turn to me.

"Um, I'm Jackson. And I was just diagnosed this year."

"Aww, a young one," Emily says warmly. "How are you feeling?"

"Well, yeah, it's supposed to be my senior year of high school, but with everything, I fell so far behind and had to take the semester off. And everyone's just so *sorry* about it, but no one seems to understand what is going on. Some days I realize that I don't even get exactly what's wrong with me. I wish we knew more about *how* or *why* this is happening to *me*."

Someone in the circle snaps in agreement.

"I guess, um, I'm still learning what my day-to-day looks like now. Recently I felt good enough to go out and try running again, but I'm nervous about playing soccer this spring. We almost won state last year, until I . . . Anyway, it's just hard not knowing what I can count on my body to handle anymore."

"Have you tried a cooling vest?" Emily asks. "It might help you manage soccer, especially outside in the heat."

I shake my head. "What's that?"

"I'll show you the site I buy from later," she says.

"This group is so innovative," the nurse says, beaming. "If you think of any questions, we've got lots of experts here to help."

"Thanks, I'll look into that. It could at least help solve one of my problems."

"What else is bothering you?" Emily asks.

"I don't know, with this girl I was seeing, and—" I stop myself. "It's probably just high school stuff you all don't want to hear about."

"That's a rough time to be figuring all this out, for sure," another woman says.

"Has she not been supportive?" another asks.

"No, it's not that. I mean, she seems to get it. More than anyone else in my life does. But she's had a rough year herself and seems to finally be finding her place and her people, and I don't know where I fit into that. Especially because I don't know what comes next with all this," I say, gesturing to my body. "So maybe I should just end things now, you know?"

Emily shakes her head. "All those same thoughts were swirling around in my head when I was diagnosed right after getting married, but with the right partner, it's all worth it. Don't limit your happiness now because you're afraid of what the future could be."

There are snaps from others again.

"Thanks, that does help a little." I sit up straight in my chair.

The introductions continue around the circle. There's equal parts similarities and differences in each story. MS affects everyone in their own way. While it can't exactly shine a light on what my own path will be, it does help to talk to people who have the same diagnosis.

After everyone speaks, the nurse leads some discussion about mobility aids, managing stress, meal preparations, and more. It's so much to take in that I sit there quietly, absorbing it all, wondering how I'm possibly going to remember or manage life and this disease. Especially since my parents won't always be able to navigate the complicated healthcare system for me.

Before leaving, Emily pulls up a link on her phone to show me the company she bought her cooling vest from.

"It's pricey," she warns. "But it really makes such a difference, especially in the summer."

I scroll through the options. "Yeah, some of those styles look intense," I say with a nervous laugh. They're bulkier than I would've expected, since they hold multiple sheets of reusable ice packs.

"I'm not sure how it would feel to wear if you're playing sports."

"Thank you," I say, returning her phone. "I'll check it out."

"Are you going to come back to the meeting next month? Scott might be here. You'd get along well." She clasps her hands together. "I hope he's doing all right; he's missed a few now."

"Yeah, I think I'll be here."

"And good luck with your girlfriend. I'm always rooting for young love."

I'm not sure of my relationship status right now, however. We're done, I think. Yet I'm not sure how well my half-hearted attempt to end things went since we did see each other this morning. And didn't actually say we'd broken up.

We're still friends, at least; that much is obvious. I guess it's good enough for now.

CHAPTER FORTY-SEVEN

Ellie

AT SCHOOL THIS week, Pamela pulls me aside before her shift ends midday. *"Don't look too excited when I tell you this . . ."* she signs, which piques my interest immediately. *"We're switching things up next semester."*

I do my best to keep a straight face, but internally I'm leaping for joy. *"Oh, how?"*

"Kim and I are both ready to be full-time again."

"That's nice," I sign, unsure where this is going in regard to the rest of my time at Amber.

Pamela gives an understanding smile, one that conveys no hard feelings. *"Since Kim seems the better fit for you, she'll stay here, and I'll be taking a position at another school."*

I try not to wear my relief too plainly. *"Good luck."* Grinning, I wish her the best, while also sort of pitying her next assignment. Who knows? Maybe she'll end up a much better fit for someone else.

When I get home from Amber High, there's another box at the front door. This one resembles more of the care packages my parents would occasionally send while I was at Brandview. Some snacks and crackers (that I already have in my pantry), a T-shirt (with the tags still on, but it looks like something Madison might've left behind in the closet), and a ten-dollar gift card to Starlight Chili (that barely covers an entree these days, but I have very little money, so I'll take it).

This has to stop.

I don't know how we're going to repair our relationship, but clearly some sort of conversation is required. I'm not sure I want to be the one to start it, but I am the one who took the step to leave home. They might not want to risk crossing a line.

"Should we hold an intervention?" Shay asks, having witnessed the whole package saga firsthand and understanding how I feel about it just from the expression on my face.

"For my parents?" I'm not sure how that would go over.

"Well, my parents could use it, too," Kayla adds, getting up from the couch to join us standing in the kitchen.

"Want my Deaf parents there?" Izzy offers with a smirk. *"They can talk some smack to them."*

"They were very encouraging with mine years ago." Alex smiles at Izzy. *"I think it did make a difference, too."*

"Some adults have never had this." Shay gestures between us all. *"Support. Or, at least, a group that encourages Deaf culture for their kids with hearing loss."*

"Okay, let's do it," I agree. Confronting my parents like this could go poorly, but I'm out of ideas. *"On one condition . . . ASL only. I don't want them to feel like they have the upper hand."*

"*Alex, can you get your interpreter friend?*" Shay asks. "*To maybe, uh, volunteer their time for us?*"

"*Yeah, they owe me for picking a tick off their back when we went hiking last month.*" Alex laughs. "*They can pay me back with an hour or two of interpreting.*"

CHAPTER FORTY-EIGHT

Jackson

THESE WEEKS STUCK at home are a blur. Somehow it's already mid-December and time for the next MS support group meeting. It's also the next time I see Ellie. She seemed relieved when I texted asking for another ride, and she's standing on the driveway now, bundled up in a poofy winter jacket, waiting for me in this flurry of snow.

Seeing her again, I can't help but greet her with a hug. Her forehead is cold as it presses against my chin. *Friends hug, right? Maybe not for this long . . .* Neither one of us wants to be the first to let go, but I lean back and grin. "It's good to see you."

Her cheeks are adorably red. "Am I just your personal driver now?"

"Oh, do you need me to cover gas?" I step back.

"No, no, it's fine." She waves a hand and walks over to get in the car. "I mean, it's nice to see you, so I don't mind."

"How has school been?" I ask, getting in the passenger seat and adjusting the dials to turn down the heat blowing toward me. My body can't handle this abrupt change in temperature.

"Well, boring without you. But!" She smiles wide. "I did find out that the interpreter I didn't vibe with isn't coming back next semester. What a relief."

"That's good. It'll just be the one you like?"

"Exactly."

"I'm glad."

We turn into the parking lot, and I curse how short this drive is. Why isn't there anywhere farther that I need a ride to?

"Actually," I say, hesitating before walking away, "I know it's freezing, but do you mind sticking around? There might be coffee inside."

"Of course." She beams ear to ear and rushes out of the car to meet me. I go slowly, avoiding any icy patches, and she sticks by my side. In the lobby, she points to a chair by the window. "I'll meet you here when you're done."

"Thanks, Ellie."

In group today, there's a guy in his late fifties who introduces himself as Scott Rodriguez, so he must be the guy Emily was talking about at the last meeting. In the circle introductions, he mentions being out with a relapse and that his neurologist wants to try switching treatments. His disease is more progressed than mine. He's been using a manual wheelchair regularly, and he sings praises of how helpful it's been.

Tapping his fingers along the side of the chair, Scott says, "I used to think something like that meant you were stuck and limited." With a shake of his head, he continues proudly, "I didn't realize that a wheelchair meant freedom to go places and do things. I leave my house more now than I have in the last few years."

Once we're dismissed, when everyone is still hanging around for a while, Scott notices my eyes lingering on his wheelchair. "Are you nervous about this?" he asks.

"Sorry, I didn't mean to stare."

"No, I get it. I was in your shoes not too long ago. Don't worry; not everyone ends up needing one. I fought it for such a long time, but if I could go back, I'd talk some sense into myself. This chair saves so much of my energy. I can get through the day without being completely depleted. Or tripping all over the place." He gives a wide grin. "Plus, remember when you were a little kid, so, you know, like three years ago for you . . ."

I laugh, putting us both at ease.

"Don't you remember thinking that wheelchairs looked kinda fun? Well, they can be. Do you wanna try?"

"Are you sure?" I ask apprehensively.

"Yeah, why not."

He rolls beside a chair and, with one shaky step, carefully transfers himself to the seat. "Ay, Dios mío, it's a miracle," he jokes, taking a deep breath to steady himself from the exertion. "Really, though, gotta be careful who sees you get up from a wheelchair or things can get strange fast."

I take a seat, realizing I'm supposed to grab the rims attached to the wheels rather than push the wheels themselves. Around the conference room floor, it takes a bit of energy to get going, but once I've got momentum, it's fairly smooth sailing. After a spin around the room, I return to Scott. "You're right; it's not that bad."

"Come on; go faster!" He puts a hand to his hip.

During a second loop, I garner enough momentum to have some wind in my hair. "That could get dangerous going down a hill." I chuckle.

"Oof, been there, done that." He shrugs. "But only when I'm looking for a little excitement in life and with the power-assist attachment to help me get back up the incline."

I bring the wheelchair over to him and stand. I've been dreading what my future could look like if I lose functionality in my legs, but seeing how Scott feels about using the chair, I realize it wouldn't be like I thought.

"You know how some folks here really lean into that 'MS warrior' language?" Scott asks as he eases himself back into the chair. "To each their own. It can be a way to reclaim your power."

I can tell from his tone there's a catch. "But it's not for you?"

"Nah." He pauses, giving me an encouraging look, then drops some more advice. "I'm not in a war. It's a series of good days and bad days and possibly progressively worse ones. But no amount of sheer willpower will change it, right? You can do everything 'right,'" he says, with air quotes, "and yet your body won't get the memo to cooperate. So if I wake up each morning feeling like I'm fighting a losing battle, that might begin to grate on me after a while, mentally. And as hokey as it sounds, a positive attitude *is* everything."

That all makes sense. I haven't had long enough to think about the nuances of all this. I'm really glad I came to these meetings. "What's worked best for you?"

Scott holds up a finger. "Keep stress at bay." He nods and continues, "Took me too long to figure that one out. Find what makes you happy and don't waste time on things that don't. Because who knows what it all means in the grand scheme of things . . ."

"Yeah, I've got a lot to figure out."

"You've got plenty of time, kid."

I've . . . got time. At least, more or less the same amount of time I had before I found out that I have MS. The diagnosis might have stopped me in my tracks, but I don't have to have it all figured out yet. If anything, there's a fire lit under me to make sure I use my time in the best way possible.

After saying goodbye to Scott, I leave the meeting and find Ellie waiting for me in the lobby, and it's like I see everything clearer. Being with her makes me happy.

She notices and jumps up with a spare to-go cup in her hands. "It's hot chocolate! With oat milk if you can't do dairy now. I tried to time it just right, but I wasn't sure when your meeting would end, so it might be a little bit cold, but here . . ."

I eagerly take a sip of the lukewarm drink. "It's still good. Thanks."

"How'd it go?" she asks, putting back on her jacket.

"Really well. It's like things are getting back on track, you know?" The words pour out of me like I'm willing them into being true. "Maybe I'll even get back behind the wheel soon. Once this snow lets up in the spring, I'll see if my cousin can take me practicing some more."

"Oh, that's nice." But Ellie's face drops. "I guess I'll just see you at school, then."

Crap, I didn't mean it like that. "Maybe soon I can drive to you."

"Or . . ." She smiles again. "Maybe you could have a licensed driver drop you off at my place on New Year's? We're throwing a party."

I push aside the anxieties that have been plaguing me these last few months, because I'm finally feeling more at peace with myself. And if Ellie wants me there, I'm there.

"That sounds great."

CHAPTER FORTY-NINE

Ellie

I SPEND ALL Saturday morning getting ready for this intervention, wondering the whole time whether this was a good idea. It's so close to the holidays that people are all up in their feelings about family and togetherness and primed for huge, decades-long simmering resentments. What's more festive than airing out some grievances?

My sister is home for winter break and has been surprisingly supportive about this intervention.

MADISON:

> Let me know if you want me there, too. I still need to visit Cheese (and you) soon. But don't worry.
> I'll make sure Mom and Dad show up later.
> They seem nervous . . .

ELLIE:

> They're nervous? I'm nervous.

MADISON:

Summon some of that fire like when you moved out of
the house without them knowing.

ELLIE:

Are they still mad?

MADISON:

I don't know, but I think they wanna know why you did it.

And I'm ready to tell them.

I dress somewhat professionally, in a borrowed blazer from Shay, which I sort of regret when I look in the mirror and am unable to take myself seriously. But it's too late to change since everyone will be here soon. The show is about to start, whether I'm ready or not. I can't run away from this when I'm the reason they're coming here in the first place.

When my parents come to the door, I greet them with a quick "hi" and a wave, but that's the only word I'll speak out loud to them tonight.

"Thanks for inviting us," my dad says. He seems to be unsure whether he should hug me or not.

Mom gives a curt nod.

"*You can sit here,*" I sign, motioning toward our usually sparse living room that is now cluttered with as much makeshift seating as we could cobble together. A couple beaten-up folding chairs, some larger pillows on the ground, and some sturdy boxes. Izzy's parents are already on the couch, and Mr. Diaz waves for my parents to join at the chairs next to them. They exchange gestures for introductions, since Alex's interpreter friend is already waiting at the front of the room for us to start.

When Kayla's parents show up a few minutes later, they walk in carrying camping chairs in bags over their shoulders, probably having been briefed on the furniture situation beforehand. They seem chill, mostly intrigued to meet her friends' parents. There's probably nothing that could be said tonight that Kayla hasn't already expressed to them. I wonder what that must be like.

"How is this supposed to go?" I ask across the room to Shay, who's leaning against the kitchen counter.

"It can be casual," she signs back, but keeps her distance. It was her idea, but it's up to me and Kayla to facilitate for our parents.

Alex walks over to say hi to Izzy's parents, and my mom and dad watch their conversation unfold despite clearly feeling out of place here. None of this is new to them since they ran into other Deaf families at Brandview before, but it was never so close to their own turf. That was always something *elsewhere* and not at home.

"Okay," I sign, standing in front of everyone and waving for attention. The interpreter voices for me. *"I guess we should get started."*

Kayla jumps up and stands at my side, taking a more cordial approach. *"Thank you so much for coming. I know we all really appreciate it."* She motions for me to take over again, but I freeze, forgetting everything I prepared in my mind for this moment, so Kayla continues, addressing her own parents. *"Mom and Dad, I know sometimes raising me hasn't been simple for you. You had to figure it out as you went along, so I'm grateful and understanding that you have always had my best interests at heart."*

She continues on for a while, talking about how difficult it was to come back from Brandview and how moving into this house was a way to resurrect some of the community she'd been sorely missing. Her parents nod along and smile. They're clearly a family that communicates well.

When it's my time to speak, on the other hand . . .

"*Thank you for coming,*" I sign, facing my parents straight on, trying to channel some of Kayla's levelheadedness. "*I know we fight a lot. I'm not saying this to be mean, but living at home, I felt like I was more stranger than family.*"

My dad sits stiff, while my mom holds her hands tightly together. By this point, they both would be talking over me, but surrounded by other people and having to go through an interpreter, they're quiet.

"*All my life, I've felt lesser than. Like Madison was the perfect child you always wanted and I was some reject second choice who was considered a hinderance.*" I swallow, glad I don't have to speak or my voice would break. "*You always assumed you knew best. You never asked me what I needed. But you always told me what you needed from me. How you wanted me to communicate. How you wanted me to be. And by doing that, you just kept pushing me away. There was never any patience or willingness to adapt so that I could fit into the family better.*

"*I got to go to a Deaf school, but I was only encouraged to embrace that side of me there—never at home. Whether it was the intention or not, it felt like I needed to hide who I am. So I needed to move out because I think we can only hope to repair our relationship with distance between us. Coming here today was a great first step.*"

Both of my parents' eyes are welling up, and I need to look away. Mom looks at me and, with the interpreter signing for her, says softly, "I assume you want us to learn sign language."

"*Yes. Though, in the meantime, there are other ways to make me feel welcome. Don't force me to wear my hearing aid or cochlear receiver when I need to take them out. Don't get mad when I can't hear something, especially when you're all talking over each other at the dinner table. Don't try to change who I am.*"

My mom nods slowly.

Dad asks a simple question. "Can you visit home for Christmas?"

Now tears pool in my eyes. *"Yes. And maybe, for the big family party, we could get an interpreter? That way I can be included, because otherwise it's too noisy and difficult to talk to anyone."*

"We can figure that out," Mom says, brow furrowed, clearly uncertain about the logistics but not saying no.

My dad squeezes her hand. "I know this was hard. Thanks, Elliedoor." He notices my hesitation at the disliked nickname. "I mean, Ellie."

I nod, indicating that I'm done addressing the group. I walk away to get something to drink from the kitchen and take a moment for some breathing space. That was much more emotional than I thought it would be. Looking over my shoulder, I see that my parents are chatting with Izzy's through the interpreter. My mom's patting her cheeks dry with a tissue while my dad wipes his eyes with his shirt sleeve, but both are now chuckling at something Izzy's mom just signed, probably relieved that the tension has been broken. I'm glad Izzy offered to bring her own folks. Some messages get across best parent to parent.

I'm still shaking from the adrenaline of it all. This was cathartic. Like taking a weight off my shoulders that I hadn't realized had been dragging me down for so long. Who knows what my parents will take away from this experience—at the very least, hopefully we can find our way into each other's lives.

I take a deep breath, steadying myself before going to rejoin the conversation.

All these chairs will be useful for the party we're throwing soon. I'm still counting down the days until New Year's Eve.

And to seeing Jackson again. Giving him space has been harder than I thought, but maybe it's all about to change, for the better.

CHAPTER FIFTY

Jackson

IT'S ALMOST TIME to start back at school again next week. I'm not sure how simple it will be to slip back in the final semester of senior year. Who knows what rumors have spread? Liam supposedly thought I was in rehab this whole time. I don't even know if I'll be able to manage getting through all my classes without the midday nap I've grown used to.

I'm starting New Year's Eve by playing in a rec league one-day soccer tournament. Darius invited me last week. I'm nervous to be back on the field, but this low-stakes match is probably the best way to do it, especially since I know I'm not as fast or agile as I used to be. This will be a good test for how I'll be able to play the spring season at school.

My dad drives me over to the indoor sports center, giving my shoulder a soft pat once we park. "Well, take it easy out there."

I chuckle, shaking my head. "I don't think you've ever said 'take it easy' before in your entire life."

I'm half expecting a chuckle, but Dad turns away and says, "If this year's taught us anything, there's more important things than always going full speed." When he looks at me again, his eyes have a sheen to them—they contain a multitude of words that go unsaid. I've never seen him like this.

"Yeah" is all I manage to muster.

He clears his throat, looking straight ahead out the windshield, ready to drive away. "Have fun."

"I will." I give a wide smile before hopping out of the SUV. "Thanks."

The gym smells of turf and sweat. It's not too crowded, since players don't have to hang around when it's not their game time. Teams of four face off on the two small fields, with the time almost up on their games.

Darius and I are playing with two other guys from the school team. For a moment, I think I'm in the clear from the player I most want to avoid. Except it turns out Liam is on the opposing team.

I lace up my cleats and take a seat on the edge of the bleachers. I used to have a whole warm-up that I'd do, but now, doing just a few stretches, I'm more concerned about conserving my energy for the match. It's been so long since I did a scrimmage match at Amber, and even longer since I played in season last year. How much of this is going to come back to me once I'm on the field?

It's cold in here, not much heat to counteract the outside winter weather in this big boxy space. I've got the new cooling vest, frozen and ready in my bag, but maybe I won't need it.

When the last match clears out, Darius and I jog on, and I can already feel my body warming up. On second thought, the cooling vest seems like a good idea. I stop back on the sidelines to put it over my head and Velcro the straps around me.

My teammates are eyeing me and my attire apprehensively, unsure if I'll be good to play. "Wait, so were you in rehab?" Gavin asks. "You haven't been in school in, like, forever."

I shake my head. "Just some health-issue stuff. I had to take the semester off."

"That's cool, man." Karl seems jealous, not realizing that I'm downplaying this. "I wish I got to stay home when I was sick."

"You're all better now?" Gavin presses, looking me up and down.

Snark gets the better of me. "Well, no, but also kind of yes." I shrug, leaving it at that, fully channeling Ellie in my lack of desire to go over everything with them right now. It's liberating, not owing anyone a full explanation.

"You look fine." Gavin nods.

"He looks good!" Karl hypes me up while elbowing Gavin. "Relax, yo. If he was sick—" He interrupts his own thought. "You're not still contagious, though?"

No, dude, it's not cont— I shake my head. "I'm good to play."

"What's this shit you're wearing?" Liam jumps into our conversation. He's the only one to comment on the elephant in the room, which is this bulky cooling vest I'm wearing beneath the bright orange mesh pinny.

I ignore him. The referee waves us over to get the show on the road. Darius hustles over to the goal while Gavin, Karl, and I line up at the center of the field.

When the game starts, it takes some adjustment to play with the vest on. Despite how tightly I secured it, the ice packs bounce up and down along my chest and back. Liam usually plays defense, but he is now up on left attacking so he can face off against me. When he knocks into me, I'm worried the packs will crack and break. But they don't, and I'm able to stay in the game with more energy than I would if I were overheating.

I'm still very relieved when we get a halfway break.

This field is much smaller than the one I'd play varsity matches on. I'm not running as fast or far as I otherwise would. When playing for school, especially in the outdoor heat, I might need to sub out more frequently and get significantly less play time. But today, I'm realizing that I *will* be able to play this spring. After that, who knows? But if my body can stay the way it is right now for a little while, I'll be able to finish out my high school soccer career.

Knock on wood.

\/‾

Darius and I hang with Gavin and Karl after the tournament for a bit. It's a good time. Maybe I shouldn't have isolated myself from the whole team this year as much as I did.

At home, I take a cool shower and a quick nap, desperately needing to recharge before getting ready for the party tonight. Ellie texted me the official invite while I was playing earlier. Someone in her house designed a little square graphic with fireworks and their address, so they must be throwing an elaborate party. In large font, it reads *Dress up or else.*

I haven't put much effort into my appearance lately, since that takes spare energy I don't have. The fanciest I've dressed these days is wearing the itchy holiday sweaters Mom got me. But I want to look nice tonight.

My resolution for next year is to take life as it comes at me, no matter what that entails. To go beyond my comfort zone.

I know that Ellie makes me happy, and I want to be with her. In a year that was tough overall, every moment I spent with her was bright.

JACKSON:

Hey, I forgot to ask. Do you have a date for tonight?

ELLIE:

Only if you're there.

Slacks and a button-down. Combing my hair. A little spritz of something nice.

I'm ready for the new year.

JACKSON:

Save a kiss for me at midnight?

CHAPTER FIFTY-ONE

Ellie

THE DEAF HOUSE is getting pretty good at throwing gatherings, and preparations for New Year's are going like clockwork. We've scattered around some of the seating options from the parent intervention. And we've got *tons* of strategically placed mood lighting to keep ASL visibility in mind: Christmas string lights, little tabletop lamps, glow necklaces, and more. The decor creates ambiance and accessibility at the same time. And the music is blasting. The neighbors don't seem to mind, given the occasion.

I pace around the living room, waiting for Jackson to get here. Almost all the other guests, mostly friends of my roommates, have shown up already. It's a bigger crowd than I expected. I pass by the window, looking outside eagerly.

He asked me to *save him a kiss.*

Kayla is replenishing the bowl of chips, standing around with some of our new friends from the Deaf Night Out. Of course, Arun is here, laughing about something with Shay. They've been inseparable since that night. Izzy and Alex are cozy in the corner, signing with a friend from ACC. They wave toward me, so I'm about to join them when I realize that they're pointing at the door.

I turn around. Jackson is there across the room.

He looks good, dressed up for the night. Standing tall, confident, with arms wide open. I run to greet him with a hug. He staggers backward slightly but lifts me a few inches off the ground, squeezing me tight.

"You got my text?" Jackson asks, a grin growing across his face.

"Yes." I bite my lip and play coy. Slinking back down to the floor, I straighten out my dress.

"You look nice," he shouts over the music.

"So do you," I say and sign.

He motions around to all the people and folding chairs and boxes. "This is new." He's reduced his volume but is trying to carefully mouth his words.

"Oh, yeah, they're from the intervention."

"Intervention?" he asks while bending his index finger forward to punctuate the question.

I smile, appreciating the effort. "Long story," I say and sign. "For our parents."

"Now I—" Jackson realizes I'm struggling to hear him and tries to lean toward my ear, but he immediately backs up so I can read his lips. "It's loud in here."

I shake my head and shrug. "Yeah, I can't really hear you!"

"Sorry," he says and signs. He looks around at everyone else, signing. We're the only ones trying to have a spoken conversation. I'm not really making this easy. I don't want him to feel too out of place.

"*Come here,*" I sign, then reach for Jackson's hand and lead him over to my room. He walks in while I lean against the door, now closed to block out some of the noise.

"It's a cool party," he says. "I don't want to keep you from it. We can go back out there."

"It's okay; we can stay in here for a little bit." I take a step toward him, wanting to be back in his arms but not wanting to cross any boundaries. I'm not sure where things stand between us. Jackson's left it murky, and I'd rather give him space than push him away. "I've missed you," I say and sign. Next, without speaking, I reverse the signs, asking Jackson if *he* missed *me*.

"*I miss you,*" he signs. "*Really,*" he adds, tossing his finger out from his chin. He continues the movement, reaching to tuck a stray hair behind my ear, sending a shiver down my spine. I dare to tilt my head and press a soft kiss to the back of his hand, which he lets linger along the side of my cheek and then traces down my collarbone.

"I know it's not midnight yet, but—" I reach out, latching onto Jackson's shirt.

With the same urgency, he whispers, "Happy New Year," and presses his lips against mine.

Fireworks. Going off as my heart races, and I don't want it to ever slow down. I run my hands up through his hair, undoing in seconds how nicely he styled it. My knees go weak as he takes a brief detour to plant a few kisses along my neck. I draw him close, ready for whatever the night has in store for us.

As much as I love to curse the unfairness of the universe, somehow it got me here, exactly where I need to be.

CHAPTER FIFTY-TWO

Jackson

ELLIE AND I have been inseparable since New Year's. When the school year ended, we decided to make up our missed Sign Museum date. She picked me up and we drove over together for an afternoon of wandering. The neon lights here shine brighter than Times Square, drawing our eyes toward the names of pizzerias, barber shops, and hotels from years gone by. It's mesmerizing.

In the middle of the Main Street USA display, Ellie says and signs, "Let's take a picture with these ones."

"*How want?*" I sign back, motioning to demonstrate vertical or horizontal. She mimics a wide display, so I turn the phone to capture the image. "*Okay.*"

I'm not going to wow anyone with my ASL abilities yet, but at least Ellie is impressed that I'm still working at it, and there's no better feeling. I do often lose control of my hands and make absurd mistakes, just like my spoken ones, but Ellie finds it endearing.

We smile for the selfie, heads pressed together and shadows cast on our faces as the bright lights behind us draw the focus. All that matters is we're here together.

I'm proud to have made it through this curveball of a senior year. Ellie and I did *in fact* go to prom together. My parents cried when I walked at graduation, then got drunk and sappy at the party they threw for me after, but I let them have it, especially since they were good about me taking a gap year before figuring out what I want to do for college and beyond. Mom's still letting me manage my own diet, though she's always there to help with the most random recipes she finds, and Dad, while seeming to think I'll come around to the idea of working at his company again, is willing to let me forge my own path, the way he never did. Oh, and I've got an appointment for the driver's test in a few weeks to finally get that license.

For now, I'm soul-searching and spending my days with Ellie, who's starting at ACC this fall. I'm not sure much has changed with her parents yet, but she's thriving with her found family. And has booked her tattoo appointment for next week.

Looking around the museum, I chuckle to myself. Ellie immediately leans on my shoulder, asking "What?" right into my ear.

I let her know what I was thinking. "It feels like forever ago that we were going to come here."

"For a daaaaate," she says with a sly grin. "Then I thought you stood me up," she teases gently.

"Dang," I say, playing into the tone. "I should've just shown up and vomited all over the place."

"Probably not ideal." She leans in to kiss my cheek.

"Probably not. Definitely wouldn't have gone how I planned."

"Oh, so how did you plan for it to go?"

Holding her hand, I lead Ellie over to a small seat where we can rest for a moment. It's in a dim corner of the exhibit where there's only a single illuminated sign above us. "Well, I would've met you at your house."

"Right on time," she says, going along with my narrative without missing a beat.

"Hmm, a few minutes early."

"No." She gasps in fake shock.

"Okay, I would've gotten there early but had the EasyRide circle around the block so that I only got to your door right on time."

"And I would've watched from the window, wondering why you were making the driver do that."

"Then we would've taken your car for a quiet ride. Pretty awkward, actually."

She scrunches up her face adorably. "Cringing just thinking about it."

"Here at the museum, we'd walk side by side, brushing arms." I gently nudge her for effect. "And afterward, I'd have suggested we go grab something to eat. You know, making sure it was a date and not just a homework assignment."

"What was that?"

"Not just a homework assignment, but a date," I repeat more clearly.

"I didn't need extra credit *that* badly . . ."

"But after eating, I'd have chickened out, and then on the drive home, you'd suggest we hang out at a park or somewhere since you didn't want to go back to your parents' house."

"You totally get me."

"We'd find a bench and sit there most of the afternoon, chatting like we'd done most of lunch and study hall," I say, gesturing to where we're sitting now. "And you'd think, 'He's such a dork, but what if he was *my* dork?'"

Ellie laughs but refutes me. "I can guarantee I'd never be that cheesy."

"No, *never*."

She leans close to me, reaching for my hand again. "Then I'd get impatient and kiss you first."

"I wouldn't have it any other way."

Underneath the flickering neon sign, she plants a sweet kiss on my lips. When she breaks away and smiles, I pull her close for another.

"Well," Ellie says, before taking a sip of water and signing one-handed, "*What do you want to do next?*"

"Hmm." I reach a hand to my forehead to sign, "*I don't know.*"

There's a lot about my life I wouldn't recognize even a year ago. So much I wouldn't have expected. I don't know what comes next. Then again, no one ever really does.

But I'm ready to find out.

AUTHOR'S NOTE

SOMETIMES YOU THINK you've got things mostly figured out, so you write a book like *Give Me a Sign*, to help readers who are where you were a few years ago. Other times, you're thrown in at the deep end and don't see a clear path forward, so you write a book like *On the Bright Side*, to help make sense of your life right now.

Myself and others with MS are grateful for support, research, and resources from the National Multiple Sclerosis Society. If you can, please consider a donation.

ACKNOWLEDGMENTS

ON THE BRIGHT SIDE required me to write with more vulnerability than I ever have before, which was only possible because I knew this story would be safe in the hands of my brilliant editor, Polo Orozco.

I'm also grateful to have my fantastic agent, Kari Sutherland, as a supportive advocate for my work, continuing to help me uncover gems in the future stories I can't wait to share with the world.

A big thanks to the wonderful folks at Penguin who played a part in the production, promotion, and more of this beautiful book: Cindy Howle, Misha Kydd, Kaitlin Yang, Christina Chung, Natalie Vielkind, Lizzie Goodell, Amanda Cranney, Naakai Addy, Jen Loja, Jen Klonsky, Amanda Close, Shanta Newlin, Elyse Marshall, Emily Romero, Christina Colangelo, Alex Garber, Felicity Vallence, Shannon Spann, James Akinaka, Carmela Iaria, Helen Boomer, Kim Ryan, Micah Hetch, and teams.

As always, I wouldn't know how to exist in publishing without the wisdom of my talented Fork Family—I'm so lucky to know you all and to have finally met many of you in real life!

For my family, thank you for being incredibly proud and supportive. In particular, it was wonderful to celebrate the release of my debut with you all. My grandparents, aunts, uncles, and cousins for showing up to events and surprising me with how quickly you read. Mom orchestrating logistics and road-tripping again with me. Dad racing out to be the first to see it in stores. Cara doing hair (and every other supporting task!). Mark spotting the first typo (that hopefully slips past others' notice) during an overnight reread. And Luke for getting the word out to his friends (and being an adult sibling).

Mika and Zuko, who will never read this but need my love for them to always be enshrined in print, regardless.

And Gabe, for being there through the confusion, the hospital visits, the tears, the determination, the everyday, and more. Without you, none of this would be possible.